# DEEP INTO
# TROUBLE

Also by Dawn Ryder

*Dangerous to Know*

*Dare You to Run*

# DEEP INTO TROUBLE

## DAWN RYDER

St. Martin's Paperbacks

This is a work of fiction. All of the characters, organizations, and events portrayed in this novel are either products of the author's imagination or are used fictitiously.

DEEP INTO TROUBLE

Copyright © 2017 by Dawn Ryder.
Excerpt from *Take to the Limit* Copyright © 2017 by Dawn Ryder.

For information address St. Martin's Press, 175 Fifth Avenue, New York, NY 10010.

ISBN: 978-1-250-07523-9

Our books may be purchased in bulk for promotional, educational, or business use. Please contact your local bookseller or the Macmillan Corporate and Premium Sales Department at 1-800-221-7945, ext. 5442, or by e-mail at MacmillanSpecialMarkets@macmillan.com.

Printed in the United States of America

St. Martin's Paperbacks edition / March 2017
St. Martin's Paperbacks are published by St. Martin's Press, 175 Fifth Avenue, New York, NY 10010.

10  9  8  7  6  5  4  3  2  1

*To Morgan Perry.*
*The world is full of wonderful chance encounters,*
*thanks for sharing one of those with me.*
*Love the life you live!*

# DEEP INTO
# TROUBLE

# CHAPTER ONE

"You are not seriously going to take a book back to that stripper you met?"

Ginger rolled her eyes and kept a firm grip on the book in her hands. Karen was making a half-hearted grab for it, then glared in reprimand when Ginger refused to relinquish it, but there was a gleam of envy in her eyes, too. A very knowing one from years of being cohorts in misadventures.

"Yes I am," Ginger confirmed. "A promise is a promise. I'm keeping it."

Karen fluttered her eyelashes. "I really hate you right now."

"I know," Ginger replied as the elevator reached the lobby of their hotel. There was a chime before the doors slid open. She strode out of the car with a confidence she didn't get to indulge in as often as she liked. Karen was grumbling. From long years spent together devoted mostly to indulging in their passion for mayhem, Ginger knew what the root of her friend's distemper was.

"Sorry, Karen, but you"—Ginger pointed at her

friend—"have a lovely panel to do on something really important."

"Really boring, you mean," Karen mumbled under her breath as they walked past other people attending the same conference. "Why did we become librarians?"

"I'm just nosy," Ginger responded. "Next thing I knew, I had enough credits to graduate and start doing that 'adult' thing. Now I get paid to read through people's details."

Karen snorted at her. "Yeah, *research*. It's not snooping. Honestly. And there's another thing, why did you manage to snag the position with the State?"

"Like I said, I'm nosy and CPS needs to know the dirt on people." Ginger held up three fingers in the Scout salute. "It is my job after all."

"You were never a Girl Scout," Karen accused her softly.

"Cause that cookie selling shit is boring," Ginger responded. "And the boys wouldn't let me into their troop."

"The scoutmaster was scared of your mom," Karen was pressing her lips together to keep her snickers from carrying across the lobby.

"I'm still scared of my mom, but threatening to call her won't stop me," Ginger said before she tapped the book nestled in her cross-body bag. "Wild horses couldn't keep me from taking this book to Kitten."

"Fine," Karen was trailing her through the lobby, past the bar and toward the large revolving doors that led to the entrance of the hotel. "I'll look forward to living vicariously through your stories of adventure."

Now that they were outside, Ginger shot Karen a look her friend knew well. It produced a glitter of anticipation in Karen's eyes.

"Vicariously my ass," Ginger said. "I'll go scout the area and we'll have some fun tonight. We can sleep on the plane home."

Karen grinned. "The conference might be boring, but it's in New Orleans." She cast a look out toward the street, longing on her face. "Which makes up for a lot of stupid panels. I really hate you for being done first."

"Text me," Ginger said as she took off toward the sidewalk.

It led the way to Bourbon Street. Ginger smiled like a kid embarking on Halloween trick-or-treating. There was a vibe in the air, pulsing through her body and putting a spring in her step.

Adventure was calling her name, which meant she needed to ditch her librarian attire.

There was a muggy warmth to New Orleans that made it permissible to take some layers off. It was like a gate unlocking or something, because Ginger shrugged out of her sweater and hung it through the shoulder strap of her cross body bag. She was dressed like a professional librarian in deference to doing the "adult thing" and earning a living. Seriously, some people had such a hang-up when it came to the human body. Her wool blazer was completely ill-suited to the environment. Leaving it all behind in the huge, air conditioned hotel gave her a huge shot of relief that was ever-so-welcome. It was like someone had taken a concrete block off her chest because she was finally able to breathe.

She was going to savor every last moment of freedom, too. After all, she might have to toe the line during work hours, but there was no way she was going to sit around in a lobby when Bourbon Street was a couple of hundred yards away.

The mixture of people on the sidewalk was vivid and

amazing to see; the colors, the smells floating around from the restaurants, the music drifting out from countless bands playing in the bars. Her brain was on overload, in that crazy, gut wrenching tingle down her spine to her toes way.

*Fricking awesome . . .*

She turned into a little boutique. A bell rang as she pushed the door in, a charming little old-world detail that made Ginger smile.

"Can I help you?" The woman had the New Orleans drawl in her voice. She was sitting behind a counter with a huge tabby cat in her lap. The animal looked at her with one blue eye and one brown one but didn't seem to think Ginger was important enough to leave the petting the lady was giving it. The shop was filled with the sound of its purring.

"Yes," Ginger said. "I was hoping to find an outfit a little more suited to this climate."

The woman flashed her a smile that revealed two gold-crowned teeth. She picked the cat up and deposited it on the counter where it turned around in a circle before settling down to watch with a twitch of its tail. "Come here, we'll get you fixed up."

"She goes by the name of Kitten." Captain Bram Magnus held his phone out for Special Agent Saxon Hale. "Word is, she pulls in the contacts the Raven wants to see. Poses as a stripper on the street while she's on the lookout for her boss."

"That makes sense. Tells me more about why no one sees the Raven's face and still, he runs a major underground empire," Saxon Hale answered.

He considered the street in front of him. The French

Quarter never seemed to go completely quiet. Maybe the day after Fat Tuesday, but that would be about it. There were still people roaming down Bourbon Street, mostly tourists and escapees from work conventions intent on stealing a little time away from marketing seminars. They milled around with ties stuck in their pockets in an effort to unwind.

Saxon was looking for the locals, those who did their work under the cover of darkness and behind the shield of the public. He'd followed his tips there, but the residents of the community were tight-lipped.

Well, it wouldn't be the first case he'd cracked through persistence. Just because no one admitted to ever setting eyes on the underworld figure known as the Raven, didn't mean he was leaving before he had the guy in cuffs and the evidence to keep him locked up. But that wasn't all. No, he had a personal reason to be there, and it all centered on the photos Bram's team had captured of one former Special Agent Tyler Martin.

Tyler Martin was someone Saxon was very interested in taking down before Tyler took another shot at Saxon or his brother. Bram was there for the same reasons. Tyler was a rogue, one who didn't care who he sold out, so long as it got him what he wanted. He was a traitor, the worst kind because Saxon had once called him a superior among the Shadow opps teams.

"When Kitten pops her head up, we'll see what she does tonight." Saxon replied. "And just what part Tyler Martin has in it."

"You can bet it won't be pretty," Bram answered. "I've got surveillance on her taking three of the most recent victims into various bars but since half the bar owners around here swear she's one of their strippers . . ."

"It proves nothing," Saxon confirmed. "Except that the Raven should have used another girl because now we have a reason to follow this one."

"There's one major problem with being a bad guy," Bram answered. "You need to throw us good guys off your scent, while keeping the number of people you work with at a minimum so you can maintain that ever-so-important secret identity."

"Yeah," Saxon agreed. "Guess it's a good thing we're the good guys."

Bram nodded, keeping his eyes moving as well. He was a seasoned man, one who knew death only needed one little opportunity to turn an agent into a fallen hero. It was the reason they were there, risking their necks to seal up a leak that had taken down men on both their teams. Whoever the Raven was, his reach went deep into the black-market world as well as all the way to the White House. The reason was money. It made the world go round.

Time passed. Saxon kept his eyes moving. Bram shifted, taking up a new position that allowed them to have different viewpoints.

Good Guys.

Yeah, that's what they were, and it meant that they spent a lot of time waiting for the bad guys to pop up out of the gutter while making sure no one noticed them.

Saxon took a sip from his beer bottle. He was using the beer as a reason to remain in the area, watching to see who went down the alley. Their source was dead, a Russian who had gone by the name of Pratt. He'd been the Raven's right-hand man, and the number of bodies showing up said whoever the new man was, he was cleaning house. It was the chance to catch the Raven red-handed. While the blood was flowing. It was a gruesome aspect of his job, one he shouldered because it made the world a better place. Shadow opps teams took the assignments no one else wanted.

Across the way, their backup team was seated in a restaurant. Dare Servant had been working the case for a solid two months without so much as a bread crumb. Then Saxon's brother Vitus had hauled in the catch in the form of Congressman Ryland's daughter Damascus being held in one of the buildings behind the famed Bourbon Street. It wasn't the first time cases had overlapped, and Saxon intended to take full advantage of it.

Now, he just needed the sun to set so Kitten would come out to ply her trade.

"Now, you look like an 'Orleans lady."

Ginger turned to look at herself in a vintage oval-shaped dressing mirror. The wood finish was cracked, giving the thing character. The top of the dress was gathered up into a band that tied in back of her neck, the fabric falling in loose waves over her breasts to where a waist band gave her shape. As she moved, the skirt of the dress twirled up to give off a flash of her thighs. With a saucy smile, the woman had given her a pair of boy shorts to wear under it. When she turned faster, the edge of those boy shorts came into sight, so it wasn't completely indecent and really sort of sexy.

Her father would collapse if he saw her in it, but she was kind of certain her mother would laugh.

*Fine, that means you're buying it. Spicy.*

Besides, her parents were Ying and Yang. Honestly, giving them something to debate was just a little gift to help them find a reason to make up afterward.

*You're so wicked . . .*

She was, and unrepentant at that. Ginger dug into her

purse and found her bank card. She gained another glimpse at the gold crowns before the woman rang up the sale. "I'll send your clothes up to your hotel. Just write the room number."

"Thank you."

"Send your friends to see me," the woman encouraged her with a twinkle in her dark eyes.

The bell rang again when she opened the door. The cat took the opportunity to jump back into its owner's lap, a loud purring starting up behind her before Ginger stepped out onto the street and the door closed behind her.

The dress was a lot more comfortable in the balmy air. It took only a moment for Ginger to adjust to the strappy sandals the woman insisted went with the dress. The two inch heels gave her hips a sway that made her cheeks heat.

*With excitement . . .*

Anticipation was making her giddy. She passed by a restaurant that smelled amazing, deciding to wait for Karen before she ate. Up ahead, the doorways were filling up as dancers tried to pull people in from the streets to fill their bars. She contemplated her options and decided on business first.

She looked down at the book in her hands. It was a signed copy of *The Silenced* by Heather Graham. She'd stood in line for three hours to get it, and there was no way she wasn't going to deliver it. Okay, maybe the real reason she'd promised to bring it back was to have a reason to venture away from her professional venue tonight. But if Ginger was being completely honest, she needed to admit that there was something mysterious about Kitten, and, as Ginger had told Karen, she was nosy by nature.

A fatal flaw perhaps. Tonight though, it felt pretty damned fun.

*Unrepentant . . .*

Yup. Guilty as charged.

Ginger considered the bars ahead of her, they all ran together in a bright, music-pumping tapestry. She racked her memory, trying to recall exactly where she'd encountered Kitten.

She had beautiful mocha skin with black eyes that looked as deep as the night. "Stripper" wasn't the right word for what Kitten did. No, her motions were too erotic, too hypnotic for such a cheap label. She was like a burlesque dancer from the thirties, a woman who captivated her audience as she teased them and used skill to titillate. The ease that she embodied as she danced made Ginger envious. To be so comfortable in your own skin, it was something she admired and longed for.

Bet she knew how to have great sex.

Ginger felt the teasing heat of a blush but didn't chastise herself for her scarlet thoughts.

She was serious.

Sex, well, at least the sex she'd had was sort of awkward. It could be fun except Ginger realized that she lacked the confidence in her body that someone like Kitten displayed in spades. That firm, unwavering belief that every part of her was just the way it was meant to be and nothing could distract from the moment when she pressed herself against another person.

Yeah, she was totally envious as well as determined to cultivate some of the same sense of being in herself. No, she wasn't going on some sex binge, just making sure she was ready when she ran into a guy she wanted to get naked with.

Ginger looked through the open doors of the bar nearest

her, but the girl working on the pole was Caucasian. She moved a little farther down, peeking in doorways as she laughed over the fact that she was looking for an erotic dancer.

One more little thing that would give her father a fit.

Poor daddy, she did love him, but he was so straight-laced. She just couldn't help but tease him a little, at least in her thoughts. Peter Boyce was a respected member of his community. His daughter shouldn't be walking down Bourbon Street looking for a dancer named Kitten. But hey, what daddy didn't know wouldn't hurt him. In two days, she'd be back in her economy coach airline seat, bound for normality. Sure, she knew that playing on the dangerous side was bound to blow up in her face, but she just couldn't resist flirting a little with it while she had the opportunity.

Living in the moment.

"What you looking for honey?"

A bartender in a striped vest and sporting a perfectly trimmed mustache was leaning against the doorframe of the next bar she came to. He had a black hat tipped down on one side of his forehead, making him look perfectly at home.

"I'm looking for Kitten," Ginger said working to make her voice husky. "She's expecting me."

The man's expression changed, hardening a little, even if his lips remained in a small grin. He racked her from top to bottom, his lips splitting to give her a glimpse of his teeth. She felt assessed, in a purely carnal way. It was blunt and a touch seedy but she'd be lying if she didn't admit to being just a bit buzzed by the knowledge that she measured up. The glint that appeared in the bartender's eyes told her that much.

"Right then. Go on back, past the kitchen, keep going

across the alley and into the next place. Kitten is working a private party. Tell the doorman she's looking for you."

"Perfect," Ginger said as she stepped up into the bar. There was a definite contact with her bottom and a slight squeeze as she passed the guy, making her close her lips to keep from snorting at him. She heard him chuckle and ordered herself to keep moving. Sure, she should have taken issue with him for touching, but there was something about the setting that seemed to make it fit. She'd think about how inappropriate it was later.

The place was full of pub style tables. A few of the men turned as she walked between their stools. Clearly looking at her . . . *assets*. It fit with her idea of the evening . . . adventure first, lamentations and common sense in the morning.

*Worry when they stop looking, girl.*

Ginger let her hips settle into a sway that made her feel as sensuous as she'd decided Kitten had looked the night before. It was natural and exciting and a real fricking relief to be free. She felt like she was always stuffing herself into a tin can to please those around her or at least those who controlled her income.

*Sometimes, she wanted to be wicked.*

*Sexy.*

The fabric of the skirt swished over her thighs, teasing the receptors in her skin and making her feel like a woman more keenly than she'd allowed herself to feel for a long time.

It was going to be a night to remember.

"What the fuck?" Saxon mumbled. Bram looked up and made a sound under his breath.

"Just another—" It took Bram a moment to see what

Saxon had. "Uh . . . yeah, that's bad. Except, the door-man just let her in."

Saxon's eyebrows lowered. He actually blinked and looked at his drink, but there was only a small amount missing from the bottle. Nope, he wasn't impaired, but his brain felt like it had gone numb.

*She* didn't belong there.

That much, he was certain of. It was clearer than anything else he knew in that moment. Hell, it was speed-ing through his veins, triggering some sort of alarm. He set the beer bottle down without realizing it. He was acting on impulse, a fact that stunned him, on his feet, ready to go after her. Whoever she was, she had a mop of dark brown hair with copper highlights that she'd twisted into a messy knot on the back of her neck. It gave him a great look at the expanse of her nape, and damned if he didn't want to taste it. He actually took a step toward her because the attraction was so strong. He caught him-self in the last second, forcing himself to stop and assess her critically.

That messy knot of hair on her head, it wasn't the sort of thing most women wore into a bar. There was a touch of function in it, like she'd escaped from someplace she needed to be, while the messy part declared her to be made of something just a little less tamed.

That just made her hotter.

There was a little curve to her lips that matched the excitement shimmering in her eyes. Hell, the look on her face darn near took five years off his life because one good long look and he almost believed in happiness again.

And then he felt like he was kicked in the balls as he watched her walk past the doorman, into what Saxon knew damned well was a nest of underworld thugs.

"Oops, excuse me" wasn't going to keep her from getting a bullet between her eyes. The image of finding her body, seeing those eyes lifeless, made him want to pull his gun free and make sure it didn't happen. The impulse was so strong, he felt it squeezing everything else out of his brain.

"Whoa." Bram had reached out to stop him. "What are you doing?"

Saxon brushed Bram's hand aside with a motion that gained him a grunt from his partner because it was damned sharp and more than a little uncalled for when Saxon factored in that he'd failed to communicate his intentions. They were partners, and jumping into something without clueing your sidekick in was a great, textbook-perfect way to get a flag sent home to his mother. He was practically begging for a case of "DDS."

Death due to stupidity.

He was an experienced, decorated field agent, but at the moment, he felt a lot like an over-protective brother.

Okay, maybe not a sibling.

That was another red-hot flash that ripped across his brain. There was nothing, and he meant nothing, brotherly about his feelings for her.

*Shit.*

That was another fatal mistake—getting personally involved. He had a case to solve and a major underworld player to take down. There was absolutely no room for anything but professionalism.

So why was his brain trying to switch modes on him?

"What got your attention?" Bram prodded him.

"She doesn't belong here, much less back there." Saxon was sizing up the doorman. He pulled out his cell and started typing in a text to Dare Servant, but Dare was sending him a text.

*Got eyes on Kitten.* Saxon turned the phone toward Bram.

The little bit of technology vibrated as a new text came in.

*Coming down the alley with a male.*

Bram's eyes narrowed as he made a low sound in the back of his throat. "Looks like it's time to work."

Saxon discovered himself torn for the first time. Kitten was an experienced operator. They wouldn't be getting a second shot at following her, but the sight of the woman going past the doorman was burned into his memory. He couldn't dismiss her as collateral damage.

He punched in a code.

"Seriously?" Bram asked. "She might be Kitten's replacement."

"She's not." Saxon answered with more confidence than he'd felt in a long time. "She's in the wrong place."

Saxon felt the minutes ticking by. His team was moving, shifting positions for their strike. He was about to blow their cover out of the water.

*For what?*

He ignored the question because the ball was already in play. Good or bad, he'd made his choice, and there was only one thing to do now.

*Take a swing . . .*

There was a hoot as one of their female agents climbed up onto a table and started dancing.

"Hope you know what you're doing." Bram said before he moved over and blocked the bouncer while looking like he was applauding the agent's actions.

Saxon kept his attention on the man at the back door. He shook his head but people were holding up their phones now, taping the incident. He abandoned his post against the tide of repercussions that would come down from the city. There had been a time when the French Quarter operated above the law but modern-day politicians minded their reputations these days and the connected generation made that harder than ever with their Tweeting, Facebooking, and Youtubing.

People were spilling in from the street, drawn by the commotion. The doormen were crushed between bodies as two more women jerked their tops off and began scrambling up onto table tops.

Saxon used the opportunity to slip through the back door, hoping he wasn't already too late.

There was a whole different feeling in the back of the building. Ginger felt it prickle across the surface of her skin. It was more sultry, definitely on the darker side but not in a bad way. It was an instinctual vibe, one that felt like it was settling into all of her pulse points and triggering a passion for satisfaction of every appetite she had.

A couple of the men in the kitchen looked over as she crossed the doorways. Ginger kept her chin level, feeling the flop of the paperback book against her right hip where her cross-body bag was resting. There was a new feeling prickling across her nerve endings now, one of unexpected victory. Being allowed beyond the tourist areas was like scoring some sort of bonus point in the adventure category. She smiled brighter as she made it to the back door of the restaurant.

The alleyway was an eerie place. She was surrounded by noise, from the bar behind her, Bourbon Street, and the private party in front of her, but it was all muffled and mixed together while she was between the buildings. A stray gust of wind blew down, lifting her skirt and raising goosebumps on her legs. Under the partial moonlight, it was like she could feel the spirits that were rumored to inhabit the French Quarter. Whether or not she believed in ghosts was irrelevant, there was a sensation of life, one that gave her a buzz. It was as if the bricks of the buildings were imprinted with the memories of the eras they'd seen.

Another doorman stepped into her path. She had to tip her head back to make eye contact, and she felt a shiver run down her spine when she did. This man didn't mess around. He considered her with a hard expression that made the scar running through his lower lip look majorly intimidating.

"Kitten is"—Her voice sounded less confident than she liked. She swallowed as the guy frowned at her—"expecting me."

There, that was better. Ginger dug deep, connecting with her memory of the way Kitten had looked while dancing, full of confidence and the will to take life by the short hairs. Ginger smiled at the guy. He looked a little doubtful but raked her from head to toe, lingering for just a moment on where the skirt gave him a teasing glimpse of thigh.

"Right . . . inside." He waved her past but pulled something out of his pocket and tossed it to her. "You know the rules."

She was already inside before she got a look at what he'd thrown at her. It was a beauty mask, or maybe nap mask was a better way to describe it, one of those black satin things that completely covered a person's eyes.

"You lying bitch!"

There was a hard sound, one of flesh hitting flesh.

Ginger looked up, her enjoyment of the moment evaporating instantly.

A man was sprawled on the floor, clearly the recipient of the punch she'd heard connecting with his jaw.

"Kitten knows who she works for. I told her to bring you to me."

A man came out of the shadows of the room, emerging like some sort of judge. The man on the floor had sat up but he remained on his butt as he raised his open hands wide.

"Look man, I know you're the boss." He was clearly pleading, the tone of his voice making Ginger want to gag.

"Do you?"

"Hell yeah, everyone does what the Raven wants."

"Except you," the Raven said as he leveled a pistol at the man. "You took it upon yourself to order a hit under my authority."

"Well now . . . that was for your protection, had to deal with the matter immediately."

"You mean, before I had a chance to hear Cortman's side of the story. Now there is only yours."

The guy had turned ghastly white; Ginger was pretty sure she matched his pallor.

"And you somehow think I am stupid enough to not know what you are about."

"It won't happen again," the guy declared.

There was a single discharge from the gun, one that made Ginger jump. Her attention was on the falling body, the sound of his head hitting the floor, making her want to vomit. The scent of fresh blood filled the air, twisting her insides.

"I know it won't."

The guy's tone was so icy, Ginger sucked in her breath because it chilled her to the bone. Evil had never been a tangible thing in her world until that moment. Now, she was pretty sure she could smell it in the air.

A couple of heads turned as the Raven and his men caught her in their sights. A strange sort of shock went through the room about the same time as Ginger recognized both of them from online photos. Which was really interesting because Marc Grog was supposed to be dead. Very, very, dead. And he so wasn't.

"Shit!"

"What the fuck?"

As the Raven shifted the gun toward her, she turned and ran. It felt like time had slowed down, allowing her to notice how long it took to complete her turn, the way she was lurching away from the men behind her, fighting to push her feet against the floor and launch her body away from the scent of fresh blood.

"Someone get her now!" An order came out of the darkness. "She fucking saw the whole thing!"

Her insides twisted, a warning bell ringing inside her head. She turned the second she got into the alleyway, but the street seemed a million miles away. Still, she had to make a try for it.

She ran straight into another man. Whoever he was, he was far more intimidating with his square cut jaw and hard expression. There was determination glittering in his eyes, and she felt like it might just melt the flesh right off her face because he was downright deadly looking, but in his eyes she saw a difference. One that was as stark as day versus night. There was a flicker of determination in those blue orbs, one that made her want to cling to him.

He yanked a gun out from beneath his suit jacket and reached out to grab her bicep. He yanked her toward him, turning slightly so that she stumbled right past him while he placed himself between her and the men crying out for her blood.

In that instant, he surpassed every other male on the face of the earth.

*Fuck.*

Her timing was epically off, but that didn't stop the burst of realization from flashing through her brain.

"Run." It was a hard command. One edged with authority. She caught a half look behind her as he took up a position of defense, firing off a couple of bullets while backing up toward her.

"Now."

Ginger took off toward the street, the light and blur of music a promise of life. Once again, she was straining against the pull of evil behind her, ripping every last shred of strength from her flesh in an attempt to reach safety.

To touch life.

Ginger suddenly realized why the bricks of the buildings felt like they held the echoes of spirits. When life was snuffed out violently, the soul didn't want to move on. She was trying so hard, but every second was a mini eternity that tormented her with her lack of distance from the murder scene. She was going to wake up as a ghost haunting that alley, wondering what the hell had happened.

Her damned heart nearly burst as she heard more popping sounds of gun fire.

"Do exactly as I say if you want to live."

Ginger was treated to a hard shove right in the middle of her shoulder blades. The strappy sandals twisted when she pitched forward and she tried to get her feet under her. She ended up wobbling like a newborn giraffe, but she'd made it to the edge of the street and out into the crowd of people.

If she wanted to live?

*Hell yes . . .*

She surged forward, feeling her unlikely savior joining her.

She bit her lip to keep from crying out. The man came in close, looping his arm across her back so that her temple ended up hitting his shoulder.

She liked him right there.

Hell, she wanted to curl into his embrace and take shelter there against his broad chest.

*Epic bad timing . . .*

"This way," he said but he didn't wait for her to comply. He locked his hand on her hip and pulled her against his side. A jolt of satisfaction went through her, making her blush. Somehow, her damned sex drive had suddenly kicked into high gear. Shit, the guy even smelled amazingly strong.

"Who . . . are you?" Ginger wasn't sure why she was asking. At the moment, it didn't matter a rat's ass.

He sent her a glare that let her see that his eyes were blue, a beautiful shade like ocean water in some exotic location like Jamaica. "We're going to hide in plain sight. It's our only chance."

He sounded so dammed confident. She was a hairs' breath from acting like a startled chicken and darting away from the scene behind her without thinking about where she was going. He, on the other hand, was controlled. She looked into his eyes again and soaked up his steady gaze before he returned to scanning the people around them.

He made her believe she could survive.

It was the solace she needed, filling her with a confidence she hadn't known she possessed. She was just nursing off of his confidence because it was the only port in a storm.

Ginger turned her head and saw the first doorman. He was poised at the edge of the alleyway talking into his cell phone as he looked at the crowd.

"Get your face out of sight." Her companion reached right up and captured her neck, pushing her head down without a morsel of concern for how much he was invading her personal space.

Well at the moment, that was small potatoes anyway. She relaxed and looked like she was nuzzling against him.

Damn, he smelled good.

"That won't do much good if you don't get her out of those clothes."

Ginger jumped, losing her balance again when she tried to land on the two-inch-heeled sandals. Her companion snorted as he slid his arm around her and carried her through the next few steps. She looked over at the second man who had slid up beside them. He was flashing a smile and moving with the beat of the band but one look at his eyes and she realized he was as deadly serious as the man she was leaning against.

"Here," he said as he tugged her elbow.

They were all suddenly slipping into another bar and through the mass of people who were dancing to a different song. It was a little odd to just change beats, like flipping through the shuffled songs on an iPod, but with the songs starting in the middle. It was a stupid thing to notice, too, when there were more important things to deal with.

Her damned brain was still in panicked chicken mode.

Whoever her companions were, they pulled her along, reducing her to feeling like a football being carried through the opposing team. She was insanely grateful because they seemed far more in their element than she was. She ended up in a back room, which smelled of hair spray and coffee. The second man shoved the door shut and flipped the lock. Ginger stared at the deadbolt, realizing just how little comfort it gave her when she coupled it with her memory of how burly the backroom doorman had been.

"Get out of that dress."

Ginger hugged herself as she turned on the first man because her brain had suddenly decided to stop understanding the most basic English.

He was digging through a rack of clothing, yanking hangers out as he looked at the dresses on them. She realized it was a dressing room of some sort, with a makeup station against the opposite wall. What captured her attention was how in control he was. The gun wasn't in sight, but she knew he had it. Nothing about being shot at had rattled him.

"Dress off . . . now." He turned and spoke in a lower voice. She realized she was staring at him with wide eyes, likely looking about two seconds from fainting.

*Get a grip . . .*

She drew in a deep breath but got distracted by her hands and forearms. There was crimson blood splattered on her skin. The metallic scent of it was filling her senses as she tried to process this newest bit of horror.

"Ah . . ." She mumbled.

"I know. We've got to get you out of the Quarter," he said with a little too much kindness for her pride.

*Get a fucking grip!*

"Someone will notice that fresh blood on you, and I need the dress for evidence."

"Right," she succeeded in answering him.

Maybe it was the tone of his voice or the expression on his face. She didn't know, and it didn't much matter. Her insides knotted as she felt like a rope was tightening around her neck and the need to run was darn near overwhelming, but conversing with him brought her out of chicken mode and back into being a human with reasoning powers.

"Evidence?" she questioned as she reached up to work on the collar of the dress.

"Yes. You're a witness."

"Oh, yeah. Right." Three words had never been so hard to produce.

There was a flicker of approval in those blue eyes before he reached out and cupped her bare shoulder to turn her around. Something new went blistering across her skin. Some sort of reaction to the contact between their bare skin.

It was so intense, it curled her toes.

He grabbed the top of her zipper and pulled it down.

"Who are you?" Her voice was a squeak again, but at least she'd managed to get her tongue to work.

"Special Agents."

"Oh . . ." It was an expression of relief. She turned around to look at him, earning a scowl as he lost the zipper tab while it was only halfway down her body. "Where is your badge?"

It appeared to be her night for asking stupid questions, but his expression made it clear that he agreed with her thought process.

"I'm undercover," he answered with a tone that made it clear he felt she needed to get her priorities in line. His partner finished unzipping her.

Ginger clasped her arms around herself again, trapping her dress against her skin and feeling unbearably exposed with the back of it open to the night air. She was suddenly trembling, jerking her attention toward the door. Why? She honestly didn't fucking know. Somehow, she'd turned into a bundle of impulses that she was just acting on while her brain took a snooze and left her at the mercy of the circumstances she was drowning in.

"Get a grip" had never held more meaning.

The first man rolled his eyes, clearly frustrated with her. "I'm Saxon Hale, and I'll get you my badge as soon as possible. Right now, the Raven's men are getting the word out to find you and in case you missed it, kill you."

"I got that part," she replied. "Sorry, my brain isn't working."

"It's shock. Listen to me, follow my lead. Don't try to think it through, just do it. One action at a time."

It really wouldn't be hard. He had a deep tone that was so full of authority, falling into line was easy. Ginger let her dress go. It slithered down her body, leaving her in a bra and boy shorts.

Saxon actually averted his gaze as he handed over another dress. It was a tiny thing, but she grasped onto it, allowing herself to think of him as a decent guy while she pulled the new dress over her head and down her body. He held her old dress up by two fingertips and lifted it high while his partner held a bag open for him to drop it into.

"That should do it," the second man said with a heavy dose of satisfaction. He knotted the top of the plastic bag. "Some hard evidence at last."

The new dress was a soft jersey that clung to her curves more. Saxon returned his full attention to her.

"Do something else with your hair." He pointed at the makeup table. "And use some of that face paint."

It was something to do and she needed action instead of being at the mercy of her racing thoughts. Ginger pulled the pins out of her hair and looked at what the table offered. She settled for using dark eyeliner and lots of mascara. She pulled several makeup remover cloths out of a tub and wiped the blood off her arms. It didn't come off easily but smeared in bright streaks that made her belly heave.

*Remember that grip? Better hold on tighter.*

Or maybe better advice was to take her lead from her companions. Saxon Hale was in complete control. Sure, finding him sexy was misplaced, but it sort of took second place to keeping her head and staying alive

So she let herself soak up the details of the man. He was built. B-U-I-L-T. Shoulders to drool over, trim waist line, which promised cut abs, and when he turned around, his jeans gave her a peek at a very nice ass. Bundle that all together with the adorable way he'd looked away while she was in her underwear, and he was undeniably the most amazing male she'd ever come face to face with outside the pages of a book.

But he was dangerous.

Only she found that trait to be another point in his favor because he was suited to his role as a special agent. Part of her recoiled from that idea. The logical portion of her brain knew he was playing a dangerous game in his chosen profession. There in her gray matter was the fact of how many law-enforcement officers died in the line of duty. Those statistics and facts that she'd seen printed on a screen suddenly took on a very real meaning.

Along with the sharp slap of reality that came with acknowledging just how helpless she was without him. He was her only line of defense.

"She saw him," Saxon whispered to Bram. He was actually fighting the urge to look at her bottom as their unexpected eye witness bent over to apply some eyeliner.

*Sleazy Hale. Don't be a dick . . .*

She wasn't that sort of girl, he'd noticed that first off. Truth was, it had been a long time since he'd dealt with an innocent woman. His job just didn't have him rubbing elbows with them very often. Tonight was the first time he'd felt that it was something lacking in his life.

And his timing couldn't have been more off. She was a witness. One who needed her wits functioning one hundred percent.

Bram made a low sound. "Positive?"

"I think she knows who he is. The Raven sure seemed to think so." Saxon forced himself to focus on his fellow agent.

"Getting her out of here alive is going to be damned hard," Bram said.

Saxon knew it. He was nearly sick with the realization. It pissed him off because it was another emotional response, and he sure as shit didn't have time for distractions. His witness was definitely a bundle of those it seemed.

He shook his head and focused. They needed to fold back into the flow of people on the street without a single ripple to announce their presence.

That was the only way he was going to keep her alive.

Now that she was back in control, her mind was offering up little bits of information.

She'd just seen a murder.

Fuck.

And, double fuck.

Ginger bit her lip to keep from telling them that she knew who she'd seen. Who the hell wouldn't recognize Marc Grog? Well, maybe quite a few considering the guy was supposed to be dead. For the last decade. But he'd been a media giant in his time. Suddenly, her obsession with details was a really bad habit. It would be a whole lot better for her if she didn't know who the guy was, but she did.

Yeah, she knew who she'd seen, but she wasn't going to say so. Saxon Hale still had his wits about him, and, honestly, she was scared to death of distracting him from keeping her alive. Alone, she would be dead. Her pride didn't much care for that hard truth, but facts were facts.

*So? Get busy doing some thinking of your own . . . Life plays for keeps.*

She drew in a deep breath and scrounged up some composure. Ginger selected some lipstick and glossed her lips with her newfound poise.

"Finish up, we need to move you," Saxon urged her.

She stood up, her unbound hair flipping around her neck and shoulders. She thought he hesitated, but it was likely her shocked brain making her think so. There was a precision to his motions; indecision really wasn't something that fit with his overall persona. It was hypnotic, drawing her attention because it was just so polished. He used his body like a weapon, every motion practiced. There was no faking that sort of thing. She was sure of that fact because she'd seen lots of men who seemed to think they knew how to take on the bad elements of the world.

Saxon Hale put them to shame.

It suddenly dawned on her why none of the guys back home did anything for her. They were safe. The knowledge was irrefutable. It wasn't a conscious choice, just a reaction to Saxon's take-control persona. There was a strength in him, something she'd thought she'd seen in other men but actually hadn't. Now she understood the difference. It sent a tingle across her skin and tightened her insides.

And made her realize she was a complete mental case who was in the running for the all-time award for bad timing. Geez. Getting turned on while people were intent on killing her.

Her mouth went dry as the second man opened the door an inch and looked out into the hallway.

Oh hell, it was real, the people-wanting-to-kill-her part. How in the hell had she gone from buying a dress from a woman stroking a cat to needing to strip in front of two men in order to avoid certain death? It sounded surreal, but Saxon reached out and grasped her bicep, confirming that it wasn't some action-movie inspired dream.

"Let's move," he said as he pulled her into motion.

The contact between them was live once more. She took strength from the buzz, letting the way he affected her jump-start her brain.

"Bring it," she said softly.

Saxon cocked his head to one side in response, one corner of his mouth twitching into a small, half grin that told her he liked her attitude. The response warmed her.

Hell, it did more than that, but Saxon was sweeping her into motion a second later, and there was no way she was going to drop the ball.

No way in hell.

"She said Kitten was expecting her."

Kitten was shaking. She could feel the sweat running down her body. "I wasn't expecting anyone."

She fought to keep her rising panic under control. The blindfold wasn't helping. Being in darkness only heightened her awareness of just how precarious her position was. The men in the room were the dangerous sort. She knew their type, had worked with them for years because it was the only way to really make enough and do more than just scrape by. She didn't need to see their guns; she knew they lived by the bullet. Had watched them use those weapons to end life. The scent of gunpowder was still lingering along with the bite of fresh blood.

She should have settled for making do. It had been a risk, a gamble to pit herself against the darker elements of the Quarter, and only a fool failed to realize the risks that went along with games of chance.

"What's that?"

Kitten waited while someone moved across the floor.

"It's a book, by Heather Graham," one of the men in the room said. She heard him turning pages. "Signed, too."

Kitten gasped.

"So that means something to you?" The Raven asked.

"Yes," Kitten admitted. She swallowed her reluctance because she had to look out for herself. "There was a tourist yesterday, a woman who said she would bring me a signed book."

Time ticked by. Kitten was aware of every second because she knew they might be her last moments in this life.

"Get out and find her," the Raven said. "Stay with her, kill her if she fails."

Kitten knew that would be the price, to do what the Raven wanted, but she still regretted the necessity of what she had to do. Yet she would because life was precious, but it was also unfair.

They all must take their chances.

"Stay close." Saxon had her against his side again. He pulled her closer and tilted his head over so that his lips were an inch from her ear. "This is his territory. He has a very effective network, and you are the only person alive who has seen his face."

"Lucky me."

Ginger shivered. The French Quarter hadn't seemed so large, not until that moment. She felt her eyes widen as she looked at the sheer number of people between her and the safety of the rest of the city. But it was bigger than that. The knowledge of just how much money and reach someone like Marc Grog had was amazing. His son Pulse ran the music empire that came complete with private jet. As a dead man, Grog could kill her and never be suspected, because the world believed him dead.

She was going to die.

It hit her like a concrete brick in the center of her chest. She struggled to draw in her next breath. Saxon shifted beside her, the hold he had on her hand the most comforting thing she'd ever felt.

"I'll get you through this."

He stunned her again because there was kindness in his tone. The sort that she could have cheerfully crawled inside of at that moment because she believed he had the ability to shelter her.

"I'm good," she offered, amazed at how steady her voice was. Actually, it was just a touch husky, betraying how much she liked the guy.

*Beggars couldn't be choosers . . .*

At the moment, he was all she had, and inappropriate thoughts beat panicked chicken. Blushing wouldn't kill her. Besides, he'd never know just what she was thinking.

"Keep your eyes moving. If you see someone you recognize, let me know," Saxon instructed her.

"What's the plan?" She asked as she started looking at the crowd around them, trying to see faces instead of just a mass of people. Trying to be just as cool and collected as he was.

"We're going to hide in plain sight until I can get you out of here. My team needs to gather resources for an extraction."

"I have a room at the Marriott," she offered. "It's only a couple of blocks . . ."

Saxon was laughing before she finished. It was a crusty chuckle that made her feel about as smart as a block of wood. She decided that learning what she clearly didn't know was more important than getting her panties in a bunch.

"So tell me why that's amusing." She cut him a sidelong look and caught a flash of surprise crossing his face. "So I don't blow it."

"Who did you say you were?" he asked.

"Ginger Boyce." She realized the second man was listening to everything. He tapped her name into his phone as he stayed exactly two inches from her left side.

"Why don't we just call the police?" she questioned him.

"Because a man like the one you just saw has connections," Saxon informed her. He suddenly shifted, turning her around and putting her behind a tree while he looked ahead of him.

"I've got him," the second man said. He went striding off, leaving her all but pressed up against Saxon.

"Who?"

Saxon actually slid his hand over her mouth, silencing her as he watched his friend over the top of her head. "The doorman," he supplied in a tight voice. "He's up there, scanning the crowd. Put your face against my shoulder."

"Ummm . . ."

Saxon made another little frustrated sound in the back of his throat before he cupped her nape and pulled her into contact with him. "There is no personal space in safety."

She snorted in response, but after that she was swept up into a moment of pure bliss. The guy felt as amazing as he looked. She was trembling but not just from the fear. No, as appalling as it might be, she was turned on. In fact, she was pretty sure she'd never been so aware of a man before in her life. Her very skin felt more sensitive, and her nipples had tightened into hard little pebbles. She was mortified, pretty sure he'd notice them poking through the soft jersey of the dress.

"Closer," he instructed her, hovering over her ear as he tilted her neck with the hold he had on it. "When I said the guy had connections, I wasn't kidding. He has people that can tap into every security camera. Hiding in plain sight is our only option until I get confirmation that my team has a plan for getting you out of this city alive."

"All right, just remember, you asked for it," She was having trouble getting her brain to function. She shifted and fit her body against his, settling her hands on his chest and slipping one up to his shoulder as she let their legs mingle in something that was purely intimate.

She felt him stiffen and it blew her confidence to hell. For all she knew, he had a wife. Ginger pulled back.

"You were doing just fine." His voice was filtering through her hair, unleashing a ripple of delight that traveled across her skin. "Don't move."

Ginger bit her lip to keep from making a little sound of contentment.

*She was so going to hell.*

Time was kind enough to slow down again. It allowed her to soak up the feeling of being held by him. Pathetic? Maybe. But she wasn't going to be so foolish as to not enjoy the moment when there appeared to be people trying to make it her last among the living.

"Bram got him, let's move." Saxon said softly before he turned her around effortlessly and had them both heading down Bourbon Street while she was struggling to get her head back in the game.

*Right. Keep your eyes open.*

Ginger scanned the people, looking past the ones who were obviously from conventions and taking in the French Quarter. She looked up at the balconies with their unique iron work. Ginger sucked her breath in and turned around.

"What is it?"

She ran right into Saxon because he stepped to the side so he could look over her shoulder. She sort of expected him to rock back on his heels because she hit him so hard but he took the impact, remaining steady.

"Ginger?" he pressed her for an explanation.

"The balcony . . ." She was fighting off panic. They were in the middle of the street but completely exposed to anyone on the balconies. This wasn't spicy, it was lunacy. She needed to escape, felt the need overriding every other thought but Saxon held her in place.

"Don't move," he warned. "It will tip them off. Details. Tell me now."

Ginger gulped down a breath and soaked up his composure to feed her own. "The woman, her name is Kitten, I was going to see her—"

"She knows what you look like?" Saxon's voice had taken on a hard edge.

"Yes. She's—"

"I see her," Saxon said in a clipped tone. "Follow my lead."

He somehow had hold of her hand and in the next moment, he was turning her under his arm. She spun around like they were on a dance floor.

"Smile." He insisted as he slid his arm down her back and settled it there with his hand on her hip and guided her toward the sidewalk like they were a honeymooning couple.

"Head on my shoulder, hide your face."

She responded instantly because he was using that no-argument tone of his. Confidence radiated from him, and she needed to soak it up because it was the only defense she had against the panic trying to sweep her into mindless reactions.

Saxon kept her going and didn't stop until they were next to another man.

"He's a friend," Saxon said when she tensed up, recoiling from how close Saxon wanted to put her to the new arrival.

"Kitten is on the balcony, knows our target's face."

The man nodded and pulled a hat off his head. It actually turned out to be two hats, a smaller one inside the larger. He dropped the smaller one onto her head and handed the second one to Saxon.

"Bram is getting transportation. I'll deal with the cat."

He was gone a moment later, threading his way through the crowd of dancing and drinking people.

Ginger bit back the question she wanted to ask. Honestly, she wasn't in a position to quibble over Saxon's methods. Kitten was looking for her. The sting of betrayal spread through her as she was guided beneath where the stripper was standing.

*You don't know her . . .*

Karen would have a lecture and a half for her once she heard the story of Ginger's adventures in the French Quarter.

There was a ding, and Saxon pulled his phone out. "We've got a ride out of here, just a little further."

Ginger enjoyed the flare of hope that went through her.

"Let's just hope you don't get dropped by a sniper before we get to the car."

He said it under his breath like an afterthought, which gave the words more punch when they landed. She felt like the breath was knocked clean out of her. The reality of her circumstances was too horrible to make it through her brain. Things like hoping snipers didn't get her just didn't happen in real life.

Not hers anyway.

The way Saxon was gripping her arm confirmed he thought it was a real possibility. Her heart was back to hammering, her lips parting as she took little, panting breaths. Sweat was trickling down her sides, making the dress itchy.

"Don't lose it now," Saxon admonished her.

"I'm rather motivated not to," she answered back. For a second, she thought she caught a twitch of his lips that might have been a smile. They'd passed the boutique and were getting close to the hotel. Each step felt like it took a really long time, while the sidewalk looked as if it were stretching. She was straining, listening for the sound of a bullet, which was ridiculous but none the less true. She was caught between the world she'd been living in just an hour before and the one she suddenly found herself trying to survive now.

It was surreal and terrifying all at the same time, a psychedelic mixture that was spinning her thoughts around and around like an out-of-control merry-go-round.

She saw the drive-up entrance of the hotel. It was full of taxis and cars with people loading luggage.

Saxon turned her down an alleyway before they made it to the entrance of the garage.

"What—" She only got out part of her question before she saw the car. Dare was there, climbing out as they came into view. He kept his attention behind her and Ginger turned, her jaw dropping open as she noted the silk tie Bram had been wearing was looped through her teeth, her hands secured with handcuffs behind her.

"She's got a tail, we need to move," Bram informed them.

Ginger found herself standing alone for the first time since she'd met them. The trunk of the car popped open as Bram came along the side of the car with Kitten.

"Put her in the trunk," Saxon said without remorse. "That should help lose her tail."

Kitten made a muffled sound of protest before Bram leaned over and hooked her knees. He lifted her right off her feet and dumped her into the open trunk. Dare reached in and locked a second pair of handcuffs around her ankles as her eyes bulged with outrage.

"Ah . . ." Ginger struggled with what she was seeing. "You can't treat someone like that."

Saxon grabbed her by her bicep, pulling her around to face him. The expression on his face chilled her blood. There was something in his eyes that spoke of a darker taste of life than she'd ever sampled herself. It was more than words, it felt like a perception that was moving through the air between them, and she wanted to reach out and sooth it away.

*Ha! He'll bite. . .*

Problem was, she sort of liked that idea.

"I mean, she's in custody," Ginger stammered.

"She will stand by while you are killed, and if someone sees her as we pull out of here, we're made."

He bit out each word, holding Ginger prisoner when she wanted to shift back, away from the hard certainty in his eyes. Bram shut the truck with a sound that made Ginger flinch. Saxon was watching her, his lips thinning when he witnessed her reaction. His grip tightened on her, like he was trying to get through to her.

Ginger cast a look at the closed trunk and swallowed her distaste.

"It's her or you. In Kitten's world, that's all she understands. She was looking for you and there is only one reason why she would have been up on that balcony. If she'd seen you first, you'd be dead on the pavement."

He made horrible sense, and still the sound of Kitten kicking the top of the closed trunk was too much for Ginger to ignore.

"I understand," Ginger forced herself to say. She didn't accept it, just couldn't seem to make it all sink into her brain because, honestly, it was like a foreign language. Just a hundred feet away, she could hear the doorman shouting for a taxi, heard the conversation of excited people getting ready to embark on their New Orleans adventure and somehow, in a grotesque twist of fate, what had just an hour before been a source of excitement, was now a den of vipers waiting to snuff out her life.

"I do." She repeated as she realized Saxon was contemplating her with a critical eye.

Saxon made a short sound under his breath before he was moving her along the side of the car to the back door. Dare pulled it open and she was in the backseat with Saxon's help. The guy even put his hand on the top of her head like she'd seen police officers do on television shows. The door slammed shut, giving her a brief moment of privacy to try and gather up the bits of her shattered composure.

*Ha! Like that was going to happen.*

The three men got into the car in a polished motion that made her shiver. She was caught between awe at their relaxed acceptance of the circumstances and horror to discover any human being so at ease under the threat of death. The car was moving as Saxon reached over and grasped her by the back of her neck. He didn't give her an explanation as he pushed her face into the seat.

But honestly, she was pretty sure there weren't enough words in the English language to help her fully understand what had just happened to her. There was only the sense of her mind reeling as Kitten kicked the trunk and Ginger recognized just how similar their circumstances were.


"They have Kitten."

The man who delivered the information was sweating. He looked at the wall, waiting to see if he was going to see his own blood splattered across it.

"And the girl?" The question made him flinch.

"I didn't see her."

"Neither has anyone else," the Raven hissed. "But she saw plenty."

"Maybe it's time to let me do what Carl Davis sent me down here for."

The new voice belonged to Tyler Martin. The doorman knew him or at least of him. Some badge-wielding guy from Washington who rubbed elbows with congressmen and the presidential hopeful Carl Davis. He'd been lying low, waiting on the Raven's good will for the last few weeks.

"I know how to find her," Tyler Martin said in a lazy tone. "And Carl Davis has the resources to put at my disposal to make sure she doesn't slip through our fingers. It might be time to reaffirm your relationship with Davis. Make it worth his time for me to clean up this mess."

"And forget about Pratt?" The Raven asked.

"You could always remember him fondly from a cell on death row," Tyler Martin said. "Or on the run outside the US borders."

"I have people who can find a little woman like that."

Tyler slowly grinned. "Saxon Hale and his team will use her to pull your shell apart." He leaned forward. "That isn't your run-of-the-mill undercover team. It's a Shadow opps, one of the best. Experienced, seasoned, and they have already kicked your ass once with the Ryland girl. I am the only fucking hope you have. Inside of two days they will have her testimony logged in, and then, if you kill her, that will only serve as another nail in your coffin."

Tyler knew the Raven was weighing his options because he was a self-absorbed prick who actually thought he had alternatives. Tyler knew better, and, honestly, would have preferred to sit back and watch the guy fry. But Carl Davis cared because the Raven gave the presidential hopeful a ton of free air time to push his name in the faces of the voters. In the current world of media-addicted consumers, that was worth more than gold. Marc Grog had his hands on the short strings that led straight into the voter's cell phones, media centers, and gaming systems.

Getting on good terms with the underworld boss was critical to Tyler's future with Carl Davis.

"Tell Davis if he plugs this leak, I'm onboard with him. Just don't forget Kitten. She knows too much," the Raven said.

Tyler pulled his phone out and dialed Carl as the Raven left the room.

"I was hoping to hear from you sooner."

Presidential hopeful and leader in the polls Carl Davis always had a smile on his lips and in his tone, but Tyler Martin heard something else. The unmistakable ring of a warning.

"Better a little more time that allows for me to make sure the situation is the right one," Tyler answered. "I've got him over a barrel now."

"I hope so," Carl spoke slowly. "What do you have to tell me?"

"A witness got a good look at the Raven pulling the trigger and Saxon Hale managed to extract her while she was still breathing."

"Fuck," Carl exclaimed. "He's screwed without us." There was a low chuckle on the other end of the line. "Perfect Martin. That is exactly what I needed you to have to hold over that bastard for me."

"I'll have to move fast. Hale is no inexperienced kid."

"No, he isn't." Carl's tone took on a hard edge. "I'm counting on you to make sure he doesn't get the jump on me the way his brother did with Jeb Ryland."

"I need a few resources that the slush fund can't help me with," Tyler continued. "I need a badge and a team of scene investigators. Full access to the Shadow opps network."

"What?" Carl's smile had evaporated. "That would lead them straight back to me if you're not successful."

"What sort of game do you think we're playing here?" Tyler asked softly. "It's kill or be killed. The Shadow opps are effective because of their resources. The only way I will find Hale's team is if I can see what he has to draw from, and let me be clear about one thing; there is no one else who knows how Saxon thinks. I trained him."

When Tyler Martin had been a young man, he'd thought getting a badge with the Shadow opps was all he needed. The problem was, the world wasn't as large as it once had been. The times when a man could serve honorably and retire to his golden years if he was lucky enough to survive his service time were gone. Today's world was run by crime bosses that a wise man made happy if an agent wanted to be more than expendable. Justice and honor were only battle cries from eras long gone.

Carl Davis was another form of a crime boss. Just because he was going to the White House didn't change the fact that he had plenty of dirt on his fingers. He shook hands with those in the underworld because money made the world go around, and in this case, the media would make the difference with the voters.

"I'll have to arrange a new name for you."

"Good. I'll make sure the Raven knows you're expecting the deal to be honored on his end." Tyler told Carl exactly what he knew the man wanted to hear.

"You do that," Carl spoke pointedly. "I will expect his unions to be supporting me as well. Get his people working on campaign bits to flash in front of the viewers. I want my face recognized by every kid old enough to have a cell phone. You tell him that's the deal."

"I will."

"Martin," Carl said. "Don't fuck up."

The line went dead.

Tyler stood for a long moment, hearing the wind for some strange reason. He wasn't a man given to moments of reflection, but it seemed he couldn't quite escape it today.

Yeah. He'd trained Saxon and Vitus Hale. They'd worked cases together, shared personal details. That was back when Martin had still believed in honor, before he'd come face to face with how cheap it was to buy men like Saxon and Vitus.

That was it really. The people at the top of the food chain looked on those serving in the Shadow opps as men who could be purchased with medals and speeches about dedication and valor. And then, they'd go pour themselves drinks that cost more than any of those men might earn in a week. While that fine liquor was burning a path down their throats, they'd crack jokes about how rich they were and how rules didn't apply to them. Wedding vows? A fucking joke. Tax laws? Not for them. Having their asses hanging out in the wind? Well, that was where men like Saxon and Vitus came in, they took the bullet, bled out, left their families behind, and for what? For men who didn't value them and sure as shit didn't play by the same rules.

So Martin had jumped the fence. Plenty of his fellow agents would call him a turncoat. He looked at it as being a man who refused to get less than he was worth. If he was going to be someone's dog, he was going to be kept in style, not tossed bones called valor and honor. Saxon Hale was one of those who enjoyed gnawing on that Honor scrap.

Good.

It would make it easier to kill him.

Tyler heard the wind again.

Okay, maybe "easy" wasn't the right word, but he wasn't going to deliberate on the topic. He'd made his choice by selling out Saxon to begin with, so there was only one way to go.

Forward.

Right through Saxon Hale.

# CHAPTER TWO

"Doing okay?"

"Sure. Fine." For some reason, her tongue felt like it was swollen and clumsy.

Saxon wasn't impressed with her answer. He crossed his arms over his chest and considered her. The assessment made her bristle because she knew she looked like hell. Still, she finished drying off her hands and turned her back on the bathroom sink she'd just used to rinse out her mouth after throwing up the second she stepped out of the car. Getting sick under those circumstances wasn't something to be ashamed of.

But it didn't help that Saxon looked so damned in control while she was fighting to maintain hers.

"Really. Steady as a rock." Ginger fought the urge to brush her hair back. It was just a nervous gesture. She knew she looked fine. "Okay, steady as a rock during an earthquake, but everything does settle down in the end."

He snorted at her, his lips curving. "That's a wicked sense of humor you have there." His lips settled back into a hard line. "Might just serve you well under the circumstances."

It was a compliment, one her pride eagerly soaked up. They'd stopped at a small house where she'd lost her lunch into the bushes before Saxon had hauled her inside. One of his men had muscled Kitten up the cracked concrete path behind her.

"What are you?" She asked, more than a little desperate to make sense of the last two hours. She didn't recall falling down a rabbit hole, but it sure felt like she'd left reality.

"Special Agent," he answered.

And that seemed to be the extent of his explanation so she waited to see what else he wanted. His eyes glittered with questions.

"How did you get past that doorman?"

His tone was all business. It made it really easy to believe he was a Special Agent because the guy sure had an interrogation mode. She was caught in it like a tracker beam in a science fiction show, and his eyes narrowed when she didn't answer instantly.

"We can do this the easy way or the hard way, Ms. Boyce. Kitten is getting the hard way. I don't recommend it."

"A book." She was smarting at just how quickly she'd jumped to answer him but hell, he was intimidating and to be blunt, she totally fucking believed him. One of his eyebrows rose when she didn't offer anything else.

"Details," he prompted.

She drew in a deep breath and reminded herself that he'd kept her from getting killed. Seemed rather reasonable that he'd want to know the details. But she did take the time to step out of the bathroom and into the bedroom so she had a little more space to put between them. The guy sort of fried her thinking process. Saxon made a motion with his hand for her to start talking.

"Yesterday, I met Kitten—"

"Where?" he interrupted her.

"One of the bars on Bourbon Street." He remained silent. "So, anyway, she asked what I was doing in town and I told her."

"Told her what?" he pressed for details.

"That I was here for a librarian convention, but that's not why I went back to see her." Ginger held up a finger so he'd let her finish. "You should let me finish or this is going to take forever. We can do a question and answer at the end."

He grunted but it gave her a bit of a buzz to see that she had the power to set him on his heel. At least in the short term anyway.

*Right, you're delusional. The guy had a woman put in the trunk of the car. He's probably thinking about making you Kitten's roomie to teach you who's boss . . .*

*Maybe, she still wasn't repentant.*

"Ms. Boyce?" he pressed her.

She blinked and recovered her train of thought. " I told Kitten I was going to a book signing today, because she asked if I was going to have any fun while I was in town. The conference was business but the book signing was for me."

His eyes were narrowing. "I'm not following on how you ended up getting past a doorman and into a private party with an underworld crime boss."

Ginger sent him a smile and shrugged, "If it wasn't for bad luck, I wouldn't have any luck at all?"

He made a scoffing sound under his breath. "That's not funny."

"It is a little bit funny," she argued.

His eyebrows rose, making her choke back a round of giggles. Honestly, she shouldn't mess with him but he looked like he needed a good laugh. That thought sobered her because he really did deal with bad guys a lot, and she should be more focused on the fact that he was helping her stay alive.

"Kitten wanted a book, too." Ginger told him in way of apology. "One signed by Heather Graham. I got it for her and I was taking it back to her. I told the doorman she was expecting me and . . . he let me through."

She'd stunned him. For a moment, Saxon Hale, who had been a pillar of composure and trained precision, looked at her with his jaw open. The sight gave her a much-needed shot of confidence, helping to restore her balance. At least she wasn't the only one being kicked in the nuts by the turn of events transpiring around her.

"Where. . . ." he actually stumbled over his words. "Is the book?"

"Umm . . ." She looked down at the cross-body bag. The side pocket was only about five inches deep and it was empty now. "I guess it fell out."

Saxon had recovered his poise, his expression hardening as she gained a glimpse of what was likely his game face. It actually made her step back, the focus and intent chilling her blood. To be fair, she didn't doubt that he needed to be just as hard and cold as the men he was trying to capture, but she didn't care to be in the path of it. He'd said " crime boss" which sounded pretty intense. His eyes narrowed.

"The men in the room, you saw them?"

He was intent on her now, his blue eyes full of purpose. Ginger didn't want to answer. Her insides felt like they were twisting, and she felt that fate was about to drop-kick her in a major way if she gave Saxon the information he wanted.

"I can't protect you if I don't know who might be looking for you."

His tone was too knowledgeable. She cringed but leveled her chin. "Yes. It was Marc Grog and his son, Pulse, the music artist. Marc was the one who pulled the trigger."

And her mind offered up a perfect memory of it, too. But she resisted the pull of that recollection.

"Marc Grog is dead."

"I know," she answered. "But I'm telling you, that's who was in that room being called 'the Raven.' The dead guy called him the Raven, right before Marc shot him."

"The guy looked like Marc Grog." Saxon asked her.

Ginger shook her head. "I know faces. That's what I do for a living, find people through blurry snapshots. It was Marc Grog. In fact, now that I'm thinking straight, he died right before a hearing was set to launch an investigation into his dealings with Conrad Mosston over that leak of military information." She was thinking out loud but knew her facts. "Marc had a scar on his neck from a failed knife attack and that man I saw today had the same scar." She pointed to her throat. "Details. It's all in the details."

Saxon's jaw had tightened. She could see that he was recalling the case now, and the word he bit back looked a lot like "fuck."

"Thank you for getting me out of there." She dug her cell phone out, intent on calling Karen and being finished with the whole affair. It was certainly going to be far more enjoyable as a memory than a current circumstance.

Saxon plucked her phone from her fingers and killed the call.

"Excuse me?" she wished she sounded more confident than she did. "My roommate is going to be worried about me."

"She should be." Saxon confirmed in a deep tone that threatened what little composure she had left. "You're in a lot of trouble."

Her heart was starting to pound again. "Well, I'm sure the police can handle things."

"Don't be." He cut through her stammering with deadly precision. "Marc Grog, if he really is still alive, has more of them on his side than not."

She drew in a stiff breath, unwilling to be reduced to hopelessness. "Stop trying to scare me. I didn't do anything wrong or illegal. I was just trying to deliver a book. Now if you don't mind, I am going to check in with my friend."

Saxon crossed his arms over his chest, her cell phone tucked into the breast pocket of his suit jacket. She looked at it longingly and it didn't escape his notice. He moved faster than a normal person. One moment she was looking at that pocket and the next she was jumping back because he'd reached out and caught the little latch that held her cross-bodybag strap to the bag. It slithered off her when she recoiled and ended up in his possession as well.

"You're under arrest," he informed her far too casually for her comfort. The guy oozed control while she was left feeling like she was twisting in the wind.

"For what?" She demanded.

"I'm placing you in protective custody," he said, his tone informing her that he was dammed sure of himself.

"Like hell you are."

All she gained for her outburst was a raised eyebrow and a very confident smirk. He was so not impressed with her.

"Stay in here. Test me and I'll put you in cuffs." He reached for the door and opened it.

"I thought you were going to shove me in the trunk."

She'd lost it now and didn't really care if her behavior was base. He was being a dick, and she wasn't going to take it.

"That can happen, too. Be a good girl and I won't be tempted." A gleam entered his eyes and convinced her he'd enjoy it.

He pulled the door shut, and her growl of frustration ended up bouncing off its surface.

*Dick . . .*

Bram and Dare were waiting for him. That should have been enough to get him moving, but Saxon discovered himself hesitating. His witness was pissed at him. As in capitol P-I-S-S-E-D. It was hardly the first time someone hated his guts for being put into custody, but, damn it, it was the first time he found someone so adorable with her ire up. That little librarian wholesomeness shell cracked to expose a fireball like she'd spent most of her time in the erotic romance section.

A wave of heat rolled slowly through him in response to that idea. Hell, he should be ashamed of himself, but the truth was that he was downright fascinated by the idea of her reading a steamy novel as the rest of the world viewed her as straightlaced.

He needed to check himself. Fast.

Her face had been red as she paced around the room. Damned if he didn't enjoy the way she moved. She took him into territory he wasn't going to go to. She was cute and had a body that stirred more than fascination in him, which was why he left the room and moved toward his men. Focusing on the case would sterilize his emotions, allowing him to get back down to business. Ms. Ginger Boyce was helping to crack his case. That was what he needed to dwell on.

Not how damned cute her ass was.

"A fucking book?" Dare Servant said the moment Saxon was close enough to hear. "I've been chasing the Raven for months and she gets through his security net with a fucking book?"

"It wouldn't have worked for you." Bram Magnus replied with a twist of his lips. "You don't have the legs for it."

Dare grunted, his fingers opening and closing like he was fighting back the urge to flip his fellow agent off.

"Marc Grog is a mighty big fish. If it's really him, sure explains a lot about how the Raven has been able to operate under the radar." Bram voiced what was on all their minds. "He'll squish her like a little ladybug that made the mistake of landing on the windshield of his Ferrari for blowing his cover."

"Not on my watch," Saxon answered. He wasn't a stranger to dedication but he felt something tighten inside him, something more intense than normal. It gave him a moment of pause, thinking about whether or not it was a good idea to continue on the case. But that thought only led him to a wave of rejection that swept aside all of his misgivings.

He wasn't going anywhere. Ms. Ginger Boyce would just have to get used to him.

"I'll touch base with Kagan. Get background on her and Kitten. See if she really saw what she thinks she did."

His section leader was going to like having an identification on the Raven and an eyewitness to murder at long last, but Saxon knew without a doubt that Kagan would also see the information as the volatile substance it was. There were going to be a lot of people, important ones, who wouldn't want Marc Grog to go down in flames because a fire like that was going to spread to his close business partners.

"We've got to get her into a facility for certified testimony, asap." Bram said. "There were a few political families who wouldn't want Marc Grog back from the dead."

"I know." Saxon answered.

It was a mess, a fucking big one. Ginger was sitting on the pressure plate of it all. One wrong move and it was going to explode. His insides clenched in response. She wasn't the first innocent he'd encountered, not by a long shot, but damn it, she was the kind of woman he would work hard for, to make sure she could go on with a normal life. He didn't want to see her rolling with the punches, didn't want to watch her disillusionment.

He just didn't have a choice today.

Kagan answered on the second ring, making a low sound under his breath as Saxon dropped Marc Grog's name. There was a moment when all Saxon heard was the soft tapping of his section leader's fingers on a keyboard.

"My witness needs to testify immediately."

"If not sooner," Kagan said, confirming just how dire the situation was.

"I need someone to take the stripper."

"Has the stripper seen his face?"

"She's not talking," Saxon informed Kagan. "And I've got my hands full with the witness."

"You do. Marc Grog complicates the case in ways I haven't finished adding up."

Saxon heard the warning in his boss's tone. He stiffened his resolve. "I didn't come down here to quit when the case got challenging. I knew what I was taking on."

Kagan drew in a deep breath. "You know what you're biting off, true enough. Any sign of Tyler Martin?"

"No," Saxon admitted. "How soon can you get me an evac plan?"

"Our first living eyewitness," Kagan answered. There

was the sound of typing again. "It's a sure bet the airport is being watched better now since you managed to get Damascus Ryland out under the Raven's nose."

"Why do you think I'm here?" Saxon said with a fair amount of sarcasm. "I'd already have her in the air if I didn't think it would mean there would be a wet-work team waiting for us when we landed because our flight plan got hacked."

Kagan made a soft whistling sound. Saxon recognized it as his boss's method of debating an issue. "I'm going to have to call in a favor because I can't go through official channels on this one. Sit tight."

The line went dead. Saxon drew in a deep breath before turning back to his team. Dare and Bram faced him with every bit of courage and determination he expected, but there was something else—a glimmer of hope that none of them had felt that morning. It was the stuff they lived on when cases remained cold for months on end. A break that helped them all remember why they dug in and persevered against what were so often insurmountable odds.

Sometimes, the good guys won.

Now he had a witness, that thing teams like his worked damned hard to pull in. The tricky part was going to be keeping her alive.

"I'm taking first position," Saxon informed them as he started toward the bedroom.

Hard, wasn't impossible.

Not on his watch.

*Good Girl . . .*

Those two words were bouncing around inside her skull, rubbing her temper when the bedroom door opened. Saxon Hale came right in without a word.

*There is no personal space in safety . . .*

Those words didn't make her as mad. No, quite the op-posite. They were forcing her to look at the sharp teeth of her circumstances.

"We're in a holding pattern," he informed her. "Better grab some rest while you can."

Saxon pulled a chair from where it was sitting at a desk and dropped it right next to the bed. It was against the wall, with the door and the windows in clear sight. He'd taken off his jacket, giving her a look at the shoul-der harness strapped around his chest.

"You really want to take the chance to sleep," he ad-vised her when she didn't move.

Maybe she should, but there was sort of no way in hell she could make her feet budge. Somehow, the carpet had a death grip on them as she stared at Saxon settling into the chair, clearly there to protect her. A scent of fresh cof-fee teased her nose as one of the other men came through the bedroom door with a mug.

"Captain Bram Magnus." Saxon pointed at the man and offered the introduction.

Bram handed over the coffee and turned to give her a nod.

"I could go for some of that," the words were sort of past her lips before she really thought about it. But it was some-thing to do. Ginger started for the door, intent on escaping.

Bram stepped right into her path. "I'll get it."

"You don't need to wait on me," Ginger replied, but she should have saved her breath because he was gone before she finished speaking.

"We're controlling your location," Saxon said. She turned and watched him set the mug down. For a second, he looked like he was finished with his explanation. The clueless look on her face made him open his mouth again. "You'll get used to it."

"I sure hope not." Ginger sank down on the bed, but she perched on the side away from Saxon and then realized it was because his persona was just so big.

Bram came back but what he handed her was a cup of tea, herbal.

"You don't need the caffeine," he offered before he left the room.

Which left Ginger with no one to glare at except Saxon. He offered her no sympathy, just a sort of bored expression that told her he'd done this before and she was the one who would be adjusting to the circumstances.

*Great . . .*

Ginger looked back down at the mug and realized just how many pieces her life was smashed into. On one hand, it was sort of good to realize how much she had. Friends to check up on via social media. Hell, her family's incessant text messaging was suddenly so dear, she felt tears actually prickling her eyes because she was cut off from it now.

Man, she'd been taking things for granted. Sure, she'd enjoyed her life, but she hadn't really been as thankful as she should have been for all the little things it was full of. Like the ability to choose her beverage or bedtime.

Or anything.

He hated witness detail.

The damned chair felt like it was burning him as Saxon tried not to stare at Ginger. She was looking at the tea, clearly feeling the weight of her circumstances. He was doing what needed to be done, and she hated it. Maybe not him, but the situation nonetheless.

*Fuck.*

He couldn't ease her transition. Didn't dare, because that would take them both someplace she didn't need to go. He'd seen it too many times to count, the way a witness formed an attachment to her team. She'd think it was love, because it was the best way to make her world stop spinning.

He'd know it was just taking advantage of her on the worst day of her life.

He had to be better than that.


"Can you give me more details, Sir?"

Tyler shook his head. He was watching his new team poring over surveillance footage from the local airfields. It was slow, tedious work, and they were coming up dry.

Good.

Tyler looked at the team Carl Davis had delivered. In two short hours, he'd been inserted into the Secret Service ranks and had a team assigned to him. They didn't know the details, but to the Secret Service, it didn't matter. They were men who believed in justice and thought they were defending the United States with their tight-lipped dedication.

Tyler intended to let them keep their illusions. For the moment, it supported his cause and in the end, it would keep Carl Davis on his path to the White House. Just not in the way any of the men in the room suspected.

Tyler started combing through the resource list, looking for the type of rabbit hole Saxon would select. Shadow opps teams liked to use houses recently vacated by deaths that had left property vacant while wills went through probate. Hotels had security cameras that might be hacked into. Shadow opps teams would stick to residential homes and townhouses where they could bunker down until their section leaders had time to move more resources into position.

One caught his eye. It was a listing for a traffic fatality. Two victims, recently moved into the area to take a job. That meant no family to be combing through their belongings just yet. Not when the bodies were still at the morgue and unclaimed.

It wasn't much to go on, but Tyler had a gut feeling, one he wasn't going to ignore. It was a perfect place to go to ground while calling in to a section leader and getting orders.

"Let's go."

The team of Secret Service personel didn't hesitate. They closed up their computer cases and filed out of the makeshift command center they'd set up within moments of their arrival. Tyler enjoyed being in command again. He strode out among their ranks, slipping into the role of superior once again.

He was going to enjoy being in charge of Carl Davis. The man understood it took a team to get into the White House and that there wouldn't be any forgetting that fact once he was sworn into office. Carl Davis would share the meat and Tyler was planning on getting the lion's share of it.

Of course it wouldn't come free. Nothing worth having ever did. Tyler slipped his shades on, tightening his resolve because loose ends needed tying up, and it was his task to see it done.

But if Saxon Hale was involved, well, that was going to be a perk because Carl Davis had a personal score to settle with the Hale brothers. It would be Tyler's pleasure to help him achieve that goal.

It was sure worth something important, and Tyler never worked for free.

Okay, point for Bram Magnus, Ginger didn't need caffeine.

Nope. Her thoughts were churning like a river with Class V rapids. At some point, she'd decided that maybe lying down would make her feel less awkward, but that had failed miserably. All it did was make her think he was noticing her butt.

*In your dreams . . .*

Yeah, well, those sorts of mental fascinations needed to go. There was no way she was going to add slobbering over him to her list of things to deal with. The only problem was now, with the aid of her newly established cold-turkey-break from social media, she had lots of time to dwell on Saxon Hale.

Lord knew the guy had details to enjoy lingering on.

*Thought you were going to stop thinking about him?* Good advice.

Something she'd always had a challenge with following.

Ginger had rolled onto her side, facing away from Saxon in some attempt to maintain her private space. She had the room memorized now. There were a couple of books on the bottom of the bedside table. On impulse, she stretched down to reach one. It required her to lean far over the edge of the bed, her head off the side of it because she hadn't bothered to sit up.

But as she hooked one, drawing it toward her, there was a whiz and a soft sound of something hitting her pillow. A second later, Saxon came across the bed, slamming into her and shoving her onto the floor.

He pressed her into the carpet before he was levering himself up and returning fire. This time, her brain didn't freeze. It identified the soft sounds as gunfire as she flattened her hands on the ground and shoved herself back, toward the door.

*You've got to help yourself, Ginger!*

The absolute truth of that thought pushed her into action. She had to do something to help.

"They've got heat sensing goggles." Saxon growled as he came toward her and pulled her farther into the house.

The popping sounds followed them as Bram and Dare came into sight. Both agents were holding their guns at eye level as they lined up the sights.

She flattened herself against the wall as Saxon shoved her back with his body. There was a pop, and he instantly targeted the location, squeezing off two rounds from his gun.

Her heart took to accelerating again, like she was too chicken to deal with things. Ginger drew in a deep breath and ordered herself to get control. There was a sound of muffled pain before she heard Kitten's voice coming down the hallway.

"You can't leave me here to get shot!"

Bram cussed before he moved out of sight, Dare watching him and following a moment later.

"Kitchen." Saxon gave her the single-word command.

"Right." She slid across the wall and around a corner. The blinds were closed tight in what would have normally been a cheery little breakfast nook.

Now, it looked more like a potential deathtrap.

*Heat seeking . . .*

Saxon's words burst in her brain as she took in the cast-iron skillet sitting on the range.

"Fire," she said.

"What?" Saxon demanded as he turned to look at her.

"I'm going to start a fire."

He grasped her meaning instantly. "Do it."

She fumbled across the short space and turned the gas range knob to the light position. It popped as the lighter engaged and it burst into a blue flame. She shoved a roll of paper towels into it as Saxon pulled her down to the floor.

There was a pop and the paper towels went flying across the counter to land on the table, one end of it burning.

"Evac now!" Saxon yelled.

The breakfast nook windows were shattering as Saxon pulled her though the living room. They dove into the attached garage and went across the rough concrete. The soles of her feet were shredding, but she ignored the pain in favor of making a dash for freedom. Her lungs were burning as she demanded more from her body, more speed, more strength, just more . . . life.

She gained a glimpse of a car's headlights right before she was shoved into the backseat by Saxon.

The breath was knocked clean out of her, but that didn't stop her from clawing her way across the backseat.

"Get in if you want to live."

Ginger heard Dare growling at Kitten as she made a sound of protest before the agent shoved her into the trunk and followed her, yanking it closed. There was a pounding sound from behind the backseat that seemed to tell Bram Magnus to drive.

The captain took off with a peel of rubber.

Ginger went tumbling into the door, because she had stopped to take time to draw in some deep breaths. Saxon caught her arm, preventing her from getting a nasty bash on the side of her head when Bram went through the intersection on two wheels and turned them down an alleyway. The second change in direction sent her smacking into Saxon.

He absorbed the impact, clamping his arms around her and driving home just how hard his body was. Bram wasn't finished yet. He drove the car like a jeep in a war movie, heading right up and over the sidewalk at times before he finally decided that they weren't being tailed and slid into traffic.

Saxon held her the entire time. Or maybe it was more fair to say that she clung to him. When he did unlock his arms, she felt a flicker of heat teasing her cheeks because of just how hard she'd been holding onto him.

"Thanks," she managed to say, hoping it sounded mundane as opposed to personal. A look into his blue eyes gave a brief moment of her catching the guy off guard before he slid his professional mask into place.

"Still think it's funny?" he asked.

He hadn't quite shifted back into his business mode. There was something flickering in his eyes that betrayed his enjoyment of managing to escape.

"Beats throwing a pity party." The words just came out of the part of her that had seen her striding off into the French Quarter seeking adventure.

Honestly, it was a big fucking relief to feel that little thump of happiness inside her. Maybe she didn't need to get a tattoo that said "pathetic" across her forehead after all. She'd surprised Saxon Hale. Ginger watched the flare of approval fill his blue eyes while his lips curved into a grin that transformed his face into something that was drop-dead gorgeous.

That was what she needed to latch onto.

It renewed her grip on life, filling her with a confidence that made the bruises worth it all.

"Some folks might agree with you, Ms. Boyce."

His tone had a husky edge to it, telling her he was exactly that sort of man. He shifted his attention away from her, leaving her grinning like she'd won some personal victory.

Maybe she had.

At least she was no longer a panicked chicken or nursing loneliness like a kitten sitting in the gutter. Sure, there were a hell of a lot of unknowns still circling her like buzzards, but she'd chuck as many rocks at them as she could.

Because there was no way they would feast on her until she was dead.

"You're kidding me." The local police officer who had responded to the 911 call didn't seem very impressed when Tyler flashed his badge.

"What does the Secret Service have to do with this?" the cop asked. "I guess you guys don't have to fill out a multi-page report for every bullet you squeeze off like my guys do."

The police captain jerked his head toward the house behind him. His men had already started tagging the bullets and holes with little yellow markers that the members of the Secret Service were just as quickly removing.

Tyler Martin tucked the badge into his pocket. "Special Agent Herbert. We weren't here." He looked past the police officer at one of the Secret Service. "Sterilize the scene."

"Now just a damn minute," the lead officer began. "A neighbor reported the gunfire, that's not going away."

"It will," Tyler replied.

There was a squawk from across the way as one of the dark-suited men broke a cell phone in half and the resident protested. The man wasn't intimidated in the least. He finished grinding the phone beneath his polished shoe heel and flashed his badge in the person's face, all while rattling off a perfectly memorized legal threat of what would happen if they talked about what had happened. Two other black-suited men emerged from the house with several other mobile media devices in hand. The home owner was so enraged, his face was beet red and he bent over to brace his hands on his knees as he labored to pull in breath. One of the bored paramedics standing around made his way over to the guy.

The team of tight-faced Secret Service was waiting, standing behind Tyler as they watched in complete silence.

"Dust for prints on the door handles." Tyler ordered.

There was immediate action. The cops watched as evidence kits were opened and print dusting began.

"Thank you," Herbert said. "We'll take it from here. Take traffic control."

The cop growled but hiked back across the lawn to his patrol car, his men following. They were chewing on questions they knew they'd never get any answers to. The Secret Service had the privilege of rank over them. Which was exactly what Tyler had asked Davis for.

He looked at the badge, wincing at the name. Walter Herbert. Carl Davis had a twisted sense of humor, but the man did know how to come through. Tyler watched the team, waiting for results. He went back inside the house, standing in the front room as one of the members worked on a laptop.

"I have prints belonging to a Miss Ginger Melody Boyce," he informed Tyler. "But they are only on file because she works for the public social services. Research department attached to child welfare. Official classification is librarian."

"Young lady is a long way from home," Tyler observed.

"She was here," the agent answered. "Lifted prints off the bedroom door as well as the kitchen."

"Nothing else?" Tyler inquired.

The man shook his head.

"Check her bank card and credit cards for local purchases," Tyler ordered. Now that they had her name, he could start to put the squeeze on her.

The agent typed away at the keyboard, tapping on the side of the case the laptop was mounted in when he finished and waited for a response. The world was harder to hide in with its network of computers. It was a fact Tyler Martin knew well and one of the reasons he'd signed on as now-deceased Congressman Jeb Ryland. Men he'd put away would find him and send their partners after him. Crime was more organized in the modern era.

"She's registered for a convention at the Hyatt on Bourbon Street in the French Quarter. Last purchase was at a clothing shop this evening."

"Picture?" Tyler leaned over the guy's shoulder, looking at the information on the screen. Ms. Ginger Melody Boyce looked back at him, her public identification photo showing him a conservative-looking woman.

*Got you.*

He soaked up the details on display, focusing on the fact that he'd found her instead of how innocent she was. She lived in a place called Cattle Creek? Christ, she really was a mouse. Tyler actually felt a touch of reluctance to deal with her, but he needed to focus. If he were smart, he'd look at the reality of the fact that wiping her pathetic life off the face of the planet wasn't going to be very hard.

"Load up."

It took only moments for the team to climb into their black SUV. They pulled away from the curb while Tyler was deciding where to go. Tension was knotted in his gut because Saxon might not have seen him, but that in no way meant he wouldn't know who was on his tail.

"Do a search of other homes in probate inside a sixty-mile radius." Tyler heard the laptop case open. "And find me any private airstrips."

Saxon would want to move her fast. He wasn't a fool when it came to the reach that Tyler had when backed by Carl Davis. Tyler looked at the screen of the laptop as private air strips popped up. "That one. Lakefront."

The driver drove across three lanes to make a U-turn. Tyler tightened his resolve. He needed to get Saxon now because he knew just how good the man was.

Saxon had been his prized apprentice.

Saxon's phone rang. He took his hand off her neck to answer it. Ginger turned her head, gaining an interesting view of the man as he put the phone to his ear.

"Right, we're en route now. Had our cover blown at the house. Wipe it from the list."

The way he spoke was so concentrated. She might have admired it if she wasn't so determined to straighten her back and earn that look of admiration from him. Honestly, fatigue was starting to twist her thoughts around, making it easy to long for someone to lean on.

*Don't you dare . . .*

She heard a thump from the trunk that made her let out a little sigh.

"Shouldn't we let your fellow agent out?"

Saxon's gaze cut to her. "No time."

Ginger didn't care for the chill that went down her spine. She cast a look out the window. It was surreal, the way people were passing them. Just normal people going to work, the market, maybe to a movie.

They had it better than they realized.

"Lakefront airport." Saxon was also clearly used to being in command. He sent out his instructions to Bram, and a moment later, she felt the car changing direction. "We have a charter plane at our disposal."

"Where are you taking me?" She asked in an attempt to keep her brain working on something tangible. "I mean, from there?"

"Undecided" was his response.

"Mystery trip," she drawled out before she caught herself. "Sorry, that's an inside family sort of joke."

His lips twitched into a grin, but he squelched the response, his jaw tightening as if the little response infuriated him.

"Don't worry, I plan to get you settled in a place where you can go back to reading all the romance novels you like."

"Oh . . . wow," she mocked him softly. "I've never heard a male making fun of romance books before."

He cut her a look that betrayed how much he enjoyed her taking issue with him.

Ginger scoffed at him. "Careful, I'm the town terror when it comes to setting males like you on their ear."

He offered her a look that informed her how unimpressed he was with her claim.

"If I do my job right, we won't be together long enough."

"Why not?" She asked.

His features tightened like he was trying to hide something. "I don't do witness protection. We're a ground team."

"That makes sense." She nodded as it sunk in, and then she turned to look out of the window because she didn't like how it made her feel. Her musings with him had seemed harmless enough but now she realized that the stability she was feeling was about to have the carpet jerked out from under her feet, all the excitement was just a very pretty coating on what was going to be a bitter pill to swallow.

Okay, she was repentant at long last.

And regret totally sucked just as much as she'd been warned it would.

The entire team was tense.

Ginger felt the tension move through her. It left behind a residue that she really wanted to rid herself of, like oil that clung and drove you near crazy as you tried to wash it off, all the while knowing it had sunk into your pores.

It was unsettling because they had always been so confident. Maybe she didn't know all that much about them, but she was left with one firm conclusion. They didn't mess around and if they were nervous, there was a mighty good reason.

She wanted to cuss again, but "fuck" was getting a little repetitive.

"Let's do this," Saxon said softly. "Check the aircraft."

Bram got out of the car. Ginger started to open the door and earned a snort from Saxon.

"Don't make it too easy for them, Ms. Boyce." He cut her a hard look. "Even Bad Guys need their egos shined. Pop your head up and it will be like shooting fish in a barrel."

"So give me a gun to make it more challenging." She held out her hand. "You strike me as the sort who has a backup weapon."

She gained another flash of surprise from him as he contemplated her.

"You know how to handle a firearm?" he asked dryly.

"Small-town girl," she offered. "My Dad's idea of a

great Sunday afternoon is shooting up the river bed. No empty can is safe."

She heard him chuckle. Oh, it was really low, because he kept it trapped in the back of his throat, but she smiled at him, letting him know she was on to him.

There was a thump from the trunk right behind her and a muffled scream.

"I better get my man out of there."

She didn't get a chance to ask him about a gun again because he opened the door and got out. It left her there looking at a white, private plane sitting about ten feet away. Bram Magnus appeared in the doorway, stooping to avoid hitting his head. He went to descend the steps but didn't walk down them. No, he clasped the rails and jumped, sliding down to the ground in a flash.

Adrenaline Junkie.

They were all that and then some. She knew what it looked like, Cattle Creek might be small but what it had an abundance of was hands-on people.

Bram was in sight again, climbing back up the steps and disappearing into the aircraft. There was a whine as the engines started up. Ginger gained a glimpse of Bram through the small window in the cockpit of the aircraft, a pair of head phones on as he concentrated on preparing for take-off.

Saxon appeared with Kitten. She was untied and ungagged, but he had a firm hold on her arm and a look on his face that promised her a hard landing if he had to take her down. He made eye contact with her, and she felt him making some sort of choice. A second later he handed Kitten off to Dare and motioned Ginger out of the car.

Trust.

Well, maybe that was stretching things a little but, it was better than what Kitten was getting.

Ginger opened the door. Her feet were more cut up than she'd realized because the second she tried to put her weight on them, agony went shooting up her legs. It made her gasp, and she felt sweat pop out on her forehead like she was crossing a floor covered in Legos.

Ginger gritted her teeth and forced herself to remain standing by sheer force of will. She moved away from the car, calling on her reserves of self-control to keep from dancing across the pavement. Saxon didn't miss it thought. He started moving toward her, his stride so damned purposeful, it captivated her. For a moment, time seemed to slow down because he was everything she had never expected to find in a living, breathing man. Maybe she was in shock, but nothing else mattered just then. There was only him and the way she felt pinned in place by his gaze. He had a sense of persona that was gripping, binding her to him by some force that was beyond the physicality's of the tangible world.

Kitten used the moment of inattention to make a break for it. Dare had released her so she might climb the steep stairs up to the passenger section of the plane. She turned, lifted her knees, and kicked him right in the chest. The agent went sailing backward as Kitten took off with amazing speed. Saxon turned and shouted at her.

Dare flipped over almost in the same moment as he hit the ground. It was impressive on a scale she'd never seen, declaring a level of physical fitness she'd rarely witnessed. Dare was after Kitten in a flash.

As Kitten ran, a black SUV pulled around the hangar, its doors opening before the tires were finished squealing. The driver turned to intercept Kitten, making her skid to a halt as the vehicle came at her. She was panting and looking around wildly as the men came toward her. Ginger felt her heart stop as Kitten smiled, a genuine expression of relief. She went toward one of the men, her expression telling Ginger that she trusted him.

It was a fatal error.

The man reached out and cupped the sides of her jaw. He gave a hard wrenching motion, and Ginger cried out as she watched Kitten's head twist at a grotesque angle. Her face was frozen in that welcoming expression but her eyes widened with the knowledge of betrayal. It was her last thought before her life was snuffed out and she went limp like a bag full of potatoes, slumping to the ground under her own weight as the man stepped over her, reaching beneath his jacket.

A gun went off next to her. Ginger recoiled in horror as the insides of her nose were singed by the gunpowder, and she actually tasted it while the sound rang in her ears and deafened her.

There was instant reaction to the gunshot. The men scrambled for cover as Saxon pulled the trigger again. Ginger turned to look at him. If she'd held any illusions, they fell to the ground in tiny shards as she gained a glimpse of him. His jaw was set, his expression one of determination, but that wasn't what sent the shiver down her spine.

He was a dammed fine sight under the circumstances. The confidence in his expression like water in the dessert.

Kitten was lying on the ground, a twisted reminder of just how dead she was. Saxon shoved Ginger toward the plane, stepping between her and the men as gunfire started coming at them. Ginger started to run toward the plane.

It wasn't a choice; it was the only instinct in her brain. The need to flee toward the promise of those engines to lift her out of the current storm of bullets.

Dare was at the top of the stairs with a gun in his hand, and she ducked as he fired over her head. She heard someone scream before realizing it was actually her. Her brain was stuck in some weird mode where nothing made sense. But Saxon was behind her, shoving her brutally through the doorway, Ginger tunneled right between Dare's wide braced feet as he fired off another couple of rounds.

"I'm out," Dare barked as Ginger rolled over and landed on her butt in the aisle.

Saxon surged to his feet and took a position in the doorway, firing off more shots. "Let's go, Captain!"

"Secure the hatch!" Bram answered from the cockpit. "Fucking civilian aircraft won't roll while it's open!"

Saxon flinched but reached out to grab the door of the aircraft. There was a whistling sound as a bullet tore through the air. A thin red line appeared along his temple as the door sealed out the sunlight. Ginger cringed as she heard a thump and another one as bullets hit the newly closed door.

"Get us off the ground," Saxon ordered.

The plane jerked and started moving. Ginger grabbed the side of a chair because she was still sprawled on the floor. Honestly, she didn't think she could move if her life depended on it. Bram was clearly intent on getting away, his focus on speed. Comfort came second because the little plane was bouncing all over the place. Saxon had his face in one of the small oval windows, looking back at the men who had tried to kill them.

Ginger suddenly gained the strength to move. She

climbed off the floor and landed in the chair as she looked out of the window. She needed to see but felt her belly heave when she gained a glimpse of the men standing where they had left them. Two of them were hoisting Kitten's limp, lifeless body off the pavement. They carried her to the back of the SUV and dumped her inside.

They wanted her in there too, cold and just as dead as Kitten.

Hard, sharp-edged truth.

The plane turned, cutting off her view. It left her sitting in the seat, looking at the mess her toes had become. Her nails were broken and she had blood oozing from more than one cut. The scent of fresh blood teased her senses, making her need to throw up. But her stomach was empty so she sat there, letting the chair hold her up since every muscle she had felt drained. The plane surged, the engines whining as they propelled the aircraft forward. She felt pinned to her seat as they sped down the runway and pulled away from the earth, leaving her completely in the hands of Saxon and his team.

Relief surged through her, making her throbbing feet seem like a badge of victory.

Saxon was looking at her. She felt his gaze on her and couldn't seem to help flashing him a smile. He took a quick swipe at the graze on his head, looked at his fingers and dismissed the amount of blood as insignificant.

"My own gun," she said over the sound of the plane engines. "That is the last time I am going to be shot at without a way to fire back."

She likely looked like a hot mess right about then but she didn't care because she sounded like she was a fresh-from-battle Valkyrie. Saxon Hale tried to maintain his professional demeanor but his lips twitched, curving into that grin that made him look devastating.

He lifted his foot, braced it on a seat and ripped open a holster that was secured with Velcro. He tossed it to her, gun and all, with a look that told her he could relate to her need to take care of herself.

Sometimes, it was the little things that mattered, right?

Ginger closed her hands around the gun, letting the feeling of it build up her confidence.

Bram started to level out, which meant the noise in the cabin settled into something conversation could flow through unimpeded.

"Who was that?"

Saxon had hit what she was beginning to accept as his home position. Feet braced shoulder-width apart, jaw tight, eyes slightly narrowed as if he was trying to shield his thoughts from her, while he had his arms crossed over his chest, his hands resting on his lower biceps.

In short, the very picture of confidence.

"Back there. Who was that?" Ginger repeated.

"The people who will kill you to protect the identity of the man you saw," he answered in a dry tone. "You might have noticed how fast they were to eliminate Kitten, and she was one of their own."

"So, you're not going to tell me," she concluded.

Saxon offered her a twitch of his lips, obviously enjoying the fact that she wasn't going to let him skirt the issue. That fit. The guy thrived on head-on contact. "Can't taint your testimony."

It was an "ah" moment. Ginger nodded as Saxon offered her a wink.

"I did give you a gun."

He passed by her on his way to the small bathroom at the rear of the aircraft.

He'd winked?

She caught her reflection in the window and looked

at the silly smile on her lips. So the guy had a playful side. One she'd touched. It took her back to the moment when she'd first seen him and decided that he really needed a good laugh.

*Weren't you finished fantasizing about him? Repentant?*

Well, maybe she was just a glutton for punishment, because when it came to Saxon Hale, she couldn't seem to unnotice all the things about him that gave her a buzz. Of course, reality would deal with that. Her smile faded.

*"We're a ground team . . . "*

Yup, good old reality could always be counted on to bring down her house of cards.

He should be focused on the fact that he'd seen Tyler Martin clearly.

Instead, he was quelling the urge to go back and talk with his witness. Impulses were something he'd learned the danger of a long time ago. Acting on them was a good way to get killed.

He ended up scoffing at himself.

Okay, fine, looking in on Ginger Boyce wasn't exactly a life-or-death sort of decision.

She was a fighter.

He liked that and ground his teeth together when he realized what he was thinking. Now he'd crossed into dangerous territory. He couldn't get personal with her. She was his witness and not for much longer either.

*She smelled good . . . *

His cock gave a twitch, now that the rumble of the engines was making sure he knew he had her out of immediate danger.

Crap.

He didn't need it, this response from his body. He should have taken a chance to blow his load between cases. It had been the idea of catching Tyler Martin that had seen Saxon deviating from his normal down time between cases. Now he was stuck with his hormones running high while saddled with a witness who was a goddamned librarian. Maybe she read on the wild side but that would be as far as she'd ventured into the real world.

And she'd seen the Raven murder someone.

That was Fate for you. She gave you what you were pining for but with a twist that made it darn near impossible to utilize. His little witness was going to need to be protected from herself and the harder realities of being in custody.

Namely the way healthy adults reacted to one another under stressful conditions. He'd watched sex be used as an advantage, even as a tactic, when the case called for gaining trust faster than most people gave it under normal circumstances.

Fate was giving him some payback for sure. Saxon had ordered men under his command into the beds of suspected traitors and now, well, it looked like the cosmos was jabbing him with a sharpened stick. Or to be blunt, one spunky librarian, who just happened to have an hourglass figure, which was his personal weakness.

Yeah, personal. That's what it was and he needed to dig down and dredge up some professionalism. As well as a prayer that Kagan would come through with a team to take Ginger off his hands before he did something regrettable.

Saxon turned and made his way to the cockpit. Dare looked up from the co-pilot's seat.

"I gave her a gun," Saxon supplied. "Maybe I can't tell her who she's up against, but I can even the playing field a bit."

Both his men nodded.

"Seems fair enough," Bram spoke up. His hands were firmly on the controls, his attention on flying. They'd settled into a flight path and leveled off. "Maybe fate will be kind enough to let her be the one who puts a slug in that bastard's skull. I think I'd enjoy knowing a librarian did Tyler Martin in."

Saxon scoffed at him. "Tyler won't go down that easy."

"Any idea how Tyler found us?" Dare said what they were all thinking. "You can bet he's pulling our flight plan right now by the look of how much support he had."

Saxon reached for the onboard phone and dialed a number. His section leader answered.

"Tyler Martin just tried to kill our witness at the airport," he reported. "We need to cover our tracks or he'll just be waiting for us when we land."

Dare snorted. "We can count ourselves lucky Carl Davis isn't president yet or we might just get shot down."

All three of them didn't care for just how correct Dare was or how close to achieving the Oval Office Carl Davis was.

Kagan came back on the other end of the line. "I'm working on swapping out your transponder with another plane. Tell Magnus to stay sharp, he's going to have to do some fancy flying to make it look convincing." There was a reason Kagan was the section leader. He was sharper than a surgical needle.

"Martin had an impressive team backing him up, looked federal. The stripper is dead," Saxon continued.

"I'll see what I can find out," Kagan answered. "Next contact needs to come through a burner phone. You'll receive it from agents I have meeting you. The Raven has put a death mark on your witness. Ten million. You can bet you're going to have contract men looking to cash in, and I'm more convinced that she did see Marc Grog. That's too much cash for someone who doesn't give a damn about his name surfacing."

*Death mark . . .*

The line cut off, leaving Saxon with those two words echoing inside his head. It wasn't the first time he'd heard them. The Raven wasn't known for his tolerance but for his swift retribution. The one thing Saxon had found a lot of evidence to support was just how often the network of underworld people responded to the Raven's commands. Saxon and his men had been finding bodies for weeks as the man tightened his grip on the underground. The Raven didn't tolerate failure. His people would go to extreme lengths because failure meant being found dead in a back alley of New Orleans.

Now that he had a name to put to the Raven, it was all making sense. Marc Grog had headed up one of the biggest media production studios on the globe. It had been a cover for the mega underworld operation that laundered billions of dirty money. Exotic locations for films had masked sky rings and drug trafficking. Marc had been clever enough to make it all seem legitimate.

Saxon could see why Carl Davis would be interested in doing business with the man. The reason was simple: reach. People were tuned into the cyber world. Any man who wanted to win the vote needed to be able to reach that world. Marc Grog held the keys to the bridge or at least he had until his death a decade before. If he was still alive, it meant he was guilty of moving classified information; there would have been no reason to fake his death otherwise.

Ginger was the only person who could set a flame to the whole thing.

He went back into the cabin. Ginger had emerged from the bathroom, more together than he'd expected her to be. She had her hair back in that messy knot on the back of her neck that he liked.

*Professionalism . . .*

Right. He moved closer to her noticing that her eyes were more than hazel. They were green and orange and brown, like autumn on the east coast.

He wanted to roll around in a pile of leaves with her.

"So tell me what the person on the other end of that phone said."

She'd caught him off guard again, which was likely a good thing considering the direction of his thoughts. Her gaze shifted to his temple.

"You're bleeding." Her voice had become a tattered whisper, betraying her true emotional state.

"Just a graze."

She seemed to weigh his words, considering his temple. Then locked gazes with him and something went through him, like a shot of awareness. He avoided naming it because without a doubt, acknowledging the emotion would be an act of surrender to the impulses associated with it.

He wasn't going there.

"So . . ." she prompted him. "What was said? Since it was about me, it seems I should know."

Saxon slowly shook his head, but, honestly, he wasn't really sure if he was warning her or himself. She pressed her lips into a little pout.

"Tainting the witness again?" she asked. "I think I should warn you that my job is digging up dirt on people."

Ginger flashed a smile at him and it was all warning. "I *love* my job."

A half sound of amusement got past his control. There was a flicker of victory in her eyes that should have pissed him off but all he ended up with was the feeling that she was entitled to that moment. Her life had certainly taken a turn for the sucky end of the pool.

"You cracked a smile. I win," Ginger declared.

"Not a smile."

She held up her hand and peered at him through her forefinger and thumb. "Just a smidge, but it happened. I'm the witness, remember?"

"Yes." He felt his body tighten with that realization. Ginger noticed, too. Whatever else she was, she had keen senses. She was reading him like a book. It was a situation he wasn't used to encountering in anyone but his immediate family.

"Fine, I get it. It's not like it's the first time the Feds have told me to nose out because the deadbeat father I'm investigating is one of their informants." She lifted her hands in a motion that told him she was dropping it.

"This is a little more important than street-corner drug dealers." He shouldn't have kept the conversation going, but his dammed impulses were overriding his brain.

Her fingernails dug into the leather of the holster as her expression tightened. "Yeah, I'm getting that feeling all right." Ginger returned to looking out the window, making good on her word to drop the issue.

He made his way down to the bathroom, ignoring the impulse to just lay everything out on the line for her.

She fucking deserved to know what she was up against. Truth was, part of him wanted to level with her, just to see the way she'd rise to the challenge.

But he also didn't want to be the one to tell her she had a death mark on her with a ten-million-dollar bounty. It would be like crushing a hummingbird that was sitting in his hand, trusting him. For the first time, he just didn't have the stomach for it. That was a first, too, because a scared witness was a submissive one. Any man on a witness-protection team would tell you that, or at least, off the record they would. Just one of those things men like him didn't share with the outside world, another fact that allowed most of the population to go on with their lives in peace. There was a cost and someone always had to pay it, and most of the time, fate wasn't very fair about where she handed the bills.

He didn't want to see Ginger crushed down to that position, even while he knew it would be safer for her.

But he was left with cold reality turning his insides because the Raven didn't have any problem stepping on the innocent. Neither did Carl Davis. Their subordinates would carry out those orders because in their minds it was merely business. Keeping her alive was going to be hard.

A lot harder than he wanted to admit to himself, much less her.

# CHAPTER THREE

God, he felt good.

Ginger let out a little sigh, shifting as she felt the way Saxon Hale moved beside her, behind her, guiding her with a touch on her hip that was shockingly erotic. Man-oh-man, she'd never guessed that a simple grip on the curve of her hip might send a bolt of excitement down her body. Only that wasn't the end of it. The current of sensation came zipping back up her legs and landed in her core, making her feel like everything inside her was warm and molten. Her clothing was bugging the tar out of her because what she really wanted was to strip.

She felt Saxon turn her again, only this time, she was face to face with Kitten. The eyes that had fascinated Ginger so much were full of something horrible. It burned right through her, leaving her fighting to escape, only she couldn't seem to get any traction. She was digging her feet into the ground, felt her skin tearing beneath her toes because of how hard she was struggling and still, Kitten was there, slowly lifting her hand and pointing at her.

Ginger tried to scream, but no sound came out of her

throat. Instead she heard Kitten's neck breaking and felt her own throat tightening with the knowledge that she was next . . . next . . .

"Ginger."

She came awake with a start, pulling her knees up and kicking out at whoever was shaking her. Her brain escaped the hold of the dream just in time to absorb the look of surprise on Saxon's face as she planted her bare feet in the center of his chest and sent him tumbling into the aisle of the plane. Shock froze her as he landed on his backside and stared at her incredulously.

There was a choking sound from farther up the aisle, where Dare Servant stood in the doorway between the cockpit and the cabin.

"I'm really sorry . . ." she sputtered. "I was dreaming."

Dare was still choking and hiding his lips behind a coffee mug. Saxon turned to look at his fellow agent as he climbed to his feet. Dare was unimpressed with the look Saxon sent him. Dare lifted two fingers to his temple in a mock salute before he turned around and ducked down to enter the cockpit.

Saxon looked down at his shirt, where her feet had left three bright red blood spots from her cut-up feet.

It was a sobering sight, one that combined with the way her skin was tingling from the nightmare.

*Real . . .*

It was all so . . . bluntly . . . real.

She felt like circumstances were trying to kick her butt.

*Well, I'll just kick back.*

"We'll get you some shoes when we land."

"Which will be when?" She asked mostly to get her brain chewing on another topic.

"About an hour, I would have let you sleep but it was clear you were having a nightmare."

He was back to being in control and seeing far more than she was comfortable with. Ginger stretched out her legs and froze when her muscles protested. She felt every scrap and strain now. In fact, her shoulder was killing her. She reached up to rub it but regretted it when pain went stabbing through her.

"Looks like the shock has worn off," he said knowingly.

*All in a day's work . . .*

It was harrowing to see how accustomed he was to the situation. She was back to feeling like he needed a good laugh, which was funny all in itself because Saxon Hale wasn't the sort of man who needed her to fix his life for him.

*Get a grip on those mental fantasies girl . . .*

She felt a chill touch her nape. "I'm fine." Ginger turned to look out the window but snapped her attention back to him when she heard the little grunt he gave her in response.

"F-I-N-E." She spelled out the word. "Because I am not going to cry over it."

His eyebrows rose, and he nodded approvingly.

He was suddenly close again, leaning against the seat across the aisle from her. "I know exactly where you're at, Ginger Melody Boyce. You can kick it in the teeth or crumble. So far, you're kicking the shit out of it. Not bad." He turned and walked back toward the cockpit while his words bounced around her brain.

*Not bad.*

Crap.

She liked the sound of that way too much for her own

good. Especially for how clear he'd been about the fact that they wouldn't be staying together.

*You are heading for a really bad case of getting burned while playing with fire.*

Oh, that much was true, but all she seemed to notice was what a great set of buns Saxon Hale had. He was wearing business slacks that were a little worse for wear and stained with grass. Somehow, they were sexier than tight jeans. The little bit of additional fabric just made her want to watch him as he walked, waiting for the wool to pull tight and give her a glimpse of what he had under it because he didn't go around flaunting it. Naw, he saved it for the right girl.

*You're going to hell . . .*

No she wasn't. There was no way God was so spiteful as to deny her a little enjoyment considering what she'd just been through. Fine, she was negotiating, and somewhere in her brain were the fragments of a psychology lecture on shock and the responses of the human brain to sudden trauma.

Screw it.

She was suddenly really done with everything and everyone. Saxon had given her a gun and she was going to crawl inside that morsel of trust and take the comfort she could.

Saxon was coming back, making her fight to hide how uncertain she was. His approval of her was the only thing going right at the moment, and she wasn't going to blow it. He handed her a tray.

"Now that shock has worn off, you're likely hungry."

Her belly decided to rumble as the scent of the food touched her nose. Saxon flipped the toggle latch holding the fold-down tray to the back of the seat in front of her to drop it, and placed the tray on it.

"You'll get mad next," he said. "Not that I blame you. Life kicked you in the teeth. Still," he reached down and plucked his gun off her waist band. "I can't hand you over armed. Sorry."

And just that fast, her house of cards came down.

It was indeed an epic crash and burn.

She looked at the food and did her best to be interested in it. It beat letting him see what a mess she was dissolving into. At least it wasn't very hard to dredge up an appetite. The tray held a cold sandwich, but she was suddenly so hungry she could smell the bread and cheese and even the mustard like it was ten times as much. Her belly rumbled again, low and deep as her mouth actually started watering.

Saxon had retreated to one of the front seats, giving her only a view of the back of his head and neck. Even if he'd been watching her, she doubted she could have stopped herself from shoving the sandwich into her face and gnawing on it like a starving dog. Hell, it took a lot of effort to pull her head back and take a breath of air before going in for another chunk of it.

She felt like she'd stretched her throat because she hadn't chewed her food enough. Her mouth was dry since she hadn't even taken the cap off the bottle of water. A little package of painkillers caught her eye, reducing her once again to feeling pitiful.

Hell, the guy was taking care of her. Her adventure had turned into a Stephen King version of an expedition. A horror story.

She finished off every last scrap of her meal and drained the water bottle before the painkillers kicked in. She picked up the package the pain medication had come in but it was clearly labeled as Aleve. Nothing out of the ordinary, but she was shutting down, slumping against the side of the plane as her body refused to soldier on. The vibration of the aircraft rocked her to sleep even as she tried to argue with herself about staying alert.

"This is turning into a mess, Martin," Carl Davis hissed.

"It was already a mess," Tyler retorted. "I'm the man trying to clean it up. Marc Grog would already be in front of a judge being read the list of charges against him if I hadn't been there to offer him an alternative."

"You shouldn't have let a witness see the Raven working in the first place," Carl countered. "Why do you think I sent you down there?"

"To make the most of the right opportunity," Tyler replied. "Which was not going to be as simple as me telling Marc what a fine service I'd provided by dropping that little mouse in front of him. A man like him wouldn't understand the full implication of just how big a service that would have been. That's why I watched it all go down and didn't move until he understood how much he needed me."

There was a moment of silence before Carl answered. "Got it. You're right. Marc is a prick with an ego the size of Lake Ontario. Since he faked his death, he thinks he's untouchable. What do you need?"

"Flight plan on that plane," Tyler said. "And a team to meet it, one you won't mind me getting rid of."

There was a snort on the other end of the phone. "You're a cold-hearted bastard, Tyler."

"That has nothing to do with it," Tyler responded. "This is about not leaving strings. As soon as the campaign heats up, there will be a thousand reporters all intent on finding anything to bring you down. My job is to make sure there is nothing to find."

"It's a sure bet Vitus Hale will ask questions if his brother comes up dead." Carl warned.

"So long as the witness is dead, there will be no one to tell him what he needs to know to link it all back to Marc Grog," Tyler informed him. "So long as Marc learns from his mistake and stays the hell out of New Orleans."

"Right," Carl responded. "Let's hope he plays it safe."

"At least until after the election." Tyler remarked. "After the votes are cast, it will be useful to have him disappear. For real this time."

Carl was chuckling. "Cold hearted. You have no idea how hard it is to find a man with that quality these days, Martin."

"Glad to hear you understand my worth." Tyler killed the call, content with the outcome.

Now, he just needed to close the case.

Air-tight.

Saxon Hale wasn't the sort of man you got the jump on twice with the same thing. Ginger smelled him before she woke up completely. Her brain was still caught in a haze of anxiety, and she was lifting her legs to kick him before sleep released her completely.

Only this time he was ready. He had an arm locked down in front of her that she banged with her knees. Pain went shooting through her shins, banishing slumber instantly. Her eyes opened wide, locking gazes with him, which sent another blow to her system, only this one was purely internal.

"Sorry," he offered as he snapped her seatbelt closed. "We're about to encounter some turbulence. Hold on."

She'd actually forgotten to breathe while he was

looming over her. Crap, the surface of her lips was tingling, too.

*Are you bat-shit-crazy?*

Maybe desperate was a better word. It certainly stung
more. Which was exactly what she needed, a good slap
back into reality. Saxon had taken a seat, only closer to
her this time. She considered him suspiciously. There
was something bugging her about the way he was making sure he was closer to her. The truth wasn't pretty, but
she realized he was there because he expected her to
freak out.

"Turbulence? As in a storm?" she asked.

His lips curled just a bit and she realized her question was
far too mundane for the world he operated in. Mother
Nature's fury didn't make him hunker down, no, it was
going to be caused by something he'd initiated.

"Are we swapping flight paths?" She was racking her
brain, thinking out loud. She dealt with deadbeat parents,
but her job also introduced her to a great many ways to
track people that most folks didn't really know about.
Planes had to have flight plans now, since the attacks
on New York City. Federal agencies could access those
plans.

"The guys at the airport were Federal . . ."

Saxon jerked his head toward her, betraying the fact
that she'd touched on the truth.

"Your bullet bounced off the SUV window . . ." She
hadn't thought it through, and it was replaying across her
mind now with amazing clarity.

And Saxon was a street team.

"Oh . . . shit." She muttered. "Just fuck, fuck, *fuck*. This
in interdepartmental."

"You don't know—"

She locked gazes with him. "Think before you lie to me, Saxon Hale. No man crosses that line in my book."

Fine, she was getting personal with him and didn't give a rat's ass what he thought about it. The look she aimed into his eyes made sure he knew it. For a moment, he hid behind a guarded expression, but it broke beneath the weight of her stare.

"I can't confirm what you just said."

Which meant she was spot on.

*Fuck* . . .

When it came to the federal government agencies, they had more resources and authority than most people knew. For a moment, she actually sort of wished she was one of those ignorant souls.

But she wasn't. Which returned her to cussing, because it was really hard to distinguish between the good guys and the the bad guys, but both sides would easily cover up her death as a "regrettable" accident.

Fuck.

"Hold on. We're coming up on the plane now."

She looked out the window and discovered herself looking at a military fighter jet.

*Fuck and double fuck. She wasn't wrong.*

She'd never wanted to be wrong so bad in her life. But no such luck.

The pilot had a helmet on and a black face mask that had a hose attached to it. The sunlight reflected off his mirrored eyeglasses. The jet was even with them as another plane came up beneath them, another white, private jet like the one she was in. The pilot of the jet flipped a thumbs up toward Bram Magnus before pulling up and away in a graceful arc that afforded Ginger a view of the underbelly of the fighter and its missiles.

A second later, the plane she was on was nose diving.

It was an abrupt change in direction that made the seats rattle and her insides clench. She flattened her feet on the floor and gripped the arm rests. It was like that first drop on a rollercoaster, designed to titillate.

Only all it did was confirm just how right she was.


So she wasn't as much of a mouse as everyone thought. Damned if she hadn't made the hair stand up on the back of his neck with her warning.

Hell if that didn't give him a buzz. It was a jolt he really could have done without. Life would be a lot simpler if he didn't find anything about her that touched off more than a need to see his duty done.

He was past that now and knew it.

Kagan would have a nice team waiting for him to turn Ginger Boyce over to when they landed. Not because he'd requested it, but because Kagan wanted Tyler Martin and Saxon was a hunter.

He'd have to shuffle his memory of her away where it would live under the label of "the witness" and the type of girl his mother would be thrilled to have him bring home with a ring on her finger.

He was way past that, too. His mother was going to have to be content with the fact that his brother Vitus had managed, against the odds, to make his lapse in mission protocol into a relationship that was going to last. It was too rare a circumstance for Saxon to hold out any hope for a second occurrence.

Ginger's survival lay in complete obscurity.

It didn't matter if he found her warnings intoxicating because there wouldn't be any opportunities to investigate what other sounds he might be able to elicit from her that would please him.

No lies? He really wished he didn't feel the nip of an

impulse to test her by telling her exactly what he'd like to do with her.

And he hated the fact that he never would get the opportunity to let her tell him what she liked from men.

He had the feeling she could handle the sort of truth he lived by.


Tyler Martin was waiting. It was something that went along with his occupation, but he wasn't comfortable with it. His team was poised around him, waiting for a signal. He looked at the scene on his laptop, watching the in-flight information coming in from the flight transponder on the aircraft Saxon had lifted off in. It was going down in Dallas now. The team he'd selected was on the ground, their body cameras giving him a live feed.

His phone vibrated. He pulled it out of his suit jacket breast pocket and answered.

"You haven't called," Marc Grog hissed.

"I have nothing to report," Tyler informed him. "I am working the case."

"I don't suffer fools," Marc threatened.

"Neither does Carl Davis," Tyler answered. "I suggest you put your energy into meeting his demands, before he pulls me off this case."

"Every man has weaknesses," Marc replied. "That's one of my specialties, finding them."

"So I hear."

"The man has a brother," Marc suggested.

"Who was a Seal and managed to grab a girl from under your peoples' noses just a few months ago. We don't need him knowing we're hunting his brother. That will only bring another asset into play on their side, and if you think it's just one man, you better check yourself. Seals run in packs for life. Saxon used to be my man. I know how to track him, know how he operates. Don't make the mistake Jeb Ryland did and dick around with me by trying to tell me what to do. You have plenty of thugs. I'm not one. That's why I work for Carl Davis."

Marc grunted on the other end of the line. "You've got a solid spine, Martin. I like that in a man. Bring in that mouse and I foresee a bright future for you. Because you're right, if a man wants to be the best, he has to work with the best. Call me when you have something."

The line went dead. Tyler enjoyed the warm glow spreading through him. It was part satisfaction, part accomplishment. Two things no one got out of a man like Marc Grog without earning them. He didn't let the knowledge of how many bodies were littered on the ground in his dealings as the Raven bother him. This wasn't the Boy Scouts. He'd known what the stakes were from the moment he'd signed on with moving classified Intel. He'd had plenty of partners along the way, but the last one had blown up in his face because Jeb Ryland had insisted on taking out the Hale brothers.

Tyler shook his head. Jeb Ryland was dead now and Vitus Hale was enjoying the man's daughter. Even if Tyler had lost his place with the congressman, he couldn't help but enjoy the fact that Vitus Hale had outsmarted the old bastard.

*"Every man has weaknesses."*

Marc Grog was correct about that. The difference was, Tyler knew better than to alert Vitus Hale to the fact that his brother was running for his life. One Hale brother was trouble enough to catch now that Saxon knew Tyler was gunning for him.

No, the way to deal with catching a mouse was to hunker down and wait for her to cross his path. She would because Saxon would hand her off, thinking it the best course of action. A tactic Tyler had taught him.

And just to make sure of that, Tyler was going to give Saxon a whiff of bait, all in the interest of making sure he took to the trail and left the mouse where she'd have enough wiggle room to pop up on his radar. Witness teams weren't trained on the same level as Shadow opps. The second Saxon handed over his witness, Tyler would have her in check.

Kagan had his network set up just the way he liked it, with lots of triggers. He watched a blinking icon on his tablet flicker and tapped on it. The modern era had its pitfalls, one of which Tyler Martin had been only too happy to illuminate to him—that was that there was no way to hide. It was the reason Tyler Martin was still alive or at least why Kagan hadn't shot him when he'd had the chance. Kagan had had the reason sure enough, two of Saxon Hale's men were dead thanks to Martin being part of a plot to sell out military positions in Afghanistan. Well, more than two when Kagan considered how many men had died in ambushes.

Kagan slowly smiled. Today, he was going to be able to repay Tyler Martin by catching him in his own little trap. The world was a very hard place to slip off the edge of and Carl Davis had just tipped his hand by pulling information on Saxon Hale.

Kagan tapped his finger tip on the desktop and made a decision. He backtracked on Carl's secure password and went looking to see what else the good presidential hopeful had been doing. What he found made him reach for his phone.

Tyler Martin might think it impossible to survive

without selling out to the high and mighty of Washington, but Kagan wasn't willing to see the world in such black-and-white terms. There were still cracks in the woodwork, and Carl had just exposed a large one that Kagan had every intention of widening. Kagan put his neck on the line for one reason and that was his belief that even though the good guys only won sometimes, it was worth the struggle.

And when it happened, that was when hope had a chance to grow. If Marc Grog went down, Carl Davis would, too. Maybe, just maybe, that might translate into a fair presidential election.

It was going to be his pleasure to try and help that happen.

They touched down with a little skid of the aircraft tires. Honestly, it was a smooth landing, but Ginger felt like it was a gavel pounding. More than sound, she felt the impact and the vibration move through her body while they taxied from the runway to a small building. Bram didn't pull up to it. He stopped the plane in the middle of the expanse of cement while Dare and Saxon began moving through the cabin, bending over to peer out the windows of the aircraft.

"Looks like we gave him the slip," Dare said.

"If we did, it will be a momentary lapse," Saxon replied. "One we need to exploit."

On one hand, Ginger didn't care for the way they just talked, as though she wasn't there. On the other hand, listening had its merits and beggars couldn't be choosers. At the moment, she was reduced to taking whatever handouts fate was in the mood to cast her way.

Just so long as that included ways to survive, she wasn't

going to complain. A gift horse was an opportunity to live. She needed to focus on what was important.

"Let's move." Saxon turned around and hooked her bicep.

He guided her down the aisle and held her back from the doorway as Dare made it to the bottom of the steps and scanned the area. Then Saxon allowed her into the sunlight. She'd lost track of what day it was and no one had told her what time zone they were in. She felt sluggish but strangely alert as she went down the steps with Saxon's help.

His hold suddenly bothered her and she realized it was because he was closed off.

"I can follow directions," she offered. "Really."

His expression was unyielding. She didn't get even a flicker of response before he was pushing her toward an open door. It was an abrupt change, one that felt like it reached out and slapped her.

They walked into a building that gave way to a private terminal. The people in it were either trying to avoid notice or giddy with the excitement of embarking on a private jet. There was a rustle as a couple came in, the woman wearing her wedding dress. Unlike other airport terminals, this one lacked the rather pathetic looking seats. In their place were wide, padded chairs and tables. Privacy screens were placed throughout, and muffled conversation floated around them from the people who didn't want to be seen.

Saxon took her behind one.

There were five people waiting. Saxon deposited her in the corner, placing himself in the only escape route before releasing her. She felt like circulation was restored to her arm now that he wasn't holding it. The man had a grip and an unfair amount of strength. Her eyes narrowed when she realized how much that fact impressed her.

"Agent Powich." One of them offered Saxon his hand. Saxon firmly shook it before a woman offered him a phone.

"It's clean," she said. "We have other resources for you."

The female agent went on to list them. Burner phones, cash, paper maps with safe houses, oh, and they had a house that had just come up due to the couple being killed in a car accident over the weekend.

Ginger turned a little green at the callousness of how that tragedy was being laid out as an opportunity.

*You're jealous, too . . .*

Okay, she was, but not only because the female agent was drop-dead gorgeous. She was willow thin, with a button nose and thighs that were worthy of a bikini. She was also completely at home with the male agents, offering them a composed demeanor and even a few flutters of her eyelashes. Ginger felt grubby by comparison and totally out of her league, as well. It was depressing as all hell, no matter how hard she tried to remind herself that really, she'd rather be back in her normal life. It might be vanilla but it didn't include people shooting at her.

Ginger's eyes suddenly widened. "What about my family?"

She'd just blurted it out, and the agents all turned to look at her. "I mean, does that guy from the airport know my name?"

She was a rotten excuse for a daughter. Horror had a choking grip on her and Saxon started to turn his head back to Agent Powich without answering her.

"Don't you dare ignore me," she hissed. "Seriously, answer the question."

Her tone stunned Saxon. She witnessed the flash of surprise in his eyes before his expression cracked, giving her a glimpse at the man she'd gotten to know. Relief went through her because this was someone, a person, not the hard-muscle agent man who had taken her into the building.

"For the moment, your identity is unknown. We have a team in place, watching your parents."

She'd expected relief, but all she felt was a tingle of dread. Saxon's expression was tightening up again as she got the distinct feeling the second shoe was making ready to drop.

He broke his gaze away from her and sent a look toward Agent Powich. "Good luck."

Saxon looked her way a last time before he ducked around the screen and disappeared from her life. His jaw was tight, making her think he didn't like leaving her.

Street Team.

Yeah, it was what he was, what she actually admitted to preferring him as. It was terribly unfair of her but she scanned the agents surrounding her and found them all watered down versions of Saxon Hale and his team. Sure, they were likely all very good at their jobs, but there was no edge and she didn't get the same sense of control from them. Her confidence took a direct hit because she was pretty certain they wouldn't be as capable under fire.

It made her feel like she'd just been abandoned at the animal shelter. Sure, they'd do their job as best they could, but she had a higher risk of leaving the place dead than alive. Saxon was the only one she felt safe with.

And he was walking out of her life.

Fuck.

Saxon let out a snort, forcing himself to think about Po-wich and his team as a much-needed rescue for Ms. Gin-ger Boyce from the blunt way his team operated. They didn't know how to preserve sensibilities.

*The woman had a streak of fire in her.*

He snorted again, cursing his fickle emotions. He didn't need to notice things about her, at least not traits that he found attractive.

*Irresistible.*

He shook his head and dialed a number that was on a sticky note on the back of his badge. His section leader answered on the second ring.

"Congratulations on getting her there in one piece," Kagan said. "She's a lucky girl to have you watching her."

"It worked out," Saxon answered as he rotated his neck. For some reason, it was as tight as a slingshot. "Powich will have his hands full with her. Warn him to keep his guard up. My guess is Tyler won't give up so easily."

"Tyler is up to something. Got a fresh sighting on him heading back into the Quarter," Kagan said. "Sending it to your phone."

Saxon waited for a moment before he tapped the screen and looked at the picture. It was blurry, likely from a traffic camera.

If his neck hadn't been tight before, it was now. Saxon let out a little growl. Bram was looking over his shoul-der and made a gun with his forefinger and thumb, fir-ing off a silent shot at the screen.

"Don't know what he's going back in for, but you can

bet it will involve cleaning up what our witness saw." Kagan said. "In any event, he's being sloppy."

Saxon had the phone pressed to his ear again but his mind was seeing the picture and the word "sloppy." It stuck in his throat, impossible to swallow.

"It's bullshit."

Kagan was silent, waiting for Saxon to explain. "A picture just happens to surface now?"

"That's what drew you to the Quarter," Kagan responded. "A slip up that let you know Tyler was there."

Saxon was thinking, and he was getting a mighty bad feeling. "No. Not with that Federal team he was riding with. It's bait. Tyler doesn't know how to be that sloppy."

"That thought crossed my mind as well."

There was a long moment of silence from Kagan, proving that the section leader was waiting to see what Saxon would do. A test of sorts, one that held Ginger's life in the balance.

"I want the witness," Saxon informed Kagan. "Tyler's trying to draw me away from her."

Bram's eyebrow rose. He was suddenly snapping his fingers at Dare, who was nursing a cup of coffee. He set it aside after one long swing.

"That might be a stretch," Kagan replied.

"Except that Tyler trained me and knows procedure," Saxon responded. "And he'll have less trouble taking down a protection team than he will with me."

"True," Kagan grunted. "Babysitting isn't in your nature. You know the realities of an assignment like this one."

"I also know that Tyler Martin likes to steamroll through innocents." Saxon was avoiding thinking about anything beyond the immediate moment. Sloppy and Tyler Martin didn't belong in the same sentence.

His section leader made a low sound on the other end of the line. "Fair enough. I agree that no one understands Tyler Martin like you do. No one else will know what to look for," Kagan cut back, his tone having gone deadly.

"Take her and bury her, until I can arrange a testimony hearing."

It was what he wanted and satisfaction filled him but there was something else, a very distinct sting of guilt. Just because he had valid reasons for taking her back under his control didn't change the fact that he knew he was pleased for personal reasons.

"If anyone can resist the urge to hop into her bed, my money is on you."

Saxon narrowed his eyes at Kagan's comment. "Handing out double-edged compliments today?"

"So it seems. I'll be in touch."

Saxon killed the call. Shadow opps was a deal-with-it sort of world. He thrived on it, but that didn't mean there weren't times he would rather decline. It was one of the traits that so often separated adventure junkies from true agents. A lot of special opps men came through the ranks. Marine Recon, Army Rangers, Seals, and so on. They signed up, thinking it would be a thinned-down version of active duty, and in some ways it was. But there was another side to it. There were the seedy details, the times when even the best self-directed lecture on duty and the greater good taking precedence didn't do squat.

You still ended up feeling like shit, and what was worse was that you knew you deserved it. He moved back so that he got a glimpse of Ginger Boyce.

She was mouthwatering. She could satisfy a man like him, a man who hadn't tasted purity in way too long. But it would be bitter, would leave a taste in his mouth that he wouldn't be able to wash out. The sort of woman he invited into his bed was one who knew it was for the moment and nothing more.

Ginger didn't know the meaning of that. For a moment, he allowed himself to enjoy that idea, the concept of her take on the world, the idea of hope. Sure, he kept working to catch men like the Raven because he wanted there to be a brighter future, but his concept of hope was more of a "holding back the darkness" sort of thinking opposed to Ginger's view that included home, family, and growing old together.

He wanted to taste her though.

He let the thought roll through his mind and linger for just a moment, long enough for him to recognize how dangerous it was before he ordered himself to pull together his professionalism. At least he was practiced enough in being in the field to know when his face was tightened into a mask. He trusted the feeling, pushing himself into motion and into the case that he was assigned.

It was time to do what needed doing.

Tyler wasn't going to add another notch to his gun belt while Saxon had breath in his body.

Saxon was still there when she woke up the next morning.

Ginger had thoughts about that but shoved them down, way deep, into a dark hole and slammed a door. Sure, it likely wouldn't last but for the moment, she was succeeding in avoiding thinking about him at all. That was a victory of sorts, really it was. The guy radiated some sort of allure that she found hypnotic.

And since he had walked back around that privacy screen and taken control of her, she'd realized just how bad an idea it was to let her thoughts run wild.

*Like that's ever stopped you before . . .*

Ha! There really should be some sort of law about her inner voice using her own sarcasm against her.

She needed a diversion.

They were in another house. There was a kitchen that was painted green, giving it a happy glow. There were California poppies hand-painted around the large picture window that was at one end of a breakfast nook. Even with the blinds closed, she felt a sense of welcome, like the walls were radiating years of happy memories or hopes for a full future. She felt the sting of oncoming tears for the couple that had never made it home.

*Boy, you're really losing it . . .*

*Shut it.*

She wasn't losing it, but it appeared she was talking to herself. The cabinets offered a nice selection of dishes. Ginger considered the pantry, trying to decide if any of the canned goods went together.

"Snooping, Ms. Boyce?"

Saxon filled the doorway. Somehow, she hadn't really noticed how big he was. Six feet and change, and his shoulders were wide and bulky with muscle. So much for not thinking about him. The door she'd slammed shut inside herself came flying open and right behind it were all the mental musings she'd indulged in.

She shrugged "You said the owners were deceased. Must sort of suck to always be one step behind the Grim Reaper."

"Better than having him behind you," Saxon answered. "Trust me on that one."

She leaned against the kitchen counter. She'd never been so uncertain and no matter how much her logical brain tried to argue that she should just categorize their relationship into a professional one, she just couldn't seem to stop thinking about him in a very personal way.

Right then, she would have sworn he was battling the same issue. Watching her with those blue eyes, trying to decide what to think of their situation.

*Right. He's done this before.*

That fact gave her back a chunk of her poise.

"So, snooping, exploring, it's something to do," she offered with a shrug.

Ginger turned around and opened another cabinet. What she needed was boring things to look at, not the very fascinating visage of Saxon Hale, eye candy, and all man-meat. Because she was so tempted to mess with him.

*Soooooooo tempted . . .*

And that wasn't right. The guy was taking care of her. He didn't need her using him as entertainment. Honestly, he really might have a wife or girlfriend, and she didn't have the right to ask. She was his job.

Professional. He was that, all right, and she was, well, her thoughts were inappropriate.

"My section leader is working out the details of getting you before a judge to testify."

"Great."

She felt like she sounded lame.

She turned back to face him and found an expression on his face that she hadn't seen before. This one was curiosity, like he was trying to peel her bland, professional response aside and get a look at her thought process.

"I mean, seems like some good should come of all of this. You guys have been shot at."

Saxon's lips twitched. She knew that look. It was the male grin of "bring it on."

"Okay, so it was nothing you couldn't handle."

Ginger settled back against the edge of the tile countertop, staring at the glitter in his eyes. More of his personality was on display, and she felt privileged to see it. She chose her tone carefully because she didn't want to spook him. She had the feeling Saxon Hale didn't share his private persona very often. "But beyond the rush, it's a damned dangerous game."

He offered her a single nod. "They were shooting at you. I just stepped into the line of fire."

"But you were there." Now that she was taking time to think about it, she recalled the look on his face when she'd explained how she made it past the doorman.

"I solved something for you," she said. "By seeing Marc Grog."

Her comment sobered him. He stepped into the kitchen, making her feel like it had shrunk. It was just ridiculous the way she was in tune with him. Awareness was rippling through her as he moved closer. He racked her from head to toe, considering her.

"I wish you hadn't."

Something flashed in his eyes that looked like pity and that stirred her temper.

"Don't think about me that way." She really should have kept her mouth shut but didn't.

His eyebrow rose.

"Like you feel sorry for me," Ginger clarified. "Don't."

"You'd prefer I was a real hard ass who didn't recognize how your life has been smashed to bits?"

"I'm not going to let life get me down." She looked straight into his eyes as she spoke and made damned sure he knew how serious she was. For the first time, she felt her confidence holding steady under his direct gaze. "Plenty of people have to deal with crap flying at them. I'll deal with my share. Life isn't fair. I'm not planning on crying about it."

Something flickered in those blue orbs, a concession that soothed her wounded pride. It was an unspoken thing, and for a moment, she felt like her breath was lodged in her throat because he was contemplating her so intently. She thought she noticed his gaze settle on her mouth, but he recoiled, backing away from her.

"Enjoy your scouting. We're going to be here for a while."

He disappeared through the doorway, and she heard conversation start up in the outer room again. But she didn't move. She was too busy feeling like she'd missed out on his kiss.

*Oh man, she was so going to hell . . .*

The kid was good.

Tyler watched him work with a laptop while guzzling a soda. His tie was a knotted mess and his shirt half untucked from his pants because he was all of seventeen. But what he lacked in experience with dress clothing, he sure made up for in cyber hacking skills.

"See . . ." The kid realized Tyler was watching and launched into an explanation. "Even burner phones have to connect with cell towers. Sure, there are zillions of prepaid phones out there, and it all just ends up as a mass of numbers, but when you embed a photo into a text, that cuts down on the number of records to shift through. When you have a tracer on the photo, it's like looking for a glow stick at midnight."

The kid was typing harder, peering intently at the screen as his excitement grew. There was a slam as he hit the keyboard and shouted with victory. "Got it!"

Tyler looked past him at the screen. "Can you track that phone now?"

"Sure," the kid assured him with pride. "Just as soon as the sucker uses it, his ass is mine."

Tyler nodded. "Good." He walked away caught between a mixture of pride and frustration. Saxon hadn't taken the bait. It was impressive to see his previous trainee proving his worth by thinking outside of the box. Frustrating because he needed to wrap up the operation.

Still, Tyler found himself smiling for the first time in a long time because there was one thing that Saxon and Vitus Hale had always provided him with.

And that was entertainment.

He didn't give a rat's ass over anyone's bleeding heart reaction to that either. Saxon and Vitus had known what they were signing up for. To play with the big dogs. Saxon was every bit as much of a killer as Tyler was. The only difference was how they took their pay.

Ginger woke up before dawn and grumbled at the ceiling. The bed was a tangled mess, and so was her hair. She flounced into the bathroom and jerked a brush through the mess on her head as she tried to understand why she couldn't get Saxon out of her thoughts.

No one else seemed up, but there was the soft sound of a television. She moved toward it and discovered Agent Dare Servant watching a movie. He saw her before she made it into the living room, his attention jerking over to her. He nodded as he recognized her and looked back at the screen.

"You're an early riser," he offered. Dare had black hair. She found it sort of fascinating because not many people actually had midnight-colored hair. She realized she was staring at it and felt a nip of shame because she doubted he missed it.

"Got a lot on my mind. Seems stupid to lay in bed when I'm not sleeping," she answered as she caught sight of the computer sitting on a desk against the wall.

There was a dust cover on it, but she could see a little blue light shining through the hazy plastic of the cover, telling her the system was active. She plucked the cover off and laid it aside.

"You can't check your email. Or use the Internet since the house is supposed to be vacant."

Dare was on his feet, the relaxed man she'd just spoken to gone. As in, he'd transformed into an Agent who was ready to muscle her if she didn't give him a response he approved of.

*"There is no personal space in safety . . . "*

Saxon's words rose from her memory and she realized it was some sort of code among them all. One that she actually discovered herself grateful for.

"Sorry," she offered.

"New territory for you," Dare said as he watched her put the dust cover back on the computer. He gave her a nod.

Ginger looked at the closed drapes and fought back a wave of pity. It hadn't been that long since she'd seen sunlight. There was no reason to get her panties in a twist. She and Karen had been sitting at a breakfast table and sharing inside jokes just the day before. Actually, a little less, so there was no reason for throwing a pity party.

*Except there is a hitman trying to kill you . . .*

The scene from the airport rose from her memory like a cloud of smoke. It enveloped her, choking her with its fumes. She wanted to shove it aside, but it didn't have anything solid for her to brace her hands against. There was just the replay of the way the guy had gotten out of the black SUV and the look of relief on Kitten's face as she ran toward him, clearly believing him to be her rescuer.

Saxon's face came through her thoughts on the heels

of that idea. He was hard and sharp edged and exactly what she'd needed. He really had saved her life. A chill touched her nape as she absorbed just how real her circumstances were. Yesterday, it had just all been a haze of surreal events. Now, everything seemed to be settling inside her, a full night's rest bringing her a new perspective on it all.

If possible, she was more horrified now than she had been when the bullets were flying. The unshakable reality of Agent Dare Servant sitting a few feet away and the securely closed blinds was tunneling into her like termites. She was going to end up being eaten.

Her stomach was knotting, her insides feeling like they were twisting as she actually began to feel like she was going to throw up again.

Except Saxon's face was still there in her memory, the look he had leveled at her more than once staring at her from her recollections.

Yeah, the expression he gave her when she rose to the occasion. She wasn't going to lose it now and blow the idea of knowing she'd impressed him. Even a little.

It was thin reasoning, but it worked well enough. Okay, it felt a lot like she was poised on a surfboard, but she would just have to adjust to the pitch and roll of the wave her life had suddenly been hit by. Surfing was better than being rolled.

It would end at some point, and Saxon Hale would move on to something else. That was a trifle sad, and she avoided thinking about why she thought so.

*Because you were wishing he'd kissed you yesterday . . .*

There wasn't any point in denying it. She'd spent the night hot and bothered by the idea of having a taste of the guy.

*So . . . going . . . to . . . hell . . .*

Yup, more than likely. Only, she couldn't help but feel a sort of comradery with him. Loneliness sucked, and it seemed like he embraced it as part of his duty. That was sad because the guy deserved better for his level of dedication.

*Now you're trying to justify getting your hands on him as some sort of favor to him . . .*

Pathetic.

However, still undeniably true.

Life sucked.

Waiting was an art.

It was a skill that often separated the living from the dead in the world of shadow operations. Tyler Martin considered the blinking link on his phone. He took a moment to enjoy seeing it before he tapped on it to see just where Saxon had snagged a cyber space trip line.

Maybe electronic wires didn't have as immediate an effect as ones laid out in a war zone, but that didn't make them ineffective. In this case, it would mean the difference between bringing in what Carl Davis wanted and having to suffer failure. The Raven wasn't really someone Tyler considered very important. His value was wrapped up in Carl Davis's opinion of him. Tyler had his eye on the ball he wanted to keep in play and that was being part of Carl Davis's personal security team when the man became President of the United States.

Gaining a position like that would take very specialized skills, one he was about to demonstrate in spades. Personal security meant handling details, personal ones, which could often be translated into dangerous opportunities for people to get at elected officials.

And Saxon wanted to take Marc Grog down. That meant he needed Kagan to set up a testimony hearing.

Tyler waited for the trace-back link he had on the line to deliver his location. Every second was one too long because he knew Saxon wouldn't keep the line open long. Tyler tapped his finger against the side of his phone, intent on the screen. It flickered and displayed an address.

The mouse had just crossed into the open.

# CHAPTER FOUR

"Any news you can share with me?"

Saxon had come back inside from the backyard after making several calls. He was still tucking the phone into his pocket when she asked her question.

"Knowing things can be dangerous," was all he offered.

Ginger choked on a snicker and winked at him. "Right."

It was three in the afternoon, but Saxon reached for the coffee pot and poured himself a double cup. Bram Magnus had taken over for Dave Servant in the early morning, making her think that Saxon had been up most of the night. His silent stare was making her nervous. He knew something, a something he didn't think she'd like.

So she turned and pulled a pan from the back burner. It was a heavy cast-iron one, the kind her mother favored because it was truly impossible to wear them out.

A pang of homesickness went through her, making her sigh, but she was determined to not spend her day in the pity pool.

"How do you like your eggs?" She asked.

Her offer gained a response. His lips twisted into a

sarcastic grin as he set the mug down. "I'm not here for you to practice your homemaking skills on."

"You know something," she turned back to face him. "I make a mean glass of lemonade. Now, you can enjoy my attempts to make the best of things, or I can drown you in my lemonade."

He snorted at her reprimand. Ginger enjoyed the way his eyes glittered like there was nothing he'd enjoy more than testing her threat.

"You are such a man-child." It was another one of those personal comments. It came sailing across her lips, common sense kicking in after the fact to slap her with how inappropriate it had been. "Sorry, that was way personal."

She turned her back on him, determined to keep her attention on the pan. She felt exposed. It was her own damned fault, too. She didn't have any right to feel like he shouldn't leave her twisting in the wind.

It seemed she was way too dependent on him saving her.

She needed to ignore him, and deal with her own emotions but she ended up losing the battle and looked over at him anyway.

He hid behind his coffee mug, considering her through the steam rising from it.

"So . . ." She offered him what she hoped was a look equal to his own. "I've never done this before. Are we supposed to ignore one another, since offering to cook is some sort of breach of protocol?"

He set the mug down and seemed to be considering his response. "It's just best not to get personal."

His tone was meant as a warning, but what she heard was lament.

*You're hearing what you want to . . . and thinking*

*of pouring sugar all over him and licking it off was likely stepping over a line, too.*

*Just a smidge . . .*

Her mom was going to have something to say about that one. Right after she got done laughing. Ginger bit her lip to keep from grinning.

"What?" he demanded when she sealed her lips.

"Oh, now who's curious? Wouldn't telling you be getting personal?" She replied in a tone that was far more husky than she recalled ever sounding before. "What's good for the goose is good for the gander."

He stood, sending a ripple of awareness across her skin. "Doesn't mean I'll take it from you."

There was a dark promise in his tone, one that touched off something deep inside her. She was getting a glimpse at that personal part of him once more and she smiled with the knowledge. She wasn't the only one fighting to maintain boundaries.

*Playing with fire . . .*

It was like he knew what she was thinking, his eyes narrowing as his lips thinned, tiny little motions that she noticed keenly. It was unsettling on an epic scale, knowing how in tune she was to him. Maybe it was the situation, but even if that was so, it didn't change how she felt punched in the gut by the way he affected her. He was looking at her mouth again, and she really wanted to know what his kiss was like.

*Oh . . . shit . . .*

She was getting in way over her head. They'd just met. She knew next to nothing about him.

And all those facts somehow measured up short against her mounting fascination with him.

Ginger whirled around and grabbed the frying pan.

She lifted it up and started to turn back toward him. "Never let it be said that I intimidate easily. Speak now or take what I dish out."

She heard another snort from him, a sound she was beginning to associate with his personal nature and a victory on her part for touching it. Ginger brandished the pan in the air like a warning, but a second later, pain went shooting up her arm and into her shoulder with enough force to make her cuss. There was a loud "bing" that got mixed up in the sensation of being taken to the ground by Saxon Hale.

He'd knocked the breath right out of her, as well as flattening her beneath his much larger body.

"What . . . was that?" She flattened her hand on his shoulder, trying to push him up so that she could fill her lungs.

"A bullet," he informed her in a deadly whisper, giving her not even a millimeter.

He actually sealed her mouth beneath his hand, the side of it going right between her lips. She felt her eyes bulge as she became aware of him. As in, every hard bit of him.

It would have stolen her breath if she had any.

"Listen to me." His words were clipped, and there was no mistaking the urgency in his tone. "We're dead if we stay here."

He'd been looking over her head, toward the direction that the shot must have come from. Now he shifted, locking gazes with her.

"Stay on my side, and I mean right the fuck on my side."

Ginger nodded because he still had his hand in her mouth. The motion made her conscious of just how intense it felt to have his skin in contact with her lips. The timing was epically bad but that didn't seem to matter a wit to her brain. Her nervous system seemed to be short circuited into some sort of weird reaction cluster of responses, all firing off like the grand finale of a fireworks show. She wasn't in control of it, just the recipient.

In the next second, Saxon had her half off the floor and was pulling her toward the breakfast nook window. There was a round of gunfire, some of it behind them but more of it coming from the front room. She heard one of the other agents returning fire, and there was a discharge next to her head as Saxon aimed at the window and shot it out.

The glass shattered with a pop and slithered to the ground like sand running out of a broken hourglass. It horrified her because it felt like it was some sort of example of her own life, about to be smashed, her remaining years scattered onto the ground and wasted.

Saxon wasn't in the mood to let it happen, at least not without a fight. He pulled her through the window, sweeping the blinds aside with one powerful motion of his arm. He tugged her to the ground on the other side, the glass crunching beneath their knees and feet but thankfully, it was safety glass and didn't cut into her. It was still damned uncomfortable, but she huddled there next to him, sort of enjoying the stabbing feeling because it meant she was alive.

"We're going to make a break for it." He was right next to her. "Over the fence . . ."

There wasn't time for more explanation. The neighbor's door opened as a guy appeared in a pair of shorts. "What the fuck—"

Bram Magnus was suddenly vaulting up and onto the porch as he shoved the guy back into the house. "Get down!"

Ginger felt Saxon's grip tighten a moment before he

surged forward. She was ready, her heart pumping with the need to live. It was pulsing through her, taking control as she dug her feet into the ground and pushed herself faster. For a moment, she was lagging behind, Saxon's grip on her wrist pulling her forward, but then her body was responding and she was sprinting alongside him, keeping pace. She caught a quick glance from him, but it was long enough for her to notice the approval on his face. He stopped next to the fence, intending to help her up but she jumped and caught the top edge of it, somehow vaulting over it in a tangle of limbs. It was a concrete wall that left scratches all over her but adrenaline was surging through her helping her ignore it. When she dropped onto the other side of it, she landed on her butt but didn't stay there.

"That a girl." Saxon came down beside her, landing on his feet, looking capable and so damned strong. She was struck with just how much strength he had in him.

"Small town . . ." She was up and keeping pace with him with ease. "We spent a lot of time outside."

She heard a chuckle from him and a hint of acceptance.

"One more." Saxon pointed at the back wall of the yard they were running through.

Ginger took it with as much ease as the first, managing a bit more graceful landing.

"Where to?" she asked when he looked over to see how she was faring. He considered her for a moment, deciding if she was panicking or not. Ginger returned his gaze without flinching, shooting him her best attempt at a ready-to-go look. Surprise flickered through his blue eyes with something that looked a lot like admiration.

"The Strip."

With her thoughts buzzing, it took her brain a moment

to process his answer. Ginger looked up and blinked as she absorbed what she was seeing.

"We're in Las Vegas?" She asked.

"Observant of you," he remarked as he scanned the area in front of them and tugged her onto the sidewalk. "And we need to be somewhere very public and very heavily watched to hide while my team finds us. The Strip boasts one of the tightest security surveillance zones in the world plus it's packed with people taking pictures."

"So we're going to hide in plain sight." Impressive. In a she-really-hoped-it-worked sort of way.

He cut her a side look, one that showed her a gleam in his eyes. "They want to kill you but without witnesses."

"That won't happen here," she muttered as they got closer. There were people everywhere, and they were only on the far end of the strip, the towers of the major resorts still several blocks away.

"As long as they don't get too close. In a crowd, that would be hard to catch."

He came around her at a corner and controlled her with an expertly placed hand along her hip. She shifted, uncertain of being so close to him. Sure, she knew he was doing it to protect her, but that didn't stop the flood of responses being so close to him unleashed.

"Easy," he said, low and soothing. "We've got to blend in."

They'd crossed a street and were moving along with a surge of people making their way along the strip. "There are plenty of non-couples here."

The hand on her hip stayed exactly where it was. "We're in deep and on our own for the moment. Trust me on this. I know what I'm doing."

He looked toward her, a warning flickering in his eyes,

but he caught something over her shoulder and tugged her around in a hard motion. They went spinning into an entryway and then through a door marked "private."

Saxon didn't give it a second glance, propelling her through it before shoving it shut while he considered what was on the other side of it.

"Perfect."

Saxon was looking at the clothing in the room. There were racks of Hawaiian shirts and a rolling rack of ladies' dresses from the fifties. There was also a couple passed out on a sofa, the scent of booze rising off of them. Saxon considered both of them and nodded with satisfaction. He cast a look her way and pointed at the rack of dresses.

"Get one of those on."

He was already ripping through the buttons on the front of his shirt and pulling it open.

Her mouth went dry.

*Oh my . . .*

He reached out and cupped her shoulder, spinning her around to face the rack of dresses. "Now, Ginger, while we're still alive."

Ginger reached out for the dresses but her thoughts were very much still on the sight of Saxon's bare chest. God he was lick-able, from those hard shoulders, across amazing looking pectorals, and down to a sculpted abdomen. Man meat, eye candy, and well, scrumptious.

But looking at the dresses gave her enough time for her brain to engage. "Wait, how did you recognize anyone?" She'd flipped around, a dress in her hand but honestly, she hadn't really looked at it beyond the size. She was busy thinking through the way his face had looked right before he took her through the doorway.

He didn't like her thought path. There was a tightening of his jaw as he worked the last few buttons on the Hawaiian shirt. "We need to prioritize. Getting back with my team is in the number-one slot. Get changed, it will make us harder to spot."

He checked his gun and swept the room before he tucked it into a holster he had clipped to his belt. The shirt was one that hung free, covering the weapon.

He was right. She needed to focus but that didn't mean she was going to forget. She shrugged out of her clothes and found him holding the dress out. He wasn't looking away this time, and she felt her cheeks get warm as she recognized the look of reprisal in his eyes.

"Good for the goose . . . good for the gander . . ." he offered along with the dress.

"Ah . . ." She pulled the dress down with a rustle of fabric and netting.

"Maybe I'm trying to help you make lemonade."

Saxon offered her a grin as he reached out and cupped her shoulder once more and turned her around so that he could grab the zipper of the dress. There was a whoosh as he pulled it and the garment became snug at her waist and breasts.

"Oh . . ." There was a full-length dressing mirror in front of her, giving her a glimpse of herself. The dress had a flared-out skirt that was supported by tulle, a snug little waist and a cross-over top that afforded a plunging view of her cleavage. The way the bodice was cut, it hugged her shoulders, making her look like a mega hourglass.

"That will get the right kind of attention," Saxon said.

She turned around and caught Saxon surveying her from head to toe, darned if it didn't look like he was enjoying the sight. As in, really liking the view, which made her darn toes curl.

"Come on." He'd caught her watching him and cleared his throat before hooking her bicep and making for the far side of the room.

"Hold on." She stopped near the door where a shoe rack was and slipped a pair of pumps on. There was also a selection of little hats, cleverly mounted on headbands so they would stay on without hat pins. Ginger picked one up and put it on her head. It matched the dress and had a little piece of netting attached to it that complemented the vintage era of the dress. "Now the picture is complete."

But it actually wasn't. The moment Saxon pushed open the door, a girl turned around and smiled at them. "You look lovely," she said as she handed a bouquet of flowers to Ginger. "And the groom . . ."

Ginger was still staring at the flowers in her hands as the girl scooped up a corsage and turned around with the intention of pinning it onto Saxon. He was as close to panicking as she'd ever seen him. He had one hand out and was trying to wave the girl off when the doors in front of them opened and let out a blare of music. Saxon looked up, momentarily distracted, and the girl swooped in. She had the star lily pinned to his chest in a flurry of motion before she retreated beyond Saxon's reach.

"Good luck!" she said as the sound of "Blue Hawaii" was filling the area. Ginger looked up and realized they were facing an Elvis impersonator in a room decorated like a nineteen fifties Hawaiian resort. The fact that it was a wedding chapel slapped Ginger right across the face in that you-thought-it-couldn't-get-any-worse-and-somehow-it-did way. The passed out couple suddenly made perfect sense.

"Side door," Saxon muttered under his breath.

"Right on your tail," Ginger answered as they both tried to shimmy toward the door in question.

It opened before they made it even two steps. The man the sunlight flickered off of made Ginger recoil. Her blood went icy as the memory of him snapping Kittens neck replayed across her mind with a sickening clarity.

"Go." Saxon was shoving her through the open double doors, her heels pounding on the tile floor as she ran.

"Well now . . ." the Elvis impersonator said into a microphone. "Here's a couple in a hurr-rr-y!"

There was a round of laughter, drawing Ginger's attention to the people watching. The room had stands that faced in so people could sit and watch. Beyond them, she caught a glimpse of a casino floor. People were moving from the gaming tables and into the stands as waitresses offered them free cocktails. The far side of the room was just glass, allowing people on the strip to look in.

Both she and Saxon were looking behind them but the man from the airport had stopped in the double doorway, his hand under his jacket. He was wearing a set of mirrored shades and a dark suit, but just as Saxon had said, he seemed to not want to kill her with so many witnesses on hand. Saxon was looking at their options and ended up coming to the same conclusion she did. He held her steady as he stood right in the middle of the room.

"Well now . . ." the Elvis impersonator drew out to the delight of those watching. "Is that the best man stuck in the doorway?"

"No," Ginger said.

"He's her ex-boyfriend," Saxon declared.

There was a round of snickers from the audience.

"Hey, hey, hey . . ." Elvis declared. "This is a chapel of love. Looks like the lady has chosen and it isn't you. Shove off before I call the heat."

The man stood in the doorway, clearly not wanting to

budge. He locked gazes with Saxon, but the flashing of the cameraman made him back up.

"Well now . . . let's get this wedding started," Elvis declared.

"Not a chance," Saxon bit out.

The tone of his voice stunned her, and she felt her cheeks turning red as the crowd hooted with amusement.

Elvis cocked his head to one side and shot Saxon a look. "Well then my man, make way for the next couple."

"Gladly," Ginger growled as she started to move away.

But Saxon reached out and caught her elbows, pulling her to a stop as he jerked his head toward the window. The man was there, talking into his cell phone, but the look he aimed at her was pure intent. He wanted her dead.

She stumbled as she stepped back toward Saxon. He looked up, and she followed his example, seeing the cameras ringing them.

"Are we getting married?" Elvis pressed. "There's a line of happy couples just a' waiting . . ."

"Yes," Saxon informed him.

Her eyes must have bugged out because he stepped toward her and grabbed her wrists. "Just breathe honey."

She dug her fingernails into his forearms in response. Saxon's eyes narrowed and he gave a jerk of his head toward the man waiting to kill her. The crowd was chanting at them now.

"Tie the knot . . . tie the knot . . . tie the knot!"

They were working themselves up into a frenzy, the cocktail waitresses flocking in to take orders and make tips while they were in the mood to party. Sensing a profit opportunity, Elvis hit a pose and cupped his hands around the microphone.

"I think these folks need a song!" There was a round

of drums as the band kicked in. "Well it's one for the money . . . two for the show . . . three to get ready . . . now go . . ."

The crowd surged to its feet, shouting encouragement, as Elvis worked his moment of fame. Ginger scooched back, giving the entertainer room, but Saxon didn't let her go far. He pulled her up against his side, locking her in place with an unmovable arm. "We move and we're dead. The only thing keeping us alive is all these people. My men will find us, I've got a tracking beacon on me," he whispered in her ear.

"Great, I hope Elvis has a second song."

But she wasn't going to get that lucky. Elvis finished up with a flourish to the delight of the crowd. The room was full of applause and whistles that the impersonator enjoyed before it died away. He watched as people tossed money into his tip jar, flashing them his killer smile before he returned his attention to them.

"So now . . . let's tie the knot."

"Why don't you sing again?" Ginger suggested.

Elvis flashed her a smile and a grin. "One song a wedding," he declared. "But if you've got cold feet, there's another couple waiting behind you."

The crowd made it clear they expected a show. Elvis pointed a remote at the two doors that opened onto the strip and they popped open when he pressed the button. "Thanks for dropping in!"

"We're getting married," Saxon said.

Ginger felt her eyes bugging out again. "Are you crazy?"

"I'd say he's smart . . ." Elvis cooed. "Because you have it going on!" he made an hourglass with his hands, and the crowd hooted with delight.

Saxon was still beside her. She felt his breath in her

hair and felt his arm tighten around her waist. "Got a better idea?"

She didn't.

"Well now, let's get this party rollin'."

Elvis smoothed back his hair, the black wave settling back into place, proving his hairstylist was worthy of whatever price they were getting.

"Just step over here . . ." Elvis instructed Saxon.

It meant putting his back to the windows, and Ginger watched him flinch. She wasn't sure when she decided to do it, answer the impulse to ease the tension in him but she stepped over to the spot and faced Saxon.

The impersonator didn't say a word, just winked. "Take hands."

They both froze, staring at each other like a pair of startled raccoons.

"Dearly beloved . . ."

Saxon looked beyond her, his jaw tightening, telling her the man was still there. Her mouth went dry when she realized they were in fact getting married.

"Now . . . hold hands . . . Here come the vows."

Elvis was completely in his role, drawing out the words in Southern, king of rock-and-roll fashion. She really should have been able to laugh it all off or at least take it in stride, but the topic of "marriage" was stuck in her throat like a rock. He looked beyond them, tilting his ear as he listened to someone talking into a small security earplug.

"Seems we don't have a license folks . . ."

The crowd booed. Elvis lifted his hands. "Never fear . . . the King has everything you need."

There was a fanfare from the band as a man came forward. He had a bemused look on his face as he reached them. "Identification."

He had a tablet in hand and looked far too official for Ginger's fraying nerves. She chanced a look over her shoulder but tall, dark, and murderous was still there.

"Have we changed our minds?" Elvis asked. "Because—"

"You've got a line," Saxon cut the impersonator off. "I heard you the first three times."

"Hey man, just doing my job," Elvis said under his breath. "It's dammed hard to hold onto work in this town. Now are you two doing this or not? I get paid by the ceremony."

The gloves were off. Saxon's jaw was tight, and she was pretty sure she would have heard his teeth grinding if it hadn't been for the strains of "Blue Hawaii" playing in the background. Elvis wasn't intimidated. Saxon looked past her and bit back a word as he dug out his wallet. The clerk checked his identification as the crowd applauded.

"He's good," the clerk announced, earning another burst of approval from those watching.

Ginger felt her belly do a flip. He wasn't married, but he was about to be, to her.

She was rotten to the core, a flop of a human being. He was protecting her.

"She's good."

Ginger snapped back into the moment and realized Saxon had pulled her identification out of his wallet. The clerk was tapping something into his pad and a moment later, the girl who had given them the flowers was walking toward Elvis with a newly printed sheet. The clerk took it, gave it a last read before signing and sealing it.

"Is that—?"

"A marriage license?" Elvis interrupted her. "It certainly is!" He held it up to the delight of the audience.

Elvis let the crowd hoot and cheer for a long moment

before he sang a few notes into the microphone to quiet them down.

"Well now . . . let's get to the main event," he cooed.

Ginger recoiled, her pumps banging against the polished floor. Saxon reached out and clasped her wrists, pulling her to a halt.

"Repeat after me . . ." Elvis address Saxon. "I, Saxon Norman Hale, take thee, Ginger Melody Boyce to be my lawfully wedded wife . . ."

*He couldn't actually say it . . .*

But Saxon opened his mouth and spoke his vows. He had a near death grip on her wrists, holding her still as his voice filled her ears. She honestly thought she was going to pass out because she was holding her breath. It wasn't the grip; it was the look in his eyes. A glittering, intense light that made her feel like he enjoyed knowing he was binding himself to her.

Which was ludicrous.

"Now, repeat after me . . ." Elvis put the thumbscrews to her.

Saxon's eyes narrowed when she didn't speak up. There was something in his eyes that slapped at her, making her jump and draw in a deep breath. She avoided thinking too closely about just what exactly she'd seen because in her shocked state, she was imagining things. Like the fact that he looked hurt by her hesitation.

She felt tongue-tied and nervous in that moment, like she was taking a leap and just hoping the net would be there to catch her.

Saxon slowly stroked the back of her hands, sending a jolt up her arms as she absorbed how strong and steady he was. At some point, he'd stepped closer, making her tip her head back to maintain eye contact.

"Marry me, Ginger."

She drew in a second breath and used it to speak. Her voice was less than smooth, but her vows came out anyway.

"So sweet . . ." Elvis cooed. The crowd had settled down, several soft sounds of approval coming from the women.

The blood was roaring in her ears and her gaze was glued to Saxon's. It felt like his grip on her wrists was like a set of jumper cables and Elvis was making ready to turn the juice on.

"You may . . ." There was a rumble from the drums. "Kiss your bride!"

The room exploded into a frenzy of cheers while Ginger felt her heart stop. Seriously, the damned thing just froze in her chest as another look she hadn't seen before crossed Saxon's face. This time it was a heated one, one that made her gasp and caused her heart to jump back into rhythm.

He'd wanted to kiss her. She'd gotten that right because now she watched as he let his professionalism go. She saw the same desire she'd been trying to keep hidden from him.

She saw the desire glitter in his eyes a moment before he held her steady and stepped toward her, using that solid grip to keep her in place. He tilted his head, perfectly angling it so that he could press his mouth against hers, but he didn't rush the moment. He slid his hand around the side of her face, setting off a jolt of sensation that rocked her to her foundation.

She had no idea what she was expecting, only that the soft touch surprised her, because he wasn't pushing her around. No, he was coaxing her lips into a response, teasing them with a gentle motion that made her tremble while he grasped her nape and kept her exactly where he wanted her. It was the perfect introduction to intimacy, one that melted her heart. Her lips parted, a little gasp escaping them as she trembled and reached for him.

"Come on . . . kiss her!" Someone yelled.

Saxon opened his eyes, their gazes meeting for a moment, allowing her to see the stunned surprise in his blue eyes before he looked over her shoulder and his expression tightened. A moment later, he was wrapping his arm around her, binding her into an embrace that was inescapable. His fingers tightened on her nape, sending a torrent of sensation coursing down her body with the skin-to-skin contact. But he didn't smash her lips beneath his. She half expected him to, but he used that control she'd noticed in him, pressing his mouth against hers in a kiss that was demanding but not bruising.

It was soul shattering.

She twisted against him, not out of a need to escape, but the opposite. She was trying to get closer. His lips were moving against hers, pressing them apart as she reached up and gripped his shoulders, shivering at the feeling of having her hands on him. He was hard and hot and everything she craved at that moment. Nothing else seemed to matter. What were details compared to the way he tasted? She wanted more and rose up onto her toes to kiss him back, feeling more alive than she ever had.

She surprised him, she felt him quiver, just a tiny reaction that had the effect of tossing gasoline on the fire burning inside her.

But someone cleared their throat. Saxon lifted his head away, leaving her staring into his eyes when she opened hers. What she saw in those blue orbs stunned her. It was only a moment, but it felt like it lasted for an hour, leaving her knees feeling weak and her heart thumping so hard against her breastbone she wondered if it was going to end up bruised.

"Charming," Bram Magnus said from beside them.

Saxon stiffened and sent his man a cutting look. "Your timing sucks."

And with that comment, the bubble of bliss that she'd been suspended in burst, leaving her back in the grip of the riptide of reality.

What the fuck had she just done?

"Roof," Bram said.

Elvis had opened the doors that lead to the strip but Saxon wheeled her around and took off through the casino. Ginger heard the crowd hooting at them and making colorful remarks about making it to a room, but it got mixed up in the wash of noise from the slot machines. A man in a suit was standing near an elevator, not allowing anyone to step into it. Bram flashed him a two-finger salute as they dove inside it and he punched the button for the roof.

"Got a helicopter," Bram said as the elevator jerked and slipped into motion.

"Nice work," Saxon responded.

"Glad you think so. It's Dunn's." Bram's lips lifted into a sarcastic grin. "So you can thank him."

"It will be worth it," Saxon growled as he plucked the star lily off his chest.

The doors slipped open, revealing Dare Servant. The agent was off to their right, using an air conditioner as cover. He was mostly behind it and had his gun leveled at the elevator. Ginger recoiled, but Saxon slipped his arm around her waist and pulled her through the open doors while she was still trying to absorb all the details.

"Where'd you find them?" Dare asked as he moved the

gun. The agent didn't actually put it away, he just stopped aiming it at them. He was on guard, his eyes covered by dark sunglasses.

"Getting married," Bram offered with a flip of his hand.

"It beat joining Tyler Martin on the sidewalk," Saxon growled.

Bram was already halfway into the pilot's seat. "Agreed." He held up a piece of paper before letting it slip into the seat beside him. "But you're actually hitched, and it's a sure bet Martin will pull her information off the net since you have an official license. Better get her family hauled in."

"Shit," Saxon grunted.

"That's my line," Ginger said right before Saxon gripped her waist and lifted her into the helicopter. She landed in a puddle of netting and fabric as Bram started up the rotor of the aircraft and it whipped up the wind. Saxon was climbing in beside her, so she scooted across the backseat, half falling into it in her haste.

Saxon was on his phone. "You heard me, they're compromised. Pull them in now."

Ginger bit her lower lip to keep back the protest. Her brain understood, even if she didn't like it.

"My mom's a pistol," Ginger warned.

"I believe it," Saxon had stuffed his phone back into his pocket. "You get it from somewhere."

"In that case, your parents must be Spartans," she said.

The helicopter lifted off, filling the cabin with too much noise for any further conversation. It left her looking at the pleased expression on Saxon's face before he leaned toward her and buckled a harness around her.

"Your devotion to duty is admirable." His section leader was smothering his amusement, poorly. Saxon had such a tight hold on the phone, he heard a crack and then cussed as he realized he'd broken the glass.

"I can get it annulled."

"That can wait until after this case is finished," Kagan said smoothly.

"Explain," Saxon asked.

"We've got more important issues to address first. Like getting a judge and jury together for her to testify. With Carl Davis mixed up in this, I have a feeling that just might prove to be a challenge."

"Right." It was a solid truth, and he needed to focus. Tyler knew him, had trained him. It was time to deviate from his normal protocols and keep his damned mind off the fact that they were, in fact, married. "But it's getting annulled."

Saxon realized Ginger had paused in the doorway and heard him. It was just a refueling stop, a dot on the map in the desert, so there really wasn't any place other than the tiny restroom for her to go. He liked knowing she was close. She was watching him with those autumn colored eyes, his words like a slap in the face. The tone he'd used was the worst part. He watched the impact, unable to take the words back.

It made him feel like a turd. No girl deserved to be scorned on her wedding day, even if it wasn't a real wedding day.

*Hell* . . .

It was real and not real but that was the part that was making him feel like a turd. She'd rolled with the punches and deserved better than a situation that was nothing but a web of lies. Ginger Boyce was everything he'd first thought her to be, a good girl, one who deserved the best a man could give her while that same guy got up every day with the intention of doing even better.

The struggle would be worth it because those eyes of hers would be full of love. Even now, he found himself struggling to look away from her because he just liked the view so damned much. She made him believe in things he'd written off as romantic dribble and that was a dangerous place to go because without a doubt, he'd crush her heart.

Not on his watch. He left the burner phone behind, determined to cut any connection between his team and the outside world.

Of course he wanted an annulment. That made total sense.

So why did it hurt?

Ginger fluttered her eyelashes and made sure she didn't make eye contact with Saxon on the way back to the heli-copter.

It didn't really hurt. Her pride was just stinging, which she needed to get over immediately.

Her well-composed self-directed lecture didn't really lessen the impact of Saxon's words. He was pacing back and forth as he talked to whoever it was he reported to. Ginger moved back to the helicopter, intending to climb back into it. Saxon surprised her by ending his call and turning around to offer her his hand. She stared at his palm just knowing that she didn't dare touch him or she was going to lose it completely.

Why was he the guy who could kiss her like that? Like every dream she'd had of the man who would one day show up and sweep her off her feet? Take her past the awkward reality of sex and into smoldering passion, maybe even to that thing known as making love?

*Why him?*

*And why the fuck was she alone in the weird connection?*

She started to climb into the helicopter. Unfortunately, her pumps slipped on the skiff, sending her nose-first into the seat. Ginger got snared in the fabric as she struggled to gain her footing.

Saxon lifted her up, proving just how much strength he had in that tight, hard body before he righted her and held onto her arm to help her get back into the dammed aircraft. She ended up in the seat, sitting in a disheveled mess of cotton fabric and netting. One pump was on the floor and she just left it there while she aimed her attention out of the window to avoid catching the glances Bram and Dare sent her.

The tension was thick enough to cut and as she'd noticed before, these men were keener than most. So of course they picked up on it.

*Just . . . lovely.*

Ginger felt her cheeks turning red as Bram started up the helicopter. She was not going to think about that kiss.

Nope, wasn't going to happen, because she refused to pin her heart onto her sleeve or even her sexual libido. Saxon Hale wanted nothing to do with her? Fine. She would make sure she met the man in the middle and do her best to make it seem like she didn't care.

Life wasn't done with her yet.

Bram Magnus flew them down the state of California. Ginger was snapped out of her temper by the familiar sight of Cattle Creek. From the air, she did a double take, making sure she was really seeing her home town. Unlike a jet plane, the helicopter was at a lower altitude, allowing her to see the landmarks and buildings more completely.

The sight gutted her, leaving her fighting back tears until she slipped into sleep.

Kagan was done thinking. It was something Saxon had learned to respect but he started pacing as he waited for his section leader to inform him of what he'd decided.

"I'm going to let a little slack out on this case, let the details out on the hearing. You won't be bringing her anywhere near it," Kagan announced. "I want to see who has an interest in protecting the Raven."

"The good presidential hopeful Carl Davis would be a very likely candidate if I were looking for men who could get someone like Tyler Martin a badge and a team of federal resources," Saxon supplied.

"Tyler Martin has some pretty good friends. You might want to remember that."

"Why do you think I'm still carrying the package?" Saxon used the benign word for "witness" but it didn't seem to have any effect on just how much he wanted to kiss her again. "You want his head on a platter as much as I do."

"True," Kagan agreed. "It won't happen if Carl Davis is shielding him. That's more of a mountain to climb than we have resources for."

His section leader didn't care for it, either. Saxon heard it in Kagan's voice, but he wasn't stupid or short sighted. That was the reason Kagan was still alive.

"Carl Davis won't be able to gain a lead with the voters without Marc Grog's help. That's the only reason for Carl to put Tyler on my tail. It's a hell of a risk to be giving out Federal teams. Leaves a trail."

"I've got people trying to dig it up," Kagan confirmed.

"When this case lands, it will rip the cover off Marc's identity. Carl will backpedal away from him so fast, Marc won't have time to avoid the wave. We've got to catch them just right or settle for only taking Marc Grog down."

"And Tyler will suck up to Carl Davis as the bastard moves into the White House," Saxon finished up.

Quitting wasn't in his vocabulary, but logical thinking was, and he couldn't avoid facing the facts. The data was clear but it was surging through him in a far different manner than he was accustomed to. There was a definite flare of determination that had nothing to do with duty. It was personal and becoming more deeply rooted by the second.

A whole lot of people who wanted to be part of Carl's baggage train would be lining up to make sure Ginger never testified.

"Right, play time is over." Kagan's voice had turned hard. Saxon recognized the mission mode. It gave him a rush of satisfaction that was way out of line because logically, nothing was accomplished yet. In his line of work, you never counted actions until they happened. That didn't seem to keep him from feeling like he'd succeeded in throwing up a shield around Ginger.

That pleased him.

It shouldn't have, and he tucked the phone into his pocket with a frown on his face. He couldn't get caught up in personal emotions. He wasn't the guy for her. Normally he let facts rule his world, so he should be smart enough to wrap his brain around that one and hold tight.

But it slipped right through his grasp, leaving him thinking about the way she'd kissed him back. It sat on his brain like a live coal, just sizzling and burning a nice little crater for itself. Making itself at home.

He couldn't allow that. He needed to scrape it off and let it settle into the bin of memories associated with missions that were all stored under the heading of "necessary actions." Things he'd done to ensure the world was a brighter place.

Kissing her a second time hadn't been a necessity.

Fine, he'd wanted to do that. It was the truth, and he knew that lying to himself was a one-way ticket to complications. So, he'd pulled Ginger against his body and kissed her the way he'd wanted to, and he hadn't been disappointed.

That had been a conscious choice, one made with the best of intentions. He needed to focus on his motivations for that, for the dedication to duty that was the backbone of his life. Cold and hard? Maybe, but there was structure and solid foundation, too. With Ginger in his arms, there had only been impulse and reaction. He refused to adopt that as a mode of conduct, so he turned to look at his men, using their hard expression to find his balance. It was an operation, one he intended to succeed. So there weren't going to be any personal entanglements.

"We're in a holding pattern."

Dare Servant nodded and looked around the cabin. "At least we're doing it in style."

They'd landed at one of Dunn Bateson's properties. Located in the High Sierra Nevada, it was surrounded by timber. There was a river nearby, and the cabin itself was stunning. Built of large tree trunks, it had over four thousand square feet and every luxury a person could imagine. From the granite counter tops in the kitchen to the fixtures in the bathrooms, Saxon discovered himself wondering just what the hell Bateson did to earn the money he did.

Honestly, that wasn't the question burning a hole in

his brain when it came to Dunn Bateson. The guy had as many secrets as Kagan did. Greer McRae trusted him, and Greer was someone Saxon trusted. But Greer wasn't on his team at the moment, which left Saxon wondering just how thick the ice was beneath his feet.

He felt like he could hear it cracking, and the reason wasn't hard to deduce. Tyler Martin knew him. They'd trained together, worked side by side. Falling into routine was going to translate into a toe tag for him and his current team.

Saxon had more than his fair share of confidence, but Carl Davis was going to steamroll over him if he didn't get a team together to take him down.

He just hoped Kagan agreed with him.

They were in the forest.

It was strange the way the air smelled moist, more inviting. Ginger had always loved the rain. She peeked through a set of blinds, looking out at the trees as a light rain fell.

There was a very male sound of disapproval from behind her. She turned and found Saxon Hale shooting her a disapproving look.

Only she wasn't in the mood to be reprimanded. "I was peeking through the blinds. You don't need to glare at me."

"Innocent actions can have huge consequences."

She let out a sigh and bit back the response she'd intended to make. Her wedding bouquet was lying on a table behind him, the thing looking sad and dejected. The sight of it soured her mood.

"Say what you're thinking," he pressed her.

"To what end?" she asked. "You've made it clear how much you hate being married to me."

And she sounded way too upset about it. Saxon didn't miss it. She watched him contemplate her, like he just couldn't get a handle on her logic.

Well, at least they mystified each other. It was nice to know she wasn't alone.

"Are you saying you don't want an annulment?" he asked, sounding a lot more serious than her fragile emotions needed to notice.

She chickened out, looking away. It beat throwing herself at him.

Saxon wasn't going to take it from her though. He moved closer, looming over her. Surprise zipped through her as she locked gazes with him as he closed the distance. Damn but there was a serious buzz that went through her when he was close enough to touch. Her damned heart was actually accelerating.

"Was it really necessary to shout at your boss the second you got on the phone about getting an annulment? In front of your men?"

"It sure as hell was," he growled.

So close to him, smelling him, getting more turned on by the second by the sheer overwhelming presence of him, she didn't react well to the rejection. She reached out and tried to shove him back.

"Fine. Just . . ."

Saxon captured her wrists, jerking her to a standstill when she'd intended to push back from him.

"Because there is nothing I want to do more than play husband."

She was frozen in place as he leaned down and pressed his mouth against hers. She felt like a live current was moving between them, like jumper cables were bringing her to life. Her breath caught at the sheer intensity as she struggled to accept that it was truly happening. Saxon closed that last step between them, encasing her in his arms, trapping her completely as he kissed her like he owned her.

It was hard and carnal, sending a jolt through her system that left her unable to think. Oh no, there was nothing in her brain except impulses. She craved him, wanted to kiss him back with every bit of demand as he was unleashing on her.

But he recoiled, setting her back with a solid grip on each of her biceps.

The moment felt like an eternity, like they were poised on the crest of a rollercoaster, just waiting for it to drop as she listened to the way both of them were panting. Her belly was twisted with anticipation, and she saw a glitter in his eyes that let her know he felt it as well. Need was a pulsing, tangible thing between them, something with the power to enslave both of them. She had never needed to have sex before. Now, it felt like a necessity. A vital one.

"And that's why," he retreated, stepping back from her as he tightened his jaw.

Her brain wasn't making the switch back to logical thinking very smoothly, leaving her trying to understand what he meant.

"Is there someone else in your life?" It was way late to be asking, but at least she was getting around to it.

His lips slowly curved into a smile. Only it wasn't a happy expression, oh no, not from Mr. Agent man. Nope, this was a sensual, arrogant, solidly confident grin, one that made him devastatingly good looking. In the same way that an Orca was attractive—sleek, intelligent, but when you got close to one in the wild, you realized just how deadly they were.

"No," he offered in a tone that sent a shiver down her

back. She realized right then and there that he'd been using his professionalism like a shield. "I'm not a nice guy, Ginger," he spoke in a tone that was edged with warning. She felt it rippling across her skin, awakening a thousand little points of recognition. In short, it scared the wits out of her because of the intensity level, but it also thrilled her to the core.

"There isn't anything in my world for you except danger. You believe in happy-ever-afters, honey. Those don't exist in my world. I have a list of friends with benefits because I take sex when I'm between cases. I'm no good for you."

He went through the doorway, intending to leave her with those little gems. For sure, she should have left it there, but she'd heard the lament in his tone again, and it needled the shit out of her.

"You kiss good."

He heard her. She watched his shoulders tighten, his body flinch, before he turned into the hallway and disappeared. It most likely wasn't the wisest thing to have said, but she ended up behind the closed door of the bedroom, slipping down the door to sit against it in a puff of netting from her wedding dress as her lips tingled.

Oh yeah, she shouldn't have told him that, but she just couldn't seem to resist the urge to push him around. Maybe she wasn't as goody-two-shoes as he thought because at least when it came to Saxon, she had a real streak of devilment in her.

And Saxon Hale liked what he saw. Now that was a hell of a long way from vanilla.

# CHAPTER FIVE

Playing with fire.

It was a fascination man had dealt with since the dawn of time. Kagan grinned as he walked through the halls of the Capitol building. He didn't go unnoticed. No sir. He expected it because the crowd inhabiting the walls of the Capitol knew they had to look out for themselves. Everyone was replaceable and anyone with any sense knew they could be taken out by someone willing to go the additional mile, even if that took them through the muck and gutter.

Carl Davis fit into that category well. In fact, he thrived, feeding off the adrenaline rush. Kagan had watched him for years, noting the alliances he formed and the way he made friends with the right people. Tonight was no different. He was shaking hands and stopping for pictures with certain groups, while others went completely ignored.

Carl Davis offered his hand to Kagan. "Good to see you again."

"Happy to be of service."

Kagan knew how to play the game. He detested the

way Tyler Martin sold out, yet it was also something Kagan understood. Tyler was right about certain facts. Men like Carl Davis held a great deal of power. You could only dick with them so much and a wise man did so only as a last resort, which meant it was smart to try a private approach first. He moved down a hallway beside Carl as the man smiled and nodded.

The moment they were behind a sealed door, Carl abandoned his happy-go-lucky expression.

"You're a dedicated man, Kagan, I admire that." Carl leaned against his desk. "I am very busy."

"I never waste my time," Kagan replied. It was a calculated risk, trying to make Carl Davis think he was unconcerned about the warning he'd just issued. Carl milled it over for a moment, catching his lower lip between his teeth as he decided Kagan was worth listening to.

"Whatever it is, I'm glad you decided to come to me first," Carl said by way of an invitation to continue.

That was another warning. Kagan settled into a chair without an invitation. "Agent Hale has a witness who can identify the Raven."

Carl's face settled into a very practiced neutral expression. "Is that so? We need more men like the Hale brothers out there."

Carl was nervous. Kagan picked up the tiny details that confirmed his words were striking the target. The way Carl was tightening his grip on the armrest of his chair, the increased number of times he blinked, the tightening of his jaw were all signs.

Kagan sat forward. "The thing is this, the Raven has been causing too much trouble to ignore. The alleys have been full of bodies this year. The media is making a fuss over it. My superiors want someone brought in before they look too bad. Election year, you understand."

Carl slowly nodded. "I suppose things like that have to be dealt with." Carl dropped the act. "Cut the smoke screen. You have my attention."

"Tyler Martin has shown up twice on Saxon Hale's tail and tried to take out the girl with the aid of a very . . . Federal-looking team." Kagan stood up. "He's your man."

"He is." Carl made no apology.

"If you want to keep him, pull him in." Kagan advised.

"What makes you think your opinion matters to me?" Carl's complexion was darkening.

"I don't think it does," Kagan spoke softly. "But here's the thing; Hale is my man. If I have to start digging up how Martin keeps finding my agent team, well, I have a hunch that might matter to you, and I don't need to be on your bad side any more than you need me probing your private affairs. I think we're both better off staying on friendly terms. The Raven has attracted too much attention for me to ignore. Your choice is whether or not you want to keep your man."

"And remember that you let me have the choice," Carl cut back.

Kagan drew in a stiff breath. "He keeps killing my men. Normally, I'd just take him out. I had the opportunity."

Kagan gave Carl Davis a long, knowing look before he left the office. He knew he'd just painted a target on his back, but, honestly, he felt a little naked without one. He'd been in the Shadow opps for too long to start playing safe now.

"Your man missed her again." Marc Grog didn't mince words. "I should put a bullet through his skull."

"That would be a little harder than you think." Carl wasn't going to remain silent.

"I've brought down harder targets."

"And yet you were seen by a librarian," Carl countered.

There was a grunt on the other end of the line. "Know something? I don't have to back you for president."

"And I don't have to make sure the tax laws favor your business," Carl fought back. "Was there a reason for this call?"

"I'm getting an outside man. Contract killer. Someone who has the balls to do the job even if it means getting seen."

Carl stiffened. "That's a very bad idea. As fucked up as you sending Pratt after the Ryland girl. Do you have any idea how hard it was to bury the tie between the two of you? The scent is what drew Hale and his men down to the Quarter. If anyone gets wind of you putting money down on that girl, you are going to have a full-blown Federal investigation down there. Police department, everything. They will take it apart. You'll be useless to me with that sort of stink clinging to you."

"That's your problem. The girl is mine."

Marc hung up, leaving Carl glaring at the screen of his phone. It was a burner phone, untraceable to him so long as he didn't use it too much and got rid of it before too long.

It seemed the moment had come to part ways with Marc. He grunted out a word of profanity before he started to break the phone into pieces. He made sure to crush the data card and grind it a few times before putting it in a bin that was bound for the incinerator.

A contract killer was something he couldn't risk getting involved with. A good one was a man for sale and that meant he'd turn evidence on anyone. Carl pulled another phone from the inside pocket of his suit jacket and dialed up Tyler Martin.

"Yes?"

"Marc is hiring a contract killer to go after the girl. We're done supporting him."

"How done?" Tyler Martin asked.

"I need him to never be a problem again." Carl explained.

"I'll take care of it."

Carl killed the call, pissed at the turn of events. He paced in a circle, leaving footprints in the plush carpet of his office. He needed to make up those votes. It wasn't going to come easy either.

Marc Grog didn't get told what to do. His empire was exactly that, an empire, and he was the emperor.

Everything in his world revolved around him. Anyone who wanted to stay around needed to know that.

"It's time to take matters into our own hands," Marc informed his son Pulse. "We need someone to put a bullet in that little mouse."

His son nodded. "I'll find you a mouse hunter."

Marc didn't delegate easily, but there was one thing that helped keep people quiet even better than threats, and that was making sure they all had dirt on their hands. Didn't matter that it was his own flesh and blood and maybe, in some ways, it meant even more. Pulse stood and left while Marc struggled with the urge to do the job himself. No, he needed to let his boy shoulder the burden. Of all his offspring, Pulse was the one who had the balls to run the empire. His mother was a bitch, one that was only still alive because she'd raised up a man instead of a whelp like his other mistresses had. More than one of them hadn't been heard from in a very long time and they never would be again for their failure.

Yeah, Pulse would do what was needed.

And Marc could get on with making sure Carl Davis regretted his words.

Ginger slept like a baby.

Meaning she woke up every two hours and wanted to scream until someone removed all of the things around her that were making her uncomfortable. By the time the sun rose, her neck was knotted, her back ached, and there was something going on with her right arm because she'd slept on it wrong. She walked around the suite, opening and closing her hand as she tried to banish the tingling in her fingertips.

At least her surroundings were perfect. As in seriously, they were blissful. The lodge itself was a sprawling complex that was likely double the size of her parents' house. The suite she was in had a huge master bed, out-fitted with what had to be the best set of sheets she had ever slept in. The bed frame was made of iron and had brass flowers in it, that were all gleaming she might add. The thing was a California king if not a custom size. There was a delicious comforter that had welcomed her into it with a little poof but she'd still rolled around like she was sleeping in the back of a beat-up truck with nothing more than a sweatshirt.

She was in a pissy mood to be sure but smiled when she made her way into the retreat the suite offered. Be-tween the bedroom and the bathroom, there was an en-tire room outfitted just for relaxation, and one of the amenities was a little kitchenette. It made her morning because the last thing she wanted to do was set eyes on Saxon.

*You mean your husband?*

She filled the small coffee maker with water and grounds, inhaling the rich scent of java as it brewed and did her best to forget the word "husband." Honestly, she'd had much different expectations of what her wedding day would be. Such as a groom who wanted to be there.

*Still got the hots for him?*

Ginger snorted, pouring herself a cup of coffee and moving along on her tour of the suite before she followed that thought bunny down a path that promised her grief.

As in the sexual frustration sort.

Friends with benefits. She'd heard the term tossed around, usually by guys that looked at it as some sort of free pass to unlimited nookie. Not Saxon. She slowly drew off some of the coffee, hearing the tone of his voice again. Saxon saw it for what it was. A shallow substitution for the intimacy all humans craved.

He was a good guy.

As in golden, hero sort of material. She really should scrounge up some self-discipline, if for no other reason than he'd saved her life. There was one solid rule she had taken to heart from her grandmother and that was don't try to change a man. Saxon Hale was an agent. A really good one who deserved to be respected for the path he walked. He was the sort who would feel a twinge from his conscious when he moved on.

*Yeah, he kissed you first . . .*

*You wanted it . . .*

Well, she was an idiot sometimes. The coffee was warming her up, helping her fingers feel normal. The day crawled by. She read and paced and started to know the time by the routine checks in on her by Saxon's men. She didn't see him, though. He was a nocturnal animal to be sure. She fought the urge to nap because she didn't need to be wide awake when he was.

Truth was, she didn't trust herself.

By the time the sun set, she was bored off her gourd.

She moved around the suite again and stopped in the doorway of the bathroom. She'd been too exhausted the night before to enjoy the splendor of it. Now, the mug of coffee was forgotten as she peered into the expanse of marble-floored delight. Every one of her feminine senses was sighing. There was a large tub, like a vintage one you expected to see in an upstairs room of a historic brothel. A slipper tub with a high back and all covered in creamy enamel with brass claw feet. It sat with a view out a huge, floor-to-ceiling window that had gauze curtains drawn over it for privacy but still afforded a view of the forest and mountains. Next to it was a fireplace that lit with the simple push of a button, sending blue and orange flames licking up and over a set of glass logs inside it. The lights adjusted so that she could see the stars through the sky-light. A full moon was just beginning to brighten one corner of the glass, and there was no shade to be closed tight against her seeing into the world beyond the suite.

It was exactly what she needed.

Ginger stripped. There was a bench next to the tub that held a selection of oils and bath salts. She happily selected one and opened it up as she turned the water on and the tub started to fill. It really was like a spa. There were all the little grooming tools a girl could dream of, and she happily settled back into the warm water as she giggled and added some bubble bath. White, foamy suds were soon filling the tub and covering her completely. She scooped a handful up and blew them, indulging completely in a moment of much needed playfulness.

Reality could go suck it for the next hour.

"You're beginning to get on my nerves."

Saxon turned and thought for a moment as he stared at Dare Servant. His fellow agent only looked back at him with a steady, confident glare that made it clear he didn't give a rat's ass for how insubordinate his words might strike Saxon.

"I don't know," Bram Magnus spoke up from where he was stretched out on a sofa where he'd settled in after Dare officially relieved him of duty. "It's entertaining to watch him pace . . . .and twitch."

"You've been deployed too long," Saxon informed Bram.

Bram lifted his hand into the air and offered him a thumbs up.

"There are plenty of beds around here," Saxon suggested.

Bram let out a groan and rolled onto his feet. "Yeah, Dunn knows how to live."

"He knows how to do more than that," Dare said as Bram headed off to catch some shut-eye before he had to take another shift. "The man brings in some serious cash to afford a place like this."

"Guess I should try not to burn this one down." Saxon replied. He was contemplating Dunn Bateson, or at least he was trying to keep his thoughts on the elusive Scot in the hope it would help him stop thinking about Ginger.

His wife.

It was a hell of an idea, one he really doubted he was up to the challenge of leaving alone. He needed an annulment to keep her at arm's length, and that was a fact, because she wasn't helping the situation by giving him encouragement about how much she liked his kiss.

Hell, he'd known she'd enjoyed it. The feeling of her moving closer to him, reaching for him, kissing him back was like a red hot coal just twisting around in the gray matter of his brain. The carpet was marked from his pacing, and the damned idea was still glowing fiery red.

He needed that annulment like a vaccine. Otherwise, he was going to end up with a massive case of need for more of her.

"I'm not your man."

Pulse didn't want to hear that. He glared at the contract killer called Pullman sitting in front of him. "I thought you told me you were the best."

The contract killer flashed him a smile that revealed perfect teeth, but his eyes remained ice cold. "I am, but Saxon Hale will make me before I get within a hundred yards of his witness." The man tapped the desk top, clearly thinking. "Call Sullivan. He's got a puppy face and he's new to the game. He might be able to slip under Hale's nose. Maybe."

Pullman got up and went out of the door. It took some time to make it past the security that surrounded Marc Grog's filming headquarters in the Arizona desert. No one arrived unannounced to the complex. There was a sprawling make-shift campground outside it where the employees lived in trailers and motor homes. Pullman drove away from it, putting miles and miles of desert under the tires of his truck before he pulled into a small town and waited for his phone to ring. Tyler Martin didn't disappoint him.

"Sullivan should be getting a call. I expect my payment to be transferred. Getting in with Grog would have been good for me."

"Being friends with me will be better," Tyler Martin responded. "You've been paid."

"And?" Pullman demanded.

"I will be in touch," Tyler finished.

Tyler killed the call and Sullivan snickered at him from where he was sitting across a table from him.

Sullivan lifted up the glass he was drinking some sort of dark ale out of and toasted Tyler.

"Here's to business together," Sullivan declared without a care for how loud his voice was.

"Just remember, the deal doesn't go down until I tell you. I need Marc dead, under the correct circumstances. The mouse is our bait. I have a use for her when the first stage is complete."

"Right," Sullivan replied as he wiped his mouth on the sleeve of his shirt. "Don't you worry. I can talk a priest under a vow of silence in circles for hours."

Sullivan was an Irishman and proud of his gift for gab. He was also very sure of his capacity for holding his liquor. He stood up and happily went up to the bar in search of another ale. The barkeep was happy to serve him because Sullivan was leaning on the bar, talking to the man as though they were brothers. Before too long, Sullivan had everyone at the bar eating out of his hand like he was a local and there every night of the week.

Tyler slowly smiled before he slipped out of the door. It was the skill a contract killer needed, that ability to insert himself into the surroundings. Tyler walked down the sidewalk and onto the beach before he pulled out a cell phone and called Carl Davis.

"What news do you have for me?"

"I've got a man going in, one that will make Marc believe he's going mouse hunting."

"Good . . . good," Carl answered. "Keep me in the loop. I'm going to use the witness to back my cleaning-up-the-world image."

"I figured." Tyler ended the call, taking a moment to look at the waves crashing on the shore. He felt satisfied for the first time in a long time. It was a welcome feeling, one he'd gone to a great deal of effort to achieve. Carl Davis was the kind of man he could work with. Jeb Ryland had just been a stepping stone. Tyler didn't miss him. In fact, it was rather nice to recall how the bastard had been shot by his own wife. Sure, the media had broadcast a different tale, but that was their job, to believe what men like he and Carl Davis told them to.

Ricky Sullivan would help him make a new story, one that told the end of Marc Grog. After that was finished, he could take his place in Washington, that position he'd devoted himself to earning for the past decade. It was about damned time he got his reward.

No one was going to stand in his way. Not even an innocent like Ginger Boyce. He'd worked too damned hard and sold far too much of his soul. It wasn't personal, just the way life was.

It was a competition sport, and he intended to win.

"Interesting bit."

Saxon was used to Thais Sinclair's husky drawl of a voice. The female agent was sex appeal covered in creamy skin but today, he discovered it less noticeably. He frowned and realizing that was directly linked to meeting Ginger.

*Since kissing her, you mean.*

"What have you got?" he asked Thais to distract himself from the entire idea of what it had felt like to have Ginger in his arms.

"A hit on your witness's work file. Someone is reading up on her."

Saxon grunted and felt his temper shift but for a different reason than he was accustomed to. This wasn't about the mission goal. It didn't have anything to do with professionalism and someone's lack of attention to details. It was very personal.

"Someone is digging into Ginger's information," Saxon clued them in. The tension tightened in the room.

He was down the hallway and around the corner before he thought much about it and only gave her a quick rap on the bedroom door before he was pushing it in.

"What are you doing?"

Ginger looked up, startled out of her moment of stolen bliss to see Saxon staring at her like he'd walked in on her sacrificing a goat. She had to clamp her jaw shut so that a snort of amusement didn't make it past her lips. She'd startled him, and by now, she knew for certain it was a rare achievement. But that wasn't the real reason she fought back the urge to smile. No, the truth was, she rather liked knowing he couldn't take his eyes off her.

"I am taking a bubble bath." She spoke each word slowly and pushed one of her feet up into view above the mound of suds.

"No shit."

He suddenly stepped into the room all the way and shut the bathroom door. But he froze, clearly undecided on his next action.

"The bedroom door was closed," she offered before looking up at the stars. "And there is no shade to be pulled tight over the skylight. So, I was making the best of my circumstances."

"I'm responsible for your safety, Ginger. Any door between us will be opened. You need to be prepared for that."

She shifted, and the water moved, dislodging a portion of the suds shielding her from his view. For a moment, his attention shifted, lowering to the surface of the water, his lips thinning in a way that fascinated her because it sent a surge of heat straight though her core.

"Right," she cooed softly, drawing his gaze back to hers as he pressed his lips together so tightly they turned white. "There is no personal space in safety."

He gave her a nod of approval while she basked in the sensation of knowing she was teasing him. She liked the feeling a whole lot. It was becoming addictive and showing all the signs of blossoming into a habit.

Yup, she was going to hell, but it seemed she was going to enjoy the trip.

"You should keep your clothes on," he instructed her. "One of my men might have come in here."

"Sure thing," she said, her voice back to that husky tone that seemed to awaken whenever she was near him. Ginger watched its impact on him right before she stood up.

"Not—"

She was already on her feet, suds slithering down her body. He went rigid. Something dangerous glittered in his eyes. She recognized that fact on some deep level where instinct ruled. A shiver went down her spine in response but not one born of fear. Something awakened inside her that liked what it saw in his eyes.

It was the thing that had filled her restless night and the reason he'd taken that second kiss. No matter what, she didn't want to look back and have to admit she'd been too chicken to enjoy the time she'd been in his company.

"You have no idea what you're doing, Ginger," he warned her softly.

She believed him. Hell, it was more than that, it was more like she understood on some deep level that she'd

only been toying with him. Saxon wasn't playing anymore. He stepped toward her, and she felt frozen in place
by the heat flickering in his eyes. It transfixed her, filling
her with a confidence she'd never experienced before.

He liked what he saw.

"I don't," she answered without thinking. "And yet . . .
I think maybe I have a better idea than you do. Sometimes you have to make the best of what life hands you."

He'd stepped up close, looking down at her from his
greater height. His lips were twisted into a grin that was
one hundred percent warning. She felt it rippling down
her body, making her super aware of her bare skin. Her
nipples drew tight, her clit beginning to throb.

The guy aroused her on a scale she never even knew
existed.

"I know exactly what you're doing, Ginger," he warned
softly. "You deserve better."

Locked inside of him was something very rare, the
code of a gentleman. One that gave true meaning to the
word honor.

"You're playing with fire," he informed her through
gritted teeth.

He hooked her arm and pulled her to him, stepping
up so that she collided with him. This time, he kissed
her hard, claiming her mouth like he owned it. He was
damned strong, stronger than she'd realized, but all that
realization did was make her bold. It was a thing she had
craved without being able to put a name on it. She flattened her hands on his chest, letting her fingers slip over
the ridges of muscles beneath the pressed cotton of his
shirt.

And she kissed him back, matching him, opening her
mouth and letting her tongue tangle with his. Need went
clawing through her insides. Like a wave hitting the

beach, it crashed over her, hitting every inch of her as she rose onto her toes to kiss him even harder. She wasn't close enough, and his clothing frustrated her. She found the knot of his tie and tugged it loose, dipping her fingers into his collar and finding his skin at last.

Saxon growled softly, the sound more of a compliment than any words might have been. He captured her nape, holding her in place as he ravished her, kissing her breathless as he pressed against her and let her feel just how hard his cock was. She made a half-sound of surprise, but, honestly, it wasn't one formed in shock. It was approval and encouragement, but he pulled back, opening his eyes and letting her see the glitter of demand flickering there. But there was also a flicker of determination to resist.

"I am playing with fire." She popped two more buttons on his shirt. "Tell me, do any of your friends with benefits make you feel like this?"

His jaw tightened, but so did his hand in her hair. She felt him capturing her, making her his prisoner as his eyes narrowed.

"No."

It was a short, clipped word and Saxon acted on the admission immediately. He shifted and scooped her up. Ginger gasped and felt his chest rumble with a chuckle as he carried her to the bed like she weighed as much as a puppy.

That was the last clear thought she had as he straightened up after placing her on top of the comforter. He tore his shirt off, stilling her breath. A moment later, he was pushing her back, pressing his bare torso onto hers, a connection that felt like a collision between two locomotives.

She moaned, overwhelmed by the sheer bliss. Her

body had somehow dialed up her senses, every little touch coming across in booming, deafening high volume.

"No, I've never wanted them like I want you," he growled as he hovered over her for a moment.

He'd pressed her onto her back, and she rebelled against that, reaching for him. She flattened her hands on his chest, a little hum of appreciation escaping her lips as she slid her fingers over the sculpted ridges and up to his neck.

"Damn," he growled as he stretched his neck back, closing his eyes as he let her stroke him.

Ginger lifted up and off the bed so that she could press a kiss against his throat and once she started, she needed more, much more. Saxon groaned and rolled back as she went after him, but he gave as good as he got, cupping her breasts and teasing her nipples with his thumbs before he was twisting and capturing one of those tight peaks between his lips.

She gasped, sensation making her arch because it felt like her nipple was hardwired straight into her spine.

"That's it baby," he cooed as he looked up her body while cupping her breast. "Let's both play with fire."

Or in her case, let it consume her.

Which was just fine by her.

Saxon recaptured her nipple, drawing it deep inside his mouth. She twisted because there was just so much need churning inside her. A need to touch him and be touched in return. He was a feast for her senses.

Saxon released her nipple, sending a little shaft of frustration through her. It sharpened the edge of her need, making her feel mean. Like she needed to take what she craved.

"Not a chance baby," he cupped her shoulder and pressed her back onto the bed. "I'm in control here."

Ginger shifted, bringing her knee up so that it brushed his cock. "I don't think so."

He stiffened, and she took the opportunity to reach down and pop open his waist band. A moment later she'd slid her hand inside his pants, seeking out his length.

"Trying to get me by my tender parts?" he asked as she succeeded.

His eyes narrowed, his lips thinning as she drew her hand along his cock. It was a primal look, one that betrayed how much he liked what she was doing. So she sent her hand back down to the base and pulled her fingers along it again.

"Fuck," he whispered.

Ginger smiled with victory, but his eyes weren't as completely closed as she'd thought. His lips curled into a grin that was far from friendly. It was pure intent and there was a glint in his eyes that matched when he pegged her with a hard look.

The bed rocked as he pushed back and somehow landed between her thighs.

"You are too damned strong, know that?"

He snorted at her as he looked up her body and slowly stroked the inside of her thighs. "Fire is base, baby. Play with it and you're going to get the animal."

*Yes, please* . . .

There was a crazy twist of excitement going through her belly. She had never been so conscious of just how much she wanted to have sex before. She felt empty, so needy she would have begged for his touch, but he didn't make her. No, Saxon read her face like a book, teasing the curls on the top of her slit before he spread her folds and leaned down to lap her.

She cried out, the contact so jarring, climax almost burst through her.

"Easy," he'd pulled away just a bit, and his breath was still hitting her flesh. "Too loud and we'll have company."

Her eyes opened wide. "I forgot."

"Good," Saxon sounded more satisfied than she'd ever heard. He was teasing her sex with his fingertips. Stroking her everywhere, especially on her clit where she needed his touch the most. She looked down at him, desperate to discover why he held off. Their gazes locked, giving him a moment to show her the glitter of victory in his eyes before he leaned down and sucked her clit.

It was jarring, jolting, another collision between their flesh. Only this time, she felt the impact, clearly experienced the way she was being pushed to her limits before everything broke apart. She was clawing at the bedding and then at his hair. She couldn't breathe as the orgasm ripped through her. All she could manage was to twist as it consumed her.

It held her tight for a moment that felt like an eternity and then dropped her in a panting heap back into reality where she ended up staring at the skylight above the bed while she sucked in breath.

"I want you to forget every man but me."

Saxon was moving up to cover her. Somehow, she still needed him just as desperately as she had before, and he didn't deny her. She felt his cock teasing the wet folds of her slit, gasping as those tender bits of skin registered him slipping between them, pushing to her opening, and deeper still, until he was deep inside her.

He groaned, but, honestly, it felt like the sound came out of both of them because of how in tune she was with him.

"Every . . . fucking . . . one of them." He growled as he started to move. "Forget them all."

It would be simple. In that moment, all she felt was

the way he stretched her to fit him. How hard every inch
of him was and how close to the barrier of pain she was.
So close that it fed her needs, increasing the churning inside her, until she was lifting her hips to make sure his
thrusts slid deep and hard into her.

But he was too controlled. She opened her eyes and
found him watching her. The look on his face was primal. He wanted to command her, but he held himself in
check. She found it an unbearable barrier, one she needed
to rip away.

"Harder," she insisted.

He shook his head, denying her that lapse in self-
discipline. "I'm in control . . ."

Ginger reached up between them, flattening her hands
against his chest as he drove her near insane with the
slow pace he set. Every thrust sent a ripple of pleasure
through her but left her craving the wildness she glimpsed
in his eyes.

*"Don't . . . be . . . controlled . . ."* She cupped his
shoulders and curled her fingers into talons, scrapping
him as she drew her hands down and over his pectorals.

He growled at her.

"I want . . . *you* . . ." she demanded. "Not the agent . . .
assigned to . . . me."

She watched her words hit him. Pleasure brightened
his eyes a moment before he caught her hands and pinned
them to the bed next to her head.

"Mine," he snarled as he moved faster.

He held her in place, but she rose to take each thrust.
It was hard, and he didn't hold back, pushing them both
into another place where the only thing that mattered was
the way they crashed into each other and the friction it
created. Ginger felt herself teetering on the edge, and
she strained toward him, ready to take the plunge into

the building madness. She wanted him to be with her, so she bucked, straining up toward him to break his control. She watched it shatter in the same instant that she felt herself snapping. The wave they'd both been riding crested and crashed, rolling them in its powerful grip. The only solid thing was him, so she clung to him as they tumbled, pleasure encasing them and tossing them up onto the shore when it was finished.

She was likely half dead but didn't care.

Not one little bit.

Dunn Bateson had priorities in life.

The media liked to take stabs at defining them from time to time, and all that did was make him smile. They thought he was motivated solely by profit margins.

They were wrong. That wasn't to say that he didn't pay attention to his bottom line, because he did. Business was a challenge, one that barely fed his need to sharpen his teeth. But there was one thing he considered more important than money and that was family. He looked at the email from his aviation division on his helicopter. Well, his west coast one anyway. Having ready transportation at hand was a necessity in his business. The aircraft was accounted for and returned with a thank-you. The gratitude might turn into its own form of payment at some point and the media hounds could call him whatever they wished for thinking that way.

Favors needed to be repaid. It was just a fact, one he'd be a fool to overlook. In this case, he'd given one out, and he would expect Kagan to remember it, if the time came when Dunn needed something from the American government.

But that wasn't what snared his attention tonight. He stood and took a tumbler of Scotch with him to one of the floor-to-ceiling windows that adorned the side of his office. Aberdeen had its share of stone buildings, a testament to the history of his country. The buildings reminded him how important history was, and that meant family to him.

Saxon Hale was on the run, and his brother didn't know. Sure, it wasn't his blood, and, honestly, Vitus Hale owed him, too, but in an indirect way. It had been Greer McRae who reached out to him for Vitus Hale, and Greer was kin. Dunn took another sip of the whiskey, enjoying the burn before he went back to his desk, his decision made. He punched up a file, and dialed the number.

"Drinking alone again?" Vitus Hale hadn't lost any of his brass.

"By my choice," Dunn offered with a heavy coating of smugness.

"What's on your mind?"

"I'm going to share something personal with you." Dunn took another sip as Vitus waited. There was a soft sound near him, one that made Dunn smile because he knew he'd called in the early morning hours for the east coast of the U.S. Vitus proved himself worthy of his history as a Seal by answering the phone without hesitation.

"You were going to share something important?" Vitus prompted him.

"Family is everything."

Vitus made a sound of agreement. "Why do I get the feeling this is about my brother?"

"Because you aren't dense," Dunn offered with a smile. "I thought you'd like to know that your brother borrowed my Las Vegas helicopter and landed it in the mountains. Seems he has a witness who can confirm the Raven's identity, and Tyler Martin has almost caught him twice."

"You're right." Vitus tone had hardened. "I want to know that. The damned fool should have called me. Martin will be able to piece together that flight plan at some point."

"When you see him, tell him this for me," Dunn continued.

"I'm listening."

"Tell your brother never, ever, disturb a lady during her bubble bath."

There was a long pause before Vitus spoke. "Right. I don't want to know the details."

Dunn killed the call and wiped the file off his computer from the security camera at his mountain lodge. Honor was the only true thing that a man owned. Saxon Hale's bride would be mortified to know she'd been filmed but in this case, it might just get her husband the help he needed before Tyler Martin and Carl Davis made a widow of her.

Maybe.

Which only meant he needed to do something about helping ensure the outcome was the right one. The world was full of unfairness, and it was his personal pleasure to outsmart that reality whenever possible. He wore the scars of his own brush with that side of life.

For a moment, Dunn felt the chill that still seemed to radiate from his past. In a way, it had become a sensation he enjoyed because it meant that his heart wasn't completely dead.

He slowly smiled and took another sip of his drink, killing the shiver with the hard bit of firewater. The rest of the world didn't need to know about his weakness. As far as they were concerned, he was heartless. So he was going to insert himself into the game and make sure Carl Davis didn't win.

He pressed a button on his phone, speed dialing his flight-control manager.

"I need to fly to Vegas."

Saxon enjoyed the wee hours of the night.

The world was quiet, and pretty much only the bad guys and the badge holders were out. It also gave him the chance to look in on his witness while no one was awake to critique his interest in her.

He slowly buttoned his shirt, hating the way the fabric felt against his skin.

Ginger was sound asleep. He stood near her bed, watching her chest rise and fall. Her eyes were closed, so he allowed himself a moment of unguardedness. The sight of her in sleep did something to him, something he didn't want to define because that would just lead down a path of temptation he didn't need.

Still, the scent of her skin was teasing his senses.

She smelled good. She'd felt even better, especially her hair when he buried his face in it. That idea pushed another one of his buttons, only this one was a hot one, and his cock twitched, thickening, hardening.

He was fucking out of line, and she deserved better from him.

"Don't."

Saxon froze as she spoke. Ginger opened her eyes and pegged him with a look that was far more knowing than he was used to seeing on anyone except his brother and his men. Damned if that didn't impress him.

Just about as much as it scared him.

"Just . . . don't go there," Ginger told him as she sat up.

He'd covered her up, but the blanket slipped down as she moved.

"I knew what I was doing, so . . . no need for guilt."

He'd finished with his shirt and was shrugging into his shoulder harness. She didn't recall him taking the thing off or putting his gun on the bedside table. Heat teased her cheeks because she sure recalled the way she'd been desperate to get to his skin. That part was crystal clear.

"No you didn't, Ginger," he informed her. "An operation like this often leads to—"

"Stockholm Syndrome." She supplied the clinical term. She'd surprised him and decided that it gave her a punch of much-needed confidence. "Sorry if you feel used."

"Goddammit, Ginger." He was suddenly there beside her, the bed rocking as he captured the back of her hair. "You deserve better."

He was using that commanding tone that no doubt accounted for just how effective he was as a special agent. Ginger felt the boldness that seemed to awaken only for him stirring inside her. She really liked the way it felt. She was pushing him, and he was breaking open a shell she hadn't realized she'd been living inside of.

"You are better than any man I've ever known."

He tensed as she spoke, recoiling from her. "This is my job."

"Except that you've made it a lifestyle." And it made her mad. "You've forgotten how to have fun. I'm naked, the bedroom door is closed, we're supposed to be having . . . fun."

She grabbed a pillow, swinging it full force at his head. He'd had his gaze locked with hers but still caught the motion and raised an arm to block it. The pillow curved around his forearm. She lifted her foot and flipped over onto her side to land a good kick against his backside. With the pillow in the way, she scored a direct hit.

Saxon reacted instantly, jerking around and grabbing her ankle. She pulled her legs back out of instinct, and just that fast, he was back in the bed with her. Ginger grabbed another pillow and socked him in the back of the head with it.

"And you also . . ." she declared as she lifted the pillow up for another go, "have a stick up your ass that you've named 'duty'."

Saxon flipped over, proving just how strong his abs were before he was diving at her to prevent her from hitting him again. She ended up tackled onto the foot of the bed, in the darkness, the smell of him wrapped around her, delighting her. She flattened her feet on the mattress and used the strength in her legs to heave him upward while she shoved her hand against his jaw and pushed his head to the side.

He rolled off her, landing on the bed beside her, but she heard a deep, amused chuckle coming from him.

"What? You think a librarian can't wrestle?" She grunted with her victory and flashed him a smile. "Small town, means lots of guys who go off to the military in search of a bigger life come home and teach the rest of us what they learned in basic training. It's called fun."

Saxon stared at her from where he was sprawled on the bed alongside her. Enough moonlight was coming through the skylight to wash his face in silver.

"Fun . . . huh?"

There was a warning in his tone. As in he-was-about-to-do-his-best-to-even-the-score sort of tone. She had about half a second to try and evade him before he was on her and tickling her.

Ginger squealed as she tried to gain some leverage to escape.

"Yeah . . . this is fun!" he exclaimed as he found her sensitive spots and dug in.

She couldn't catch her breath because every time she dragged in a lungful, she ended up squealing it back out again. The man had an unfair advantage of seeming to know just where to torment her unprotected body.

The light suddenly flipped on as Dare Servant looked through the sights of his gun and down the barrel at them. Ginger was pretty sure her face went up in flames and she knew for certain she heard Saxon cuss.

"Might be a good thing all the way around that you two are hitched," Dare mumbled before he pulled the door shut and left them.

With the light on, it felt like the moment burst, leaving her in the grasp of cold reality. But that wasn't what hurt. It was the sight of Saxon withdrawing behind an unreadable mask, and it made her grateful for the fact that she'd reached for him and hadn't missed the chance.

"You bring out the best in me," Ginger said.

She stared into his blue eyes as he dropped his guard and looked at her in astonishment.

"Don't say that." He sounded like he truly meant it and kindly so. He wasn't exactly the cuddly sort, and yet there was compassion in his gaze. It wrapped around her, tugging at her heartstrings. "I've been a lot of things that aren't pretty, but I know when I dropped the ball. You're my witness. I should have been able to keep the line tight."

"Except"—she stretched out and pulled the blanket around her bare body—"you're a street team."

He scoffed at her and reached across the space between them to smooth the hair back from her face. Her tongue got stuck to the roof of her mouth as she watched the way his gaze followed his fingertips, like touching her completely captivated him.

She'd never had that sort of effect on a man and it swept her reason completely aside.

He'd settled onto one elbow. "Don't make excuses for me, Gin."

"Actually, I'm making them for me," she offered with a shrug. "This is your job. It isn't your fault I'm grasping at the moment in an effort to hold onto life."

It was a depressing little fact. One that killed the mood of the moment as she was forced to face the music. In her case, it just might be winding down.

"Don't."

His tone had sharpened, becoming commanding once again. He moved and cupped her chin, keeping her from breaking eye contact. "Don't toss in the towel, Gin. I will not let anyone take you out."

He meant it. She heard the confidence in his voice but all that did was horrify her. "Maybe you shouldn't get in the way."

"What is that supposed to mean?"

She shook off his grip and scooted out of his reach. "It means I know how far the Feds will go to protect their sources. Seems really stupid for you to get killed along with me. The odds are not in my favor, and I know it. Okay?"

He caught her up against him with a motion that was sharp and fast. The bed rocked and before it was finished swaying, she was locked against him. She was so freaking aware of him, it was like her very skin was sensitive to his presence. It felt like someone had plugged in the Christmas tree lights for the first time. Her senses were overwhelmed, the magic of the moment off the scale.

"There is no way I will leave you." His tone had deepened, stroking something inside. She felt like every muscle she had was so tight, it might just snap. Anticipation was flooding her, drowning everything except her fascination with him.

And she fucking loved the feeling of being on the edge, poised, ready, so certain, and then again, absolutely clueless because she just couldn't think. But she held back.

"I wanted to hold the line tight between us." He stroked her cheek. "You're better than I deserve. My hands are too dirty to put on you, and all I want to do is touch you."

He held back because he respected her. It was a deep compliment, showing his honor. She'd never thought she'd come face to face with true gallantry. It stunned her, leaving her silenced as she stared at the sincerity in his eyes.

It was absolutely humbling.

"You're everything I ever hoped to find in a man."

She just couldn't stop herself from reaching for him. He clamped her against his frame while he tilted his head and claimed her lips.

Ginger withered, unable to contain the sheer amount of sensation inside herself. She had to move, needed to press against him. She had never realized why her breasts were soft; it was so they could press against his chest while she kissed him back with every bit of hunger she had gnawing at her insides.

She was ravenous.

And so was he.

Saxon captured her head in his hand, holding her in place as he kissed her like he owned her. Pressing her mouth open and plunging his tongue inside to stroke hers in a blunt suggestion of the sort of no-holds-barred intimacy he wanted to demand of her. His arm had been around her waist, but he stroked her lower back right down to her bottom, curling his fingers around one cheek and pulling her into contact with his erection.

Solid, strong, immovable. Things she hadn't realized were missing until now. She felt the difference now, bone deep, and it broke something loose inside her.

"I can feel that." His tone was just as dark as the night around them, and it stroked her appetite.

"Feel what?"

He made a sound under his breath that was a cross between frustration and longing. He shifted, bringing them more in alignment and very deliberately cupped her breast.

"You tremble when I touch you."

She shivered, certain that one touch was hot enough to brand her skin.

"Stop saying that like it's a bad thing." She moved her body against his in a greeting, an enticement, something that was instinctual. Her brain was rapidly shutting down, leaving her at the mercy of her impulses. "I'm still alive, and I want to feel everything."

"I can do that for you, baby," he rasped. "Make you feel."

She honestly couldn't think of a better fate, at least not while he was there to share it with her.

She slipped her hands up his chest, feeling him quiver beneath her fingertips. "I feel you responding, too. That's not the mark of a callous man."

He drew in a deep breath, his eyes closing as she slipped her hand up and onto the back of his neck. When he opened his eyes, she witnessed the need there and something that cut straight into her heart.

She laughed under her breath, enjoying the sight just as much as the feeling of being against him.

He pushed her back and straightened back up so that

he could stroke her. Saxon Hale knew a hell of a lot about petting too. He used those strong hands to stroke her from neck to hipbones, in a long, smooth motion that made her breath catch. She was caught between the rapture his touch produced and fascination with the way he watched her.

Like he owned her.

Maybe in that moment he did. It was a willing submission on her part, sinking into the bed and letting him cup her breasts and gently knead them. Her nipples drew into hard points, proclaiming just how much she enjoyed being his pet. His lips curved with satisfaction a moment before he ventured lower and spread her thighs wide. He was sitting there on his haunches, once again keeping her exactly where he wanted her.

And once more, she rebelled.

Ginger curled up and opened his fly. She kept going until she had her thighs locked around him and his cock deep inside her. He sucked in a deep breath, cupping her hips as she wound her arms around his neck. If there was a definition of perfect, that moment was it. Ginger wanted to savor it, delay the climax that was charging toward her, but her body refused to listen. Not when he was deep inside her. Remaining still was impossible. Instinct ruled, driving them both toward the friction they craved.

Pleasure ripped through her as she felt him beginning to erupt inside her. That hot, spurting of release that somehow deepened the orgasm rippling through her insides. She forgot to breathe. Forgot everything except the need to cry out with pleasure. His or hers, there was no clear separation, so she rode the wave while clinging to him.

Saxon had dressed again while she was still only half aware of the rest of the world. She cracked her eyes and looked at him checking his gun.

"Can't get caught with my pants down," he offered softly.

"Except that you have been," someone said from the shadows.

Saxon whipped around as he yanked his gun free and leveled it at whoever was in the doorway. Ginger had to peek under his arm as she bit back a little cry of lament. Whoever was there needed to die. A light came on.

"Vitus," Saxon growled. "I almost shot you."

The man in the doorway offered them a shrug. There was a look on his face that made it clear he was amused and nothing else. "Almost doesn't count."

"Right, second place is first loser," Saxon answered with an ease and frustration that sounded second nature.

Ginger hugged the blanket close. "Friend of yours?"

Saxon grunted. "You can choose your friends."

"But not your family," the man in the doorway answered.

He was Saxon's brother and no mistake. They had the same square jaw and solid looking features. Vitus had lighter hair than Saxon but they shared the same Caribbean blue eyes.

"So . . ." Vitus was leaning against the doorframe, looking for all the world like he was relaxed, but Ginger didn't buy it for a second. There was a set to his eyes that she recognized from Saxon and she knew without a doubt this guy was ready to spring into action the second he deemed it necessary.

"So . . . what are you doing here?" Saxon was holstering his gun.

"Heard you got married."

Saxon held up a single finger and pointed toward the hallway. Vitus flashed him a devilish grin before he straightened up and winked at her before turning around and disappearing. But as a parting jab, he flipped the light off, plunging the room into darkness.

Since her night vision had been killed off by the light, the abrupt change left Ginger uncertain of her surroundings. Saxon shattered that by hooking her around the waist and bringing her back into contact with his hard body. It was lightning fast, stealing her breath. He caught the little gasp that she let out, smothering it completely beneath his lips as he kissed her hard and very, very completely. He let her go, melting back into the darkness of the room as she tried to form a complete thought. The man sure knew how to kiss. He made thinking a real chore.

"So. . . . what was that about?" She was still under the influence of him, and there was no holding back the question.

Saxon, on the other hand, was making steady progress toward the door.

"Saxon?"

He stopped at the door and turned to look at her once the light from the hallway allowed her to see him clearly.

"It means I have more resources, Ginger," he answered her in a confident tone. "Sleep while you can."

The door was closed firmly behind him. She sat there, feeling out of control and yet so protected that slipping into sleep wasn't hard.


Saxon was tense.

Ginger's taste was clinging to his lips, and her scent felt like it was lodged so deep in his senses that it was never going to be truly gone. He knew that, deep down in the center of his being, he liked it. Liked it a whole lot. But he didn't have time to dwell on it just then. His feelings wouldn't mean shit if Ginger ended up dead.

"How did you find me?"

Vitus had withdrawn to the kitchen. His brother was cradling a mug in one huge hand as he leaned against the countertop and watched the hallway for Saxon's approach.

Vitus was a Seal; the little "Ex" part didn't factor in. Just because he wasn't on active duty anymore, didn't change the man he was. That nature had been the whole reason he'd been drawn to the elite military group. It was a place he belonged, beating the odds.

"Dunn Bateson." Vitus answered his question in a tone that left it clear he wasn't happy. "You should have reached out to me."

Saxon poured himself a cup of java before facing off with his brother. "I don't call you every time I'm on assignment, so don't sound so pissed."

"Tyler Martin is more than an assignment."

"You knew I was heading out to look for him," Saxon replied. "I found him. Don't get your panties in a twist."

Vitus took a moment to contemplate that. "Fine, I'm being over-protective."

"I hear marriage does that to a man," Saxon chirped.

Vitus curled his lips back. "Makes a man soft? Yeah, over and over and over—"

Saxon's cock was still rock hard. "Right," he cut his brother off. "Glad to hear it's working out with Damascus."

"I'm the luckiest dammed soul on the planet, and I know it," Vitus replied. "But we're off topic. Dunn knows you're here and that Tyler has almost caught you twice. Is that an accurate accounting of the case?"

Saxon knew his brother, had worked beside him before, and Vitus didn't dick around when it came to mission details. That was why they were both such effective field agents.

Saxon felt the tension in his body shift away from passion and back onto keeping Ginger alive. It should have pleased him, but he was too absorbed with how hollow his insides felt as dread sunk its teeth into him.

"It is." Saxon put the mug down. Everything except dealing with Ginger was secondary now. Pushed back by the mounting need to seek out a safer location. "And if Dunn knows that—"

"Someone else might, too," Vitus finished the thought for him. "If he's got Federal resources, it's only a matter of time before someone traces that helicopter."

Saxon suddenly stiffened. "Tyler knows me too well."

"He does," Vitus agreed. "Which is why you should have reached out to me."

"He'd expect that move, so I didn't make it." Saxon locked gazes with his brother.

Vitus nodded in agreement.

Saxon considered his brother for a moment. "Maybe I need to be using your example. Take her completely off grid."

Vitus slowly nodded as understanding hit him. "You might recall I lost my shield over going off the department policy grid."

"You kept the bad guys from killing the girl," Saxon cut back. "That's the part I'm focused on."

Vitus contemplated him for a long moment. "I'm the last person who can lecture you on this idea, because I think you're spot on. Your wife has a mighty big target on her tail."

"Don't forget that someone is digging into Ginger's information." Bram Magnus added from where he'd been listening. "The Raven is no stranger to hitmen."

Saxon felt a decision take firm root inside him. Hard certainty was flooding him as he felt a rush of something else mingle with it. What was it? He honestly didn't know because he'd been determined before. This was far more intense and deeply personal.

"We need to set up some bait," he informed them. "Get Thais up here."

He honestly didn't care what it looked like on paper. There was only one way to truly protect Ginger and that was his motive, his driving focus. The idea of being able to take her with him, well that was blowing his mind with possibilities.

Ones he just couldn't seem to ignore anymore.

# CHAPTER SIX

Saxon was back in her bedroom at dawn.

Ginger enjoyed the sight, except he was fully clothed now, and he was mostly naked in her dreams. So this was reality, and yet it was a little different. She blinked, her brain starting to work and process what she was noticing. He'd always been in business attire. Slacks, pressed shirt, long sleeved, too, and a tie. The suit jacket came and went but with the exception of their wedding, he'd always been formal.

Today, Saxon was sporting a mountain look, denim jeans with a belt and attached utility pouch. She sat up as she continued to take in his transformation. There was a T-shirt peeking through the open buttons of a flannel shirt.

"I hope I meet with your approval."

That comment was more effective than a double shot of espresso. "Who are you, and what have you done with Saxon Hale? He has a serious devotion to maintaining a professional image. Even told me to cut out bubble baths."

"Very funny." He pointed at the foot of the bed. There was a pile of clothing there. "Get dressed."

He was already halfway to the door before he turned around. "Might be a while before you have access to a shower. Dress for hiking."

"Right." Ginger didn't have any real information to go on, but considering their last exit from a safe house had been under gunfire, she decided being a little hazy on the details suited her just fine.

So did waking up to having Saxon in her bedroom.

She decided to leave that idea alone, at least until she wasn't close enough to the man to do something stupid like try and touch him. But she did take a few minutes in the shower to do some personal grooming in the event she got another chance to get her hands on him.

When she emerged from the bathroom, she was dressed in layers. Her hair was still wet so she slipped a hair tie onto her wrist on the way out of the bathroom. A small bag of toiletries was dangling from her fingers as she left the suite behind. She found the entire team milling around the family room. It was interesting the way they all tended to perch themselves against solid items. The moment the thought crossed her mind, she realized it was because they were only comfortable when they felt like they had cover to duck behind.

That was a harsh fact that told her something about the lives they led. She was grateful for it and still, really sort of sad for them, too. They were never at ease.

The harsh reality of that was, he lived this life, and she was just another case. Allowing it to become anything more on her part was asking for a serious heartbreak. One she really wouldn't be justified in pinning on him. Not that any of those facts seemed to be changing her mind about getting her hand on him again.

Someone shifted, catching her attention. Ginger felt

her jaw open. It was a woman, drop-dead gorgeous. She was ultra-thin, with dark, mysterious eyes that she had expertly outlined in dark eyeliner, bringing out the slightly almond shape of them. Ginger tried not to stare, but the woman just moved in a way that was sexy, and the men in the room weren't ignoring it either.

Or maybe, the right way to phrase it was they weren't immune.

It wasn't as though they weren't trying to focus on the meeting Saxon was having, but when the woman moved, their eyes would shift toward her in that unconscious way a straight guy always got distracted by a bombshell.

"Agent Thais Sinclair."

Saxon supplied the woman's name when he caught sight of Ginger. "She's you now."

"Does that mean you are all going to take care of me?" Thais purred.

Thais's devastating effect on the opposite sex wasn't just confined to her exterior. When she spoke, her voice was a husky purr.

"Okay kiddies, life and death?" Saxon tried to prod them all back onto topic.

Thais offered him a soft laugh before she glided over to stand next to Ginger. "We're practically sisters now that I've been reprimanded in front of you."

Thais was teasing but now that she was closer, Ginger gained a look into her eyes. There was nothing relaxed about her gaze. It was just as sharp and unwavering as Saxon's.

Agent. Right. Thais Sinclair was definitely that.

"Thais will be staying here as you," Saxon took control of the conversation again. Despite his clothing change, nothing else had altered. He was the same tough, in-control guy. Even Thais felt the commanding presence, shifting around to look at her boss.

"I'm taking Ms. Boyce off-grid. Don't forget, Tyler Martin used to command us, he knows how we think, how we run a case, and the Raven, he's got plenty of hit men to call on and the fact that most of the world thinks he's dead to hide behind."

It was the first time she'd been involved in a briefing. Ginger bit her lower lip and concentrated on listening.

"Thais, please don't shoot any of my men."

Thais pushed her lips into a small pout that made her even more adorable. Even Bram Magnus was looking at her before he realized it and shook his head. The woman was the very definition of the ideal distraction. It was more than skin-deep; it was in the way she applied herself. It was an art form and completely devastating to Ginger's self-confidence.

"You're welcome to try a hands-on approach with me," Dare Servant offered devilishly.

"I need to make sure Captain Magnus is up on his medical skills first." Thais set Dare Servant down with a curving of her perfectly glossed lips. Whatever lipstick she had on was perfect, just the right amount of shine to make her lips look ready to be kissed.

*Get a grip!*

"So, does this mean I'm getting a gun?" Ginger decided to test the situation. "Since we're going out alone, it seems relevant," she added when Saxon only contemplated her from behind, offering an unreadable expression.

Vitus surprised her by reaching behind him and pulling a holster free that had clearly been clipped to his belt. He tossed it across the space between them without a hint of hesitation. "Don't shoot my brother, but the hands-on thing, that's up to you."

Saxon grunted and sent his brother a deadly look. Vitus only shrugged. "You are married."

"That would be our cue to hit the trail. The conversation is heading downhill." Saxon gestured her toward him with a couple of fingers.

Ginger ran back down the hallway to find a belt. She had to settle for a man's belt that she jabbed a hole in with a kitchen knife before she could buckle it and clip the gun onto it. Vitus had stayed behind, clearly waiting for her. He had an amused grin on his lips as he watched her, giving her a nod of approval before he pointed toward the side door.

Saxon was waiting for her next to a beat-up truck. Somewhere beneath a solid coat of mud and grime, it had faded gold paint. There were a couple of packs in the bed of it, a clear plastic tarp over them in case the weather turned nasty. The team had tightened up again, proving to her without a word that things were serious. She climbed into the truck through the passenger side door that Bram Magnus held open for her. He offered her a small box that she took before she realized it was ammunition for the gun.

It was a good thing she'd closed her fingers around it because that way, at least he didn't see her hand shaking. "Thanks."

"It will be the pair of you out there," Bram's tone was deadly and soft. "Understand what I'm saying?"

"I'm the one who asked for a weapon," she declared back.

Bram nodded, satisfaction flickering in his eyes. She enjoyed the feeling of his approval because the guy was a lot like Saxon. He didn't hand out compliments lightly, especially when it came to competency.

Saxon climbed in beside her and his team fell back.

She was biting her lower lip again, and he noticed. She realized she wasn't fooling anyone because she was giving herself away with such a blatant mannerism.

"I wouldn't take this action if I didn't think it was safer than staying with my team."

"Of course." Her voice came across a little tight but at least it wasn't a squeak.

Saxon wasn't fooled for a moment. What stunned her was the way he hesitated, looking for a moment as though he was going to say something else, something soothing.

"Almost forgot," Vitus called out.

Saxon paused with his hand on the stick shift. "What?"

"Message from Dunn," Vitus's face was a controlled mask, but Ginger caught a twinkle in his eyes, one that promised hell.

"He said to tell you, never interrupt a lady's bubble bath."

Bram cocked his head to the side in response as Vitus offered his brother a smirk. Dare Servant had his hands up in the air like he was refusing to touch that one with a ten-foot pole, and Ginger was pretty sure her face turned crimson. Vitus lifted a hand and waved bye-bye to them.

Saxon flipped his brother the bird.

Guess they really were departing from the grid. Saxon Hale truly had dispensed with protocol, first in attire and now with professionalism. The coming days were going to be interesting to say the least.

*What the hell do you mean 'least'? You're out with a slab of beefcake, who's finished playing by the rules . . . oh, and you're married, too.*

It was a bookworm's dream, even if she was practical enough to recognize the potential for the memories to become her most agonizing nightmares. Of course the part where she didn't really have a very good chance of living to see the other side of it sort of qualified as a silver lining because she wouldn't have to face up to her actions.

So she smiled and vowed to live in the moment.

It might be all she had left.

Thais Sinclair was beautiful.

Oh, there were a dozen words to describe it, and to her, most of them were as repugnant as the skills she'd had drilled into her. Sex was a skill as necessary as target practice.

She left Dare Servant behind and found herself in the suite that was going to be hers for the next few days. After she stashed her two back up weapons and hid a knife between a few of the pillows, she walked back to look at the large slipper tub. It was a perfect setting for seduction, a topic she'd been trained in to the fullest. She turned in a slow circle, locating the camera after a moment. She teased the button on her shirt with her fingers out of habit and then froze.

She wasn't on that sort of case.

And yet, she circled the tub and contemplated whether or not Dunn Bateson was watching. A man like him didn't have to resort to peeping, not hardly, and she had long since lost any sort of enjoyment out of teasing a man simply for the sake of gaining his personal attention when there was no objective.

It was sad.

She knew that. The knowledge had been burning a small hole inside her soul for some time now. She wasn't really sure when it started, only that it was becoming harder to dismiss, but there was no point in being upset about it because everyone had to do what they had to do in order to survive.

The difficulty was, all she was doing was surviving, and it left her feeling like an empty eggshell. It was only a matter of time before she was crushed because she was drying out just a little bit more every hour, becoming brittle and fragile as the elements of her life pulled the moisture from her.

She suddenly turned around and flipped the water on. It splashed down into the tub with a happy sound, surprising her because it had been a long time since something so simple had impacted her.

Well, there was another thing she had extensive training in, noticing and pressing on minute details.

She struck a match and touched the flame to the wicks of several candles that were set out on a countertop. It took a moment for them to catch because they were new and their wicks were still encased in wax. Once they sputtered to life, she turned off the electric lights, letting the warm glow radiate out and around the filling tub.

A moment of peace was something she rarely indulged in, and if Dunn Bateson was watching, she truly didn't care.

He would never see inside her mind.

No, that was her own personal hell.

"He did what?"

Kagan didn't lose his cool very often, and Vitus wouldn't exactly be fair in saying his Section Leader was shouting, but there was definitely an edge to his tone, one that carried a warning.

"And while you're at it, you can explain why you and Sinclair are there before I heard about it," Kagan finished off with a hard note in his voice.

"Since you dropped the bomb on Carl Davis, it was a

sound course of action," Vitus said without a hint of remorse for his actions.

Kagan grunted on the other end of the line. "I forget, you have a lot of buddies pulling security detail at the capitol. Carl would piss himself if he knew how much they talk."

"Might be fun to let it slip. He and his cronies forget how many men they have backing them up. And my buddies only talk to a select few. It's loyalty a number of those fat cats don't deserve."

"You got the girl in the end," Kagan responded.

"Right," Vitus agreed. "I should be humble in victory?"

"You might try not rubbing his nose in it," Kagan said. "Considering it was her daddy who was shoving her into that match with Carl Davis."

Vitus shrugged, conceding the argument. His wife Damascus was a point he would never negotiate on, but Kagan was right, her father had been the mastermind of the plot to marry her to Carl Davis. Not that Davis was clean handed in the deal. He'd planned to use her to charm the voters and hide his own personal sexual choices. Vitus didn't give a crap for the fact that Carl was gay and he even sympathized with the guy on the fact that the public would fry him if they ever found out, but the moment Carl had tried to take Damascus from him, Carl had lost whatever sympathy Vitus was going to afford him. There was only Damascus and the fact that she belonged with him.

"Carl was still trying to acquire her like a possession, which tells me a lot about his character," Vitus added.

"It does," Kagan agreed. "So your brother is more like you than he wanted to admit. Didn't think I'd live to see him embracing it."

"He's motivated, that's for sure."

Kagan made a low sound in the back of his throat. "Careful Hale, I think the pair of you might be running short on your share of luck."

"That's why Saxon bugged out. Thais found the hit on the girl's information," Vitus continued. "My guess is we have a hit man on our tail. Better to trap him here, without giving him a shot at the witness."

"Agreed," Kagan interrupted. "And there is the chance that Tyler will track Dunn's helicopter to that cabin."

"Tyler will get a surprise if he tries to make a grab for the bait."

"Glad to hear that you've taken precautions."

Kagan didn't ask for details. Vitus felt a ripple of tension go through him but it was one he was comfortable with. He knew this game, understood the risks. There was a little nibble on his conscience from guilt, a new and unexpected response that was tied directly to his wife. Risking his butt had always been his own choice to make, but now he had something he very much wanted to live for.

Saxon seemed to know where they were going. He kept the truck heading down winding roads for the entire day. The hours crept by in a blur of trees and scattered glimpses of handmade signs that marked dirt roads leading to private cabins hidden from the main road. The highway itself was only a two-lane one that had more potholes than paint on the center dividing line.

"Alright partner," Saxon surprised her by speaking at long last. "Time to pull your weight."

He slowed down and seemed to be looking for something, then he pulled a book from the door of the truck and handed it to her.

"A Tomas Brothers," she exclaimed as she took hold of the map book.

"A test of your manual skills."

She flipped it open and sent him a smirk. "I can do this in my sleep."

The lost art of looking up locations the old fashioned way.

"That's why we're using it, instead of a GPS," Saxon was creeping along, searching the trees for a sign. "If we're not on the grid, it's a lot harder to find us."

"Not bad," Ginger said as she flipped pages and found where they were. "And here I thought you were nothing without your gizmos and high-teck gadgets."

Saxon turned his attention to her. "I noticed you enjoy a hands-on sort of approach."

Her damned breath got stuck in her throat. Of course he noticed, his lips thinning in a purely male, satisfied manner before he looked back at the road.

"Let's not get distracted," he muttered.

Oh, she really wanted to disagree with him. Lord knew her body did. Distracted by each other sounded just about perfect.

"There," she pointed at the remains of a sign.

When he turned off the road, she sucked in her breath because it looked like they were heading into a wall of trees. There was a definite scraping on the windows and sides of the truck but no collusion with anything solid. The truck just bounced and rolled on its way along a very poorly maintained, unpaved road. Saxon stopped expectantly and got out.

"Need to cover our tracks."

Saxon stopped at what looked like a dead tree. He pulled on a section of the bark and a door opened up, even if the word "door" needed to be applied loosely. It was actually just a cut-out in the trunk. He pulled a rake and tossed it toward her.

They walked back toward the main road where he set about tossing dead leaves and debris over the trail their tires had left.

*Okay, simple enough.*

Ginger took to the task and they worked their way back to where the truck was. A thin trickle of sweat worked its way down her back by the time they finished. It felt good after sitting on her tail for so long. Saxon stowed the rakes, and they climbed back into the truck.

He smelled good.

She didn't need to notice that, but her hormones weren't listening. Her slightly elevated respiration was drawing in enough of the air between them to tease her with his scent.

Damn, she'd picked a hell of a time to get stuck on a guy.

On the other hand, the bulge of the gun against her waist drove home the fact that her options in life just might be limited. As in, the sand in her hourglass could be running low. Sure, it was a logical reason for her reaction to him but it didn't make her feel very good about herself.

"What are you chewing on, Gin?"

Ginger thought she'd imagined the question but Saxon cut her a glance that included a raised eyebrow.

"Why are you asking?"

He was looking at the road, but she still caught the way his jaw clenched. "Rule one of being a team. You answer my questions, but not with a question."

"I thought rule one was don't shoot you." She was messing with him but decided she preferred it to thinking too deeply about what they'd done the night before.

"That's Vitus's rule," Saxon informed her dryly.

"Ah," she conceded. "He doesn't want the duty of providing all the grand babies?"

"That's what I thought you were thinking about." He was watching the road but his knuckles had turned white.

"To be fair, I wasn't so far down the road as thinking about kids," she offered. "I'm sort of still stuck on living to see my next birthday."

His knuckles turned white on the steering wheel. "One day at a time." There was a moment of silence before he stopped and put the truck in park. He sent her a confident look. "Have a little faith, Gin. I'm good at what I do."

He'd proven that already. She didn't get a chance to tell him so because he was out of the truck in the next moment.

The sun was just a glowing ball on the horizon but there was enough light for her to see what Saxon was up to. He'd walked away from her, but when he was on the way back, she realized he'd left an empty can on a rock down field.

"Right," she said. He only stepped to the side and watched her from behind a doubtful expression. "Worried about letting me keep your brother's little present while you sleep?"

"Prove it or lose it," he replied.

Ginger reached down and opened the snap that held the strap in place over the butt of the pistol. She held it up, slipping her thumb along the side of it until she found the safety. Saxon's eyes narrowed slightly in response. She leveled the weapon, looked down the barrel, lined up the sights, and sent the can into the air.

Saxon surprised her by flashing her a smile. "Not too

bad"—he turned and reached for something that looked like a rock—"for a civilian."

"Could be worse," she said. "I could be sobbing . . . hiding under the bed . . ."

He shot her a hard look. "I think that's why they issued me a set of handcuffs."

Ginger rolled her eyes. "Now that is such a disappointing answer. My fantasies are dashed."

His features tightened, his gaze glittering. "You didn't seem to have a lack of satisfaction last night."

Heat surged through her, and it made her bold again. "Felt like you enjoyed it, too."

He let out a bark of amusement. For a moment, they were caught in a strange tension. It was equal parts buzz and uncertainty. The only thing that made it bearable was the fact that they seemed to share it.

"This will be over at some point." His tone was low, like he didn't want to say the words but did so because it was the right thing to do.

"I'm hoping we'll both be there to see it."

His jaw tightened, but he nodded, grasped the handle, and pulled on it. Dirt went flying, raising a dust cloud that tickled her nose and made her blink as it settled all around her. As the dust cleared, she got a look at a doorway that led down into the ground. It was sort of a dusty, dark hole, leading down into the earth.

"Let's get out of sight," Saxon suggested.

He was enjoying the moment. She almost didn't have the heart to crush his moment of glee, but on the other hand, she had a really great memory of the way he'd enjoyed her rising to match him.

"Thank you." She stepped right through into the unknown. Only it wasn't exactly a mystery. Her luck held and her foot connected with a step just inside the darkness and then another. She reached out and found a railing to grasp. The air inside was musty, and she'd descended a good ten steps before Saxon punched the light switch.

"So you've seen a shelter before." Saxon came down the steps behind her.

"You sound so disappointed," Ginger had made it to the main living area of the shelter. It wasn't very big, but this one was one of the better ones. She looked back at him and fluttered her eyelashes. "Sorry to burst your bubble."

"Just surprised," he corrected her.

Ginger had started to look around the structure but turned back to face him. She eyed him, giving him her best victory look. "As disappointed as a grammar school boy who got up early to catch a frog and put in in my lunch box."

He caved in and shrugged as his lips curled up to flash his teeth at her. It was a pretty good reward for being brazen, making her feel devilish to the core. Living dangerously came with a buzz, one she decided she liked, especially when the source of that spine tingling was Saxon Hale.

"Fine, a little disappointed you didn't squeal," he admitted as he moved to a control panel and started up the air-circulation system. There was a soft hum as it kicked in, and the air shifted around them.

"Small town." She began to distract herself from the fact that they were very alone. "Lots of doomsday preppers. Pandemic, super volcano eruption in Yellowstone, collapse of government, they're all getting ready. Going off grid before the end begins."

She turned and considered the living space afforded by the shelter. The ceiling was curved and she'd estimated they were a good twenty feet below the surface

of the earth. It kept the temperature down but now that
the air system was on, the mustiness was clearing up.
There was a small kitchen and table. A modest living
area with a sofa that would double as a pull-out bed and
a flat-screen against the wall. Past a double door would
be the bathroom and bedroom.

"Hopefully this one meets with your approval," he offered as he started rummaging around in the kitchen
cabinet and pulled a coffee maker out. Not exactly
Dunn's style.

"It's not the unfinished walls of a missile silo or the
inside of a cinder block lined dugout."

He flashed her a look. Ginger lifted her hands into the
air. "Small town, folks have time on their hands. I've
spent more than one Saturday helping install solar cells
and water pumps."

This shelter was one that could be purchased. She'd
seen the catalogs.

"Is that why you got into working with the Feds?"

It was the first real personal question he'd asked her.
She caught herself feeling just a tad shy as she recognized an attempt to know her better.

"Truth is," she answered, "I'm nosy by nature and the
Internet just makes it way too simple to find stuff out."

"According to your file, you're good." Saxon said.
"You've worked with more than just deadbeat parents."

"You've been doing your homework." Not that she
should be surprised.

"Maybe I'm listening to you, too."

"Right." Understanding dawned on her. "I said it was
interdepartmental."

"And you knew what that meant."

She shrugged. "Working for the Feds was just a way

to liven up an otherwise dull life in Cattle Creek. Mind you, I didn't want to leave. I guess I wanted the best of both worlds. Excitement and safety."

He was leaning against the countertop and had his arms crossed over his chest. "You aren't content to sit by and let your life happen. You want to make an impact."

She nodded.

The pull between them intensified. His approval was the sort of compliment that went straight to her head. Like she needed to be worthy and at the same time, he was letting her know that he found her to be just that. Oh for sure, it conflicted with her modern take on the world where men and women had equal rights, but Saxon had affected her on a much more primitive level.

"I want to take you to bed, Gin."

She felt her body surging to life in response. "You're getting naked this time."

His lips curled up in response to her demand.

He hooked his arm around her waist and pulled her into his embrace. She reached for him, rising onto her toes to kiss him. She felt something inside him stretching, straining against the hold he'd kept on it, the walls meant to hold it back crumbling as she flattened her hands against his chest, melting into his embrace.

It was her undoing, the moment when the leash snapped and they both willingly let reasoning go. Logic didn't have a place between them, only reaction. He cupped her nape, easing her head back so he could control her and keep her in position for his kiss.

She'd never even suspected that a man's touch could feel so amazingly good. It was bone deep and a little sound bounced off the walls of the kitchen before he broke away and took her through the door into the bedroom. She heard him place his gun on the table this time and watched as he shrugged out of his harness.

But he turned back around and caught her, returning his mouth to hers.

She'd thought he'd kissed her good before but she'd been mistaken. All of the strength was there in the way he took command of her lips, but this time, he'd made the firm choice to dispense with resisting. Now, he was claiming her.

Ginger curled her fingers into the soft material of his T-shirt, pulling him toward her even though they were already pressed against each other.

It wasn't close enough, not nearly so. She realized that she hated the fabric of her shirt. Somehow, her skin had become ultra-sensitive, to the point that she felt like the T-shirt was scratchy and needed to go immediately. She pulled it off, and he cupped the sides of her face and held her still so that he could reclaim her mouth.

This time, there was no hint of coaxing. There was only determination as he opened her mouth and teased her lower lip with a swipe of his tongue before boldly thrusting it inside to tangle with her own.

She shivered, twisting in a storm of sensations that felt like they were ripping her in too many directions at once. There was white hot need clawing at her insides so intense she couldn't stay still, couldn't focus. There was only the overwhelming multitude of opportunities to touch him and be touched in return. She was frantic to not miss an inch of him. The need to be closer to him was pounding through her, making her dizzy as she rose onto her toes to kiss him back.

"Gin . . ." He lifted his head. "You go to my head . . ."

She felt the brush of cool air against her skin. Saxon

didn't let her suffer it long. He was folding her back into his embrace, pressing his skin to hers and stealing her breath with the contact.

It blew everything else out of her mind, leaving her awash in sensation.

He knew his way around her clothing, unhooking her bra and easing it over her shoulders before it went sailing across the room to hit the floor in a forgotten heap.

"Christ." He cupped her breasts, the word coming out as he kneaded them.

The exclamation bounced around inside her head because all she could do was arch back as he leaned over and fashioned his lips around one of her nipples. She gasped, the sound echoing inside the room, certain she was going to combust.

Stripping became a priority, one she set to with a zeal. She was too damned hot to deal with clothing, both hers and his.

"Yes ma'am." He growled as he followed her lead, their clothing ending up in piles. Saxon turned away from her for a moment, setting her gun on one of the side tables. It afforded him a moment to realize she was bare. She felt exposed and proud of her choice.

"You shaved . . ." He muttered.

He moved closer, easing back against her as he smoothed his hands along the sides of her face and held her so that their gazes were locked.

"For me . . ."

He caught her hair, gripping it and sending a little tingle through her at the taste of his strength. His chest was hard and covered in hair that teased her nipples and the delicate skin of her breasts. Her clit was throbbing; her senses had seemed to turn on the moment she met him.

"Yes." It was one part agreement and another part challenge.

He chuckled, leaning down until his breath was teasing the wet surface of her lips. "I won't let it go to waste baby. I promise you that."

Her clit started throbbing with anticipation.

Ginger rose onto her toes to end the conversation. She didn't want to talk, she wanted to do. Impulses were firing off inside of her, and she longed for nothing more than to give over to them. Sure, there would be a reckoning. There always was. Honestly, what she feared more was not getting the chance to experience what she could in his embrace. Now that would be a true regret.

Saxon didn't disappoint her. He kissed her hard and completely, leaving her senseless as she twisted against him, eager to make sure she was in contact with him as much as possible. Remaining still was impossible. She wanted more, needed it. The craving was a living force inside her, melting away everything she'd been taught about behavior and its rights and wrongs. At that moment, there was only him and the way he felt against her.

The way he could make her feel if they got even closer . . .

His cock was hard against her belly. She reached for it, humming softly at the sound he made in the back of his throat. Satisfaction surged through her as she stroked him from base to tip, loving the way she affected him.

"Now, to keep my promise," he warned her before he scooped her off her feet.

For a moment he cradled her, making her feel as light as a feather before settling her on the bed. She only had a moment to feel uncertain before he was covering her and reclaiming her mouth in a kiss that shattered every little thought that had started to push through the thick cloud of sensation settled inside her skull.

"And I can't wait to toy with you . . ."

There was a promise in his voice. She caught a glitter in his eye.

"I'm really starting to enjoy the way you play." He stroked her, moving his hand down her body, across her belly and right into the curls guarding her folds.

"Ah . . . play?" It was a stupid question, but her brain wasn't working, and she didn't want it to.

He teased her bare mound, making her twist and whither as she gasped, stunned by just how intense it felt.

"You throw down, baby"—he sent one thick finger into the folds of her sex, leaning over her to keep her on her back and at his mercy—"with style."

She felt his breath before he touched her. Her slit was so very aware of every little touch. He teased the newly shaved skin, stroking it with his fingertips before he licked each side.

"Oh Christ . . ." she exclaimed.

She heard him chuckle, a very male sound that was more of a promise than anything else. She was biting her lower lip, holding her breath as he made contact with her clit. It was mind-blowing, making sweat pop out on her skin. She felt her nipples contracting as he rubbed the little bundle of nerves, drawing the fluid that was seeping from her body up and over it.

"It feels like you like it, too . . ."

"Would you stop talking?" she demanded. "I thought guys hated chicks who babble."

Saxon chuckled, choking on his amusement. "Glad to know I'm not like your other dates, Gin."

There was the ring of smug satisfaction in his tone. He liked being unique to her. He came back up her body, trapping one of her knees behind his so that her legs were spread and her clit his to finger.

"I want to make sure I blow every one of those memories out of your head . . ." He was rubbing her clit harder, grasping her hair to keep her head tilted toward his. He was watching her face. She felt his gaze on her as he drove her insane with the motion of his fingers. She wanted to say something to him in reply, but she just couldn't think. There was no way to disconnect from the motion of his fingers. Pleasure was spiking through her as every muscle she had drew tight and then tighter until she was lifting up, trying to rub against his hand. She needed just a little more pressure, just a little . . . more. She was straining toward him, her eyes closing as everything centered around his fingers. Her body was one single pulsing need, and he was the one driving her toward what she craved. It all burst like a small explosion. Pleasure snapped through her, wrenching her insides and wringing them before dropping her back onto the surface of the bed in a panting heap.

Saxon held her steady, his fingers still as he watched her.

"It wasn't one-sided. I enjoyed the hell out of doing that to you."

Saxon pressed a kiss against her mouth, following her when she tried to shy away from him. It became a hard kiss of determination, one that thrust her back into the swirling cloud of impulses.

"I wanted to watch you, learn what you like, make sure I don't come up short against your memories."

"You have control issues," she said, amazed her tongue worked.

Saxon snorted. "I know." He shifted, leaning over to

nuzzle against her breasts for a long moment. He kissed the inside of her cleavage and licked around one nipple before claiming it between his lips. She arched up, offering it to him as she slipped her hands across his shoulders. That quickly, she was being carried along once more by the current of impulse he seemed to trigger in her. It was a combination of his smell and his touch. Somehow, it just seemed to combine into something that intoxicated her to the point of complete brain function collapse. Leaving her at the mercy of her cravings.

"I want to control you," he muttered. "I want you so besotted, you don't have room to compare me to anyone else."

"I could say the same thing." She curled up and pushed him back, grasping the hard length of his erection before he'd finished falling onto the bed. He grunted, cupping her shoulders as though he meant to push her away.

"You and your control, well, I'm going to be the one calling the shots right now," she informed him before she opened her mouth and closed her lips around the head of his cock. His grip on her shoulder tightened, pulling her closer as she teased the slit on the top of his cock with her tongue.

"Oh shit . . ." he growled, slipping his hand into her hair, encouraging her as his breathing became rough.

It was the oddest form of praise, or maybe honesty was a better word. She drew her mouth off his length and opened her mouth wider to take him deeper. He shuddered, his hips thrusting up toward her as she used her hands on the portion of his cock that didn't make it into her mouth. Every rough sound that made it through his teeth encouraged her, stroking her confidence, fueling her determination.

But Saxon wasn't going to let her push him over the edge. He pulled her head back, making her leave his member behind.

"Chicken," she accused softly in more of a purr than she'd ever heard herself use.

He had her on her back, her body spread. If ever he'd been in command of their circumstances, now was a prime example, but she didn't care. The sounds he'd made while she'd been sucking him were fresh in her mind, reminding her that he had cracks in his shell. Ones she had every intention of making wider.

"No baby," he informed her in a husky rasp. "I'm just making sure I finish satisfying you before I lose my load."

He pressed a kiss against her mouth, smothering the rest of her argument. It wasn't a hard kiss, just one that blew her mind. It filled her with his taste again and let her feel his strength surrounding her. If she were able to think, she'd have wondered why her pride wasn't protesting about it but her brain was answering impulses only. There didn't seem to be room for anything else.

He was stroking her again, long, firm motions of his hands across her body, over her breasts, and over her belly. He toyed with her clit, the contact rekindling the need that had her panting beneath his touch.

She did want more.

She wanted him closer, craved his weight on her, needed to feel more than just her clit being touched. He thrust his fingers into her, and she heard her own cry bounce off the ceiling. She'd never realized the capacity of her own body to feel pleasure. It was deeper and far more intense than she'd ever imagined. Or maybe it was more correct to say, she'd only had sex before. This was something entirely different.

*It was a craving . . .*

She was pulling on him, trying to bring him to her. He caught a handful of her hair, keeping her exactly where he wanted her while he leaned over and kissed her again. There was a promise in the kiss, one that she felt on a subconscious level. It was like she could feel him shedding the last few layers of restraint before he moved over her, settled between her thighs, and drew in a deep breath.

"Now . . ." she was breathless and yet so demanding; she was almost snarling.

"Wait for it." He gave her back all of the controlling demand she was trying to give him. "Wait for me to satisfy you."

She realized how alike they were in that moment. It was a mental intimacy that stunned her because it ripped so very deeply into her soul. He settled against her, his cock slipping between her spread folds. She was so wet, he penetrated farther, his face tightening as he held back from thrusting home. She needed to have him inside her, and she lifted her hips.

"*Gin,*" he was growled through gritted teeth at her, his face a mask of strain.

She heard him growl and then he was thrusting into her body, in a smooth, controlled entry. Her body stretching once more to take him like it was the most natural thing in the world.

*Like she'd been made to be his . . .*

That was bliss on a new scale again, a feeling she was eager to explore. She shifted, seeking motion, craving friction again. She watched his teeth flash at her as he curled his lips up into a grin, one that was pure compliment.

"You're firewater, Gin . . ." He pulled free and thrust back into her as he arched back. "Intoxicating."

It was an admission, one that she eagerly soaked up. Answering him was something she did with her body, lifting to take his thrusts, cupping his shoulders, and clasping him between her thighs. His body was tense as he held himself in check, increasing his pace only when she did.

This time, climax was deeper. It felt like her core clenched with it, her body tightening around his length, intent on pulling his seed from him. She'd surged up toward him, crying out as it ripped through her. It dropped her back down in time to feel him giving into his needs, thrusting into her with a force that sent a last few ripples of satisfaction into her center. She heard him give over to it, growling as his body shuddered and he spurted inside of her.

Nothing mattered after that, only the fact that they both lay like broken dolls on the surface of the bed, their breath raspy and bouncing off the walls.

Dunn Bateson was well past the age of looking at porn on his computer. If he wanted a woman, it would be easy to get one. Between his income and the fact that he approached his personal workouts with the same zeal he did getting his profit line increased, his bed was only ever empty because he had made the choice for it to be so.

But he didn't kill the uplink that was feeding him a live shot of Thais Sinclair. He should have. It had been a hell of a long time since he'd felt any sort of stirrings from his conscience. At least when it came to a woman.

She was an agent, a very experienced, very success-ful one, but now that he was taking the time to watch her, he realized he knew very little about her origins. That was a slip up he didn't often make and it made him chuckle because he'd fallen for her ruse, at least in so much as he hadn't taken the time to investigate her.

A lapse like that could be fatal in his field. Where people came from, that was information that carried a lot of importance. It would tell you who they would kill for and whose blood they wanted staining their hands. A woman like Thais had been selected early in life for her obvious attributes and cut off from those who would have instilled anything such as virtues in her.

At least, that was the normal way an agent like her was created. There were exceptions and he discovered himself curious to see what he could dig up on her. Still, not enough so to move away from the computer. He watched her light a candle and stand for a moment as though she was enjoying the primitive light. One side of his mouth curved up because fire was something that stroked the primitive parts of everyone's brain. Those last remaining survival instincts left from eras long past when fire meant life.

Thais bathed in the light, stripping and turning so that it touched every inch of her skin before she climbed into the tub. Her hair was just long enough to be gathered up in a man's hand. Of course it was. She knew her art well.

It was a jaded thought, one that made him reach for his whiskey. The bite of the beverage seemed to enhance the sight of her lying back in the tub but not because he was aroused by her bare flesh.

No, it was due to the fact that he felt a stirring of something that he shied away from naming. An emotion awakening from the hibernation he'd put it into on purpose because things like remembering he had a heart only got in his way.

That made him kill the link. The computer screen went back to his desktop as he took another sip of whiskey.

He wouldn't name it.

Some things were too personal, which in his world translated into weakness. Thais Sinclair would not become one of his.

# CHAPTER SIX

"Take a walk with me."

Kagan had been expecting Carl Davis to say something along those lines. The man had finally run out of hands to shake and shifted his attention to Kagan. That didn't mean the man didn't have plenty of business to attend to. What Kagan was interested in knowing, and what had kept him making sure he was visible to the presidential hopeful, was discovering just where their business ranked. Carl had walked away from several movers and shakers in the Republican party. Kagan fell into step beside him. They passed debutantes decked out for the event in diamonds and perfectly tailored gowns. They were watched over by bodyguards, Secret Service, and politician wives.

Carl didn't stop until he made it to the gardens and settled into a place that was near enough to a fountain to have the water sound covering their conversation.

"I want the witness turned over to my people." Carl laid down his cards immediately.

Kagan cracked a grin. "Interesting request."

"You should put your people to better use." Carl issued

the threat in a clear tone. "I can insure she gets in front of a judge."

"You can," Kagan agreed. "The question I might ask is, will Tyler Martin agree with that?"

Carl pushed his hands into his pockets and rocked back on his heels. "You and I need to establish a solid working relationship."

"Could be a good idea," Kagan agreed.

Carl's lips twisted in a knowing grin. "What's the price of that sort of friendship?"

"It's not Tyler Martin. Like I said, if I wanted him dead, I could do it."

His answer surprised Carl. Kagan watched that emotion flicker in Carl's eyes before Carl tightened his expression and tried to decide what Kagan was up to.

Carl nodded. "He's my man? Is that your angle?"

"Exactly," Kagan agreed. "I'm focused on larger goals. Long-term ones that include my Shadow opps being in play."

Carl slowly nodded. "My point in having this conversation. No executive orders to shut down."

"Hopefully you'll see the value my teams bring to this country."

"That might be a whole lot easier if you stayed out of my affairs," Carl explained. "That includes Tyler Martin. He takes care of things for me. Hand over the witness so he can do his job."

"I still question what you're going to do with her." Kagan's tone had hardened. "She saw Martin doing his best to kill her. But you know that or Martin isn't the man for you."

Kagan watched Carl consider his next words.

"Turn her over to Tyler," Carl countered. "And I'll know you're on my side of the field. I take care of my team;

your Shadow opps would have a solid future. You're experienced enough to know you have to trade a few good horses in to keep your head above water."

It was a threat. A clear one that Kagan would be a fool to ignore.

Kagan drew in a deep breath. "I'll think it through."

Surprise flickered in Carl's eyes again. Kagan noted it before he turned and walked off into the gardens leaving the man to wait on him. Shadow Operations included a lot of bluffing, but what weighed on his mind was the hard fact that there were times when he had to make good on his bluffs. It was possible this might be one of those times.

Life wasn't fair.


His mother had raised him right.

But Ricky Sullivan's father had been a different matter. His father, Patrick Sullivan, had been at home in a riot and preferred to rub elbows with those men who believed Ireland needed to be freed. He'd taught his young son early the value of gaining what you wanted, through any means necessary, because there was nothing more important than winning.

At least that was what Rick Sullivan had walked away from his childhood with. His father was rotting in a prison, courtesy of a bombing conviction. It had left the family with few friends, at least among the sort that might have served as an example of how being a law abiding citizen could be a good way to live life.

No. After his father had loudly proclaimed his guilt in a court room, the only people who came around his mother's house were those who viewed them as compatriots. Taking up contract killing was just a way to keep a roof over his mother's head by using what was at hand.

Was it wrong? Not really, the way he saw things. The people he went after were fattened up on the things they'd stolen from men like his father. Those who never even looked down their noses at the masses they used to push their products and fill their pockets. Men who let people like his father take the fall for what they wanted done while being deaf to the cries of their families. See, his father hadn't planned a bombing on his own. No, he'd been lead down a carefully baited lane by men who had never done a day in prison for the cause they preached so passionately.

Ridding the world of those sorts, that was a service if you asked him, and as far as he was concerned, his opinion was the only one that mattered. Which was why he went hunting Ginger Boyce. Marc Grog was exactly the sort of man Ricky liked to hamstring. Punch drunk on his own fucking power, without a single thought for the people around him. Those people were like rats and a man like Marc liked to see them scurry.

Well, Ricky was going to enjoy seeing the rats feast on Marc Grog's flesh. He grinned, thinking about the way the masses would eat Marc alive, converging on him and ripping at his flesh while he felt himself being torn apart. That image was going to keep him warm through the next couple of hours while he did what he had to in order to track Ginger Boyce. He needed her to bait the trap.

Ricky wasn't gay but he could make exceptions when he needed to. Las Vegas had bars for every taste, and he'd tracked a flight controller to one that specialized in samegender seekers. The flight controller was a senior one, the man who had access to things like flight plans and ownership records for private helicopters. He was nervous, tapping a finger against the top of the bar as he leaned against it instead of slipping onto the barstool. Ricky waited for him to look his way again before he very bluntly stroked the neck of his beer bottle.

The controller's eyes narrowed, his lips thinning with hunger. Ricky picked up his beer bottle and closed his lips around the top of it before tossing down the last of the brew. When he set the bottle down, the controller was still watching him. Rick jerked his head toward the door and stood, walking out of the bar without a backward glance.

He leaned against the exterior of the building, out of the circle cast by a street lamp.

"I'm not interested in hiring." The controller had followed him.

"I don't sell," Ricky replied. "And I don't do hotels."

The controller looked at him, raking him from head to toe before he jerked his head toward the parking lot. "My place is quiet."

"Good."


"In other news today, Pulse Grog made a public announcement that he has decided to support Vice President Tom Hilliard in his bid for the White house . . ."

The picture turned to show Pulse Grog standing at a podium with a campaign poster for Tom Hilliard on it. He was surrounded by union representatives from the music and movie industry where he was a mover and shaker. He was making a passionate speech that the news anchor talked through, but Ginger felt her belly twist. Just the sight of him brought a memory crashing into her skull from the bar in New Orleans. Just a moment before, it had seemed nothing but a distant echo left to be forgotten in some corner of her brain. Now, it surged up, smothering her in horror as she recalled very precisely the way he'd ordered his men to kill her.

"Sit."

She jumped and knocked her shin against the chair Saxon had brought up behind her. The pain startled her, but, honestly, she was still locked in the grip of the memory. None of that seemed to matter as she tried to skirt around Saxon. The need to escape was pounding through her brain.

He caught her just as easily as he had in New Orleans, but there was a difference in the way he folded her into his embrace. That broke through the memory, allowing her to draw in some deep breaths.

"Easy . . ." he said soothingly. She wanted to be stronger, more capable, just . . . more. But all it had taken was a lousy news story to break her.

"I'm just clumsy. No reason to pet me," she groused as she wiggled free.

"I like petting you," he informed her in a tone she recalled from the darker hours of the night when they'd shared a bed.

That shocked her. It set off a tingle of excitement. There was a look on his face she didn't recognize, largely because it was aimed solely at her. She'd seen him determined before, this was personal.

"And no one would blame you for finding that clip alarming." His arms tightened around her, making it clear he wasn't going to be put at arm's length.

Ginger smiled at him. "Except you're a street team."

"I am."

"So is this where we finally address the elephant in the room?"

He surprised her by cracking up. Ginger stared at him,

feeling the corners of her mouth twitch because he was so damned adorable. She slipped away, enjoying the way their laughter was mixing and bouncing off the walls of the small shelter.

Saxon contemplated her for a long moment, his eyes sparkling with amusement. "Considering we've been stuck in this shelter all day, we should both be commended for managing to avoid any elephant."

"Maybe it's a little one."

His expression tightened, becoming serious. She'd seen it before and yet, this was different. It was personal. The glitter in his eyes had nothing to do with business.

"It's a damned big one, Gin," he confirmed.

It was . . . or maybe, she really hoped it was. Honestly, her thoughts were so jumbled, all she knew was that she needed him too badly to think the matter through. She was worrying her lower lip.

"I like kissing you, Gin." He closed the gap between them with that fluid, sharp motion of his, making her breath lodge in her chest as her senses went into high alert. He still had his fingers under her chin, lifting her face so that her lips were his for the claiming.

"So don't bite these . . ." he rasped as his breath hit the little wet spot left on her lower lip. He was a hair's breadth from kissing her. The delicate skin on her lower lip was registering the touch of his breath against it, all of her nerve endings lighting up, eager for more stimulation.

But he pulled back, withdrawing a step and crossing his arms across his chest. "So let's discuss what has kept you from making eye contact all day."

She was guilty as charged. As in, majorly so. She battled the urge to squirm and look away because, well, she'd had a plan to own her life, and it was time to make good on her choice. They'd had sex, and she'd wanted it. So, no avoiding the issue.

"Well . . . we should discuss . . . the fact that we failed to use protection."

His expression tightened.

"I should have mentioned that I'm not on birth control pills . . ."

He cut her off. "Wouldn't have mattered if you were, since I have all your personal belongings. I knew you weren't, Gin. You don't need to worry about it."

"Ah . . ." she wasn't going to let the subject drop. "That response is going to need a little clarification because my knowledge of biology says I'd better give the matter some attention or I'm going to get drop-kicked by reality. And for the record, I might be guilty of taking advantage of having you within arm's reach, but I will not chain you to me with a child."

His jaw clenched in response, but he squared off with her. She had a moment to absorb the fact that he was about to give her exactly what she'd asked for in spite of the fact that he didn't think she was going to like it.

"I am a field agent."

He let his words sink in for a moment as his knuckles turned white because he was gipping handfuls of his shirt over his biceps.

"Which has exactly what to do with birth control?" she asked.

"I underwent a sterilization procedure because sex is often part of gathering information."

His tone was cutting, making her think that it was the first time he'd regretted his choice.

*You're hearing what you want to . . . He hasn't just been waiting for you to drop into his life.*

"As for STDs, I get tested between assignments.

So . . ." he finished up. "Nothing on my end to worry about. I imagine that's a shock to you, but in my world, it's pretty run of the mill."

"You've actually given up ever having a family?" It was a very personal question. "Maybe I shouldn't have asked that one."

She expected him to become guarded again but instead, he grinned, like she'd done something daring that he found admirable.

"It's reversible."

"Oh."

That was as far as she got with a response. Saxon was watching her, gauging her reaction with those keen eyes of his.

"When you decide what you think of that Gin, let me know," he spoke softly.

"Why?"

He raised an eyebrow and took a step toward her, reclaiming her in an embrace that sealed her against him.

That fast, her heart started to accelerate, and she felt her flesh warming. He smoothed his hand up her back, sending little ripples of delight down her spine until he reached the skin of her nape. Somehow, the way he slipped his hand beneath her hair just made her shiver. And then he was gripping her hair, just tight enough to let her feel his strength.

God that made her clit twist.

"Because I can't keep my hands off you."

And he wasn't going to discuss it, which suited her just fine because Saxon Hale leaned down and kissed her. She reached for him, rising onto her toes and locking her hands around his neck so that she could meet his kiss with one of her own. She wanted him to feel her strength, see in her someone who could keep pace with him.

Saxon picked her up again, carrying her into the bedroom before he withdrew a step and looked like he was fighting to collect his thoughts.

"I never gave up on having a family. I just made damned sure it wouldn't happen while I was working a case." He actually opened his hands, like he needed her to understand him. "My mom and dad are . . . great, loving, and butt kicking when they had to. Every kid should have that in parents."

She ended up smiling. "Yeah, I've felt a few of those well-meant tush shots myself."

"You don't even cuss," he exclaimed. "Mind you, that sort of control puts you on a pedestal in my opinion."

"Pedestal?" she scoffed at him. "Don't placate me. I've thrown myself at you."

Ginger shifted back, her confidence deserting her as the light washed over the perfection of Saxon's chest. Well, the truth was the truth.

And she still wasn't repentant.

Nope.

She wanted to lunge at him. Tear her top off, throw her bra aside, and tackle him. But he was doing his job, and if he walked away from her, well, she really didn't have any right to be upset over it.

*Devastated you mean . . .*

She bit her lower lip, and he reached across the space between them and tugged her chin down to free it. With the light coming from behind him, his expression was just shadows, leaving her feeling unbearably exposed. Like her whole house of cards was about to get blown down.

"You fascinate me." He closed his arms around her, coming up against her back as he cupped the sides of her hips and pressed his lower body firmly against her. "I notice every little thing about you." His tone was a dark, husky whisper against her ear. "The way you smell . . ." He inhaled against her head. "The way you look at me and don't give a crap for how I snarl at you. I put you on that pedestal so that I can see you better."

Saxon scooped her off her feet, stealing her breath with both his words and his strength. At the moment it was all one thing, him, just him. He was a presence so powerful, the only thing to do was wash away with it.

But she did want more than to give him compliance. She wanted to participate, give as good as she got. When he set her on the bed, she reached for him, hooking her hands into the waist band of his jeans and popping open the first two buttons.

"You scatter my thoughts . . ." she said as she fought to free the last three buttons on his fly. "So I'm going for wild abandonment."

"Works for me," he said through gritted teeth.

She purred with satisfaction and popped the last button. His jeans sagged, slipping off his lean hips as she pulled his briefs down. His cock sprang loose, jutting out from his lower abdomen, swollen and hard.

"I'm going to make you squirm," she declared softly as she closed her hands around his member. It was hot, delighting her as she stroked it, drawing her fingers along its surface, marveling at the silkiness of the skin covering it.

"Give it your best shot," he challenged her.

There was just enough light for her to see the glitter in his eyes, but the bed was a perfect height for her to lay on her belly, rest her weight on her elbows and toy with his cock as he stood next to the bed. She licked it, drawing her tongue around its circumcised head and through the slit on the crown before closing her lips around the head.

He arched, sucking in his breath, the bluntness of the sound delighting her. It stroked something inside her, feeding it, encouraging her to stretch the boundaries encasing her. With him, impulse ruled, and she needed to dance to the beat.

It was Saxon who cut her ambitions short. She was sucking him, drawing on his length, teasing the sack of his balls with her fingertips when he threaded his hand into her hair and pulled her head away. His cock came out of her mouth with a little popping sound as she growled at him.

"Can't let you finish the job, Gin."

"I'd think you'd understand that need more than most," she groused, trying to lower her head and regain his cock.

Saxon didn't give her enough slack. She stopped when pain went zipping across her scalp. "Let loose."

He lowered himself so that they were nose to nose instead. "No. I can't let you suck me off, or I won't be able to fuck you, sweetheart."

She jerked at the word fuck. It was exactly what she craved. Saxon pressed his mouth to hers and kissed her until she was breathless. Fuck was a verb after all and Saxon's tone told her he fully intended to be a man of action.

"And you like the way I fuck you . . ." He was standing up, pulling her with him with the aid of two hands gripping her jeans. It pulled the fabric tight against her clit, driving her nearly insane.

He dropped her on her knees and cupped the sides of her face, tilted his head to the side and sealed her mouth beneath his in a soul-shattering kiss. It was more than carnal; it was pure intensity that broke down the walls between them. In that moment, they were one entity.

She pulled at his shirt and she yanked hers up and over her head. For a moment she was trapped in the soft jersey, the air teasing her bare torso. Saxon left her there as he unhooked her bra and her breasts sagged free. He ripped the shirt off her head but stood for a moment, cupping her breasts.

"I love these." His tone was rough. Enough light was coming through the open door to show her his face. Appreciation was there, etched deep into his expression.

Unguarded honesty.

"Elvis said it . . . you've got it going on, Gin."

He pulled her pants open and then sent her onto her back so that he could drag them off her body. She ended up dumped onto the top of the bed, giggling at the way he looked down at her like he'd achieved some sort of major accomplishment.

She wanted to focus on his words, wanted to savor the sound of raw honesty, but there was something she craved even deeper.

Him.

She crooked her finger at him. "Come here . . ."

His lips curled into a grin a moment before he crawled onto the bed with her. She scooted up toward the headboard and then nearly lost her mind when he lowered himself onto her. He was hot and hard and it was enough to blow her remaining thoughts into smithereens. She was squirming beneath him, the need to rub every last inch of her bare skin against him pulsing through her brain. Her thought process had shifted to impulse mode.

So she opened her legs, cradling him between her thighs as she clasped his hips. It was like she'd never realized what a true embrace should be until that moment when he thrust into her body, completing the moment while he caught his weight on his elbows.

"Goddammit . . ." He groaned as he withdrew and pressed back into her. "You're going to make me lose it . . ."

She purred. Arching up to take his next thrust, a breathless sound escaped her lips as he penetrated deeper, hitting some spot deep inside her. Thinking was beyond her grasp. There was only the smell of him and the feeling of his body moving on top of her. A full-body experience that blew her mind with just how intense it was. Like climbing to the top of what you saw as the highest peak and realizing there was an entire mountain range behind it.

Saxon took her up to their heights, driving into her, harder and faster but with a control that stole her breath. She was straining toward him, desperate for release but dreading it too because having him inside her was a bliss she was desperate to savor. But there was no holding back what her body craved. She lifted up toward him, tightening her thighs around him to bind him to her. It was the last bit of pressure that she needed to burst into a white hot flame. She felt the climax jerk through her as Saxon growled and arched back, the muscles along his arms corded as his cock jerked inside of her, giving up its hot load. Something inside her twisted as his seed coated her insides. She gasped, feeling like her muscles just might snap, but she didn't care a bit.

There was only Saxon and her need to stay as close as possible. Nothing else mattered.

"What the hell do you do for a living?" Ricky demanded. The man behind him tensed up, his hands biting into Ricky's hips.

"Let's not get personal," Brendon said, his breathing heavy.

"Bet it's some stupid thing where you have to follow the rules all the time, because you fuck like a schoolboy."

The cock that was only halfway inside him twitched. Ricky snorted and shoved back toward it. "Come on, show me what your balls are made of."

Brendon grunted, thrusting forward and gaining depth. "I'll give it to you," he rasped out.

"I'm growing old waiting." Ricky suddenly surged up, taking Brendon by surprise. He turned the man around, slamming him down on the tabletop where he had just been. His own cock was hard. He grabbed the lube that was sitting nearby and squeezed a generous portion against Brendon's backside.

"Wait . . . I want to . . ."

Ricky locked the man's arm up behind his back. "I'm going to give you what you crave, you bastard. What you can't admit you want because you're too fucking busy following the rules."

There was a grunt as Ricky thrust into the man but the sounds that followed were ones of enjoyment. Harsh, carnal, blunt enjoyment. The table rocked as Ricky used the man hard, judging by the sounds coming from him. When the time was right, he buried himself inside him and reached beneath his hips to jerk on his cock. Brendon bucked, crying out as he ejaculated across the table top. Ricky enjoyed the moment, loving the power. His cock was still swollen when he let Brendon finish with a hoarse cry before he used the butt of his pistol to knock him across the back of his skull. Brendon slipped into a heap on the floor, his eyes rolling back in his head. The front of his body glistened with his own juice while Ricky wandered toward the bathroom. He used a hand towel to clean himself off without a care for how nice it was.

He tossed it onto the floor and went back to where Brenden was snoring on the floor. His clothing was lying about where it had been shucked. Ricky went through the pockets until he found the man's work phone and held it up to the light to detect the grease marks that showed the swipe pattern. Breaking the man's password took a little longer but soon he was into his email. Ricky popped a beer and sat down to read through deleted messages, memorizing details and names to use in his search. He snapped screen shots of several before he finished and tossed the phone back down onto the pile of discarded clothing.

Ricky dressed and left. The Las Vegas air was warm enough for Brendon to sleep on the floor without a shiver. Ricky left him alive. There wasn't any profit in killing him, and he might be useful at some point in the future. Flight controllers often were, especially ones with secrets Ricky knew how to exploit.

He flipped out his phone and selected a burner phone number that would connect him with Tyler Martin.

Saxon was holding her.

It was pitch black, but they were in a shelter, so it was anyone's guess what time it was. Her head was pillowed on his shoulder, letting her hear his heart. He was toying with her hair, gently twisting a lock around his finger.

"I love this . . ." he muttered, letting her know he knew she was awake.

Of course he knew.

"I never could do much with it."

"That messy knot you fix it in is devastating enough," he informed her.

"Please." She wiggled, but he only pushed his hand into her hair and gripped it just tight enough to keep her still as he rolled toward her.

"It's sexy, Gin." He moved just a bit, letting her feel his cock. "That's what it does to me. The first time I saw it, the first picture that popped into my brain was you in bed and me being there to make sure your hair was messed up."

His tone was husky and hard, stroking her confidence as he angled his head and pressed a kiss against her mouth. She smoothed her hands over his shoulders as he rolled over completely. Opening her thighs so he could nestle between them seemed so very natural, without a hint of awkwardness. Sex, that thing that had always seemed so messy and ridiculous suddenly struck her as intimate. At least with Saxon it was.

"Talk, Gin."

He'd stopped with his cockhead just teasing the wet folds of her labia. "Huh?"

"You're biting your lip again."

She opened her mouth, earning a knowing chuckle from him. "It's not fair that you read me so easily."

He was completely unimpressed with her grousing, his lips remaining in a wide smile as he looked down at her. But he thrust forward, slowly, driving his length into her inch by inch until he was buried to the hilt.

"It's damned unfair that way you make me forget every solid reason why I shouldn't be in your bed."

Conversation fell aside as passion took over. In the dark, it was so easy, so natural to just give into it. To him. She strained toward him, the urgency building until sweat coated both of them and their cries were bouncing off the low ceiling. All of it combined into a moment of soul-shattering bliss that dropped them both back down to earth in a tangle of limbs.

Saxon turned toward her, hooking his arm around her waist as he moved up behind her and buried his nose in her hair. He was half asleep, making the motion more endearing because it lacked his normal ironclad control. There was something about being with him with his guard down that hit her straight in the heart. Oh, it was foolish and bound to land her in a lake of misery but that seemed so far away. Consequences mere peaks in the distance. Ginger let her eyes close and her thoughts quiet.

Live in the moment . . .


"You don't take rejection well."

Carl Davis didn't care for Kagan's comment. He'd been turning a pen through his fingers but stopped and pointed it at Kagan. "I don't sit still for double crossing. Marc Grog shouldn't have crossed that line. I called you in because Marc just changed the rules of the game."

Kagan heard the unmistakable warning in the man's voice. "Can't blame you for that. Got a tender spot for turncoats myself. I like to see them get what they deserve."

It was a firm reminder that Kagan didn't like Tyler Martin, or the fact that Carl Davis was shielding him. Carl's eyes lit with understanding as he went back to moving the pen through his fingers while he decided what he wanted to say.

"I need Martin," Carl said slowly. "Don't bother to try and sell me some line about there being plenty of men out there that have more integrity. I know that. Tyler Martin is loyal to me one hundred percent because he has no other place to go."

"True enough," Kagan agreed.

"I didn't have anything to do with his actions under Jeb Ryland."

"And he was only following orders?" Kagan slowly grinned and watched Carl stiffen. It was the normal re-action to his grins, one he enjoyed. Carl David enjoyed a little too much confidence in his position. Something Kagan was happy to shake at its foundation.

"Why don't we focus on the present?" Carl did his best to sound intimidating. It wasn't that he wasn't good at it. He was, but Kagan had a lot more blood on his hands and the presidential hopeful knew it.

That fact sort of made Kagan like him or at least low-ered the level of disgust he felt while sitting in the man's office and forcing himself to do business with him. It was a fact that Kagan would like to snap his neck but it would be a rash action, one he needed to quell the urge to per-form because there would be retributions. Big ones. Like executive orders to close the Shadow opps teams. Some-thing Kagan wouldn't allow to happen.

Even if the price was high.

"Why do you think I'm sitting here, instead of help-ing to put the case against Grog together?"

Carl didn't have many people raising their voices to him and that showed in the way his eyes narrowed.

Kagan grunted. "Better doing business with the devil I know . . ."

Understanding dawned on Carl, and his lips curved slightly. "Hilliard is a puss bag, isn't he? With him in the White House, you'll have plenty to worry about." Carl happily blackened his biggest opponent's nature. "Choos-ing me over him? I'm less than flattered."

"It's how the game is played. I'm choosing the stron-ger man," Kagan answered. "Still, you were in bed with Ryland. Jeb was a piece of work."

"His wife was Miranda Delacroix. I wanted the daughter. Delacroix blood. They have ties to every major family in politics. I needed the support. Jeb just happened to be part of the deal."

Kagan titled his head to the side. "Interesting explanation."

Carl laid out his demand. "I want the witness. Grog just took a very public swipe at me. If I fail to pay that back in kind, I'll get eaten by the rest of his cohorts."

Kagan only drew in a slow, deep breath, making it clear he was less than impressed. "As I told you the first time we talked, I've got to clean up a few places before it all lands on me. That witness is the key to providing the American viewers with a crime boss being taken in for his day in court. Considering Marc faked his death, it will be a media feast."

"I can ensure the case doesn't get buried by the lawyers Marc Grog can afford to man the shovels. Let me take credit for it, and I will be happy to keep the Shadow teams that made it possible. Unity, and the start of a nice, long, working relationship."

Threat and promise, the Washington special. Kagan stood, letting several moments pass before he spoke. "I'll be in touch when I make a decision."

"Today," Carl pressed the issue.

Kagan nodded.

And he'd have to make good on it, too, or risk Carl looking for other allies. Kagan knew that as he left the Capitol building. Carl wasn't stupid. He knew the game, and that he had him close to a corner. It was a rat's nest of complications and risks. Everything was fairly well balanced, which meant there was no way to ensure Saxon's witness didn't get the short end of the stick. Pulse could cover up one press conference by claiming he didn't have enough information when he allowed his passion to get the better of him. Back-pedalling wasn't a first for the music artist. Tyler would be the first to put the idea on the table since the witness had seen him kill Kitten. Keeping the witness and doing his job just might ensure that Kagan watched his Shadow opps teams get shut down when Carl was elected.

In a way, Ginger Boyce had managed the impossible. Slipping through a loophole that so many people had done their best to ensure didn't exist.

The problem was, it just might prove to be her end because dead women couldn't testify.

Tyler Martin came out once he was certain Kagan was well down the hallway outside Carl Davis's office and the door firmly sealed. Carl looked toward him. "Did you get all of that?"

Tyler nodded. "That witness saw me kill Kitten. She's got to go, even with you severing ties with Marc Grog."

Carl nodded. "I won't leave your ass out in the breeze." He tossed the pen onto his desk. "Not so long as you cover mine, that is."

"That's the arrangement," Tyler confirmed. "But we need her alive long enough to deal with Grog. She's about the only thing I can think of that will push on his soft spots. Much as I'd sleep better if I just put a slug in her brain."

"Kagan will give her to me," Carl offered.

Tyler considered the meeting he'd just seen for a long moment. "He just might. Never pegged him for having that much flexibility. He might be playing you, too."

"I know that," Carl said. "It's a risk I have to take. I can't make him turn over the girl. Make him sorry for it, sure, but that won't help us now."

"I've got a man looking for her. Pulse thinks Sullivan works for them. One way or the other, we'll get her. When a hitman takes her out, the blame will fall on Marc. Saxon Hale has to go, too. Along with his team. I'll handle it."

Carl was quiet for a moment, thinking over the situation. "Good. I need to turn my attention to making up the votes in California I just lost with Marc Grog's announcement. I'm sending a warrant team to his place to make sure he knows I'm playing for keeps."

"That will make an impression," Tyler said. "Sure you don't want to wait until we have the bait to draw him out?"

Carl shook his head. "I want Grog to feel the bite of handcuffs. His lawyers will have him out in record time. That's why we need the witness, to keep him from jumping into that plane of his and running off beyond our reach."

"Jeb Ryland was nursing a hard-on for vengeance, too. It didn't turn out too well."

"The difference is, Jeb let his personal grudges interfere with his political goals. Marc Grog is going to help me keep my lead in the polls one way or another. He seems to have chosen the hard way, and Kagan isn't going to budge while I'm on the fence as far as the public goes." There was a touch of heat in Carl's voice, one he took a moment to control before finishing.

Tyler admired the calculated effort Carl was displaying. It was a relief, too, because he didn't need to work for another whack job who would blow everything over bruised pride.

"Kagan will choose his teams," Tyler agreed. "Once we have the witness, Marc will send his hitman for her. Hitman does the dirty work, we just have to make sure

Marc is out on bail so it lands on him and I'll bury the hitman to erase the trail."

"Precisely," Carl said. "We do make a good team, Martin. I'm looking forward to a long future together."

Tyler left the office through a hidden door in the wall. It took him through passages that dated back to the Cold War era. They were all over Washington, DC. Cold, concrete-lined underground passageways that smelled of mildew and blood. He wanted Carl to get on with his campaign. That was a sign of the man's trust.

Tyler emerged through a utilities closet in an old building that had been transformed into a water district management office. It was filled mostly with computer servers, the few employees on the far side of it. He ducked through a side door, none of the workers realizing he'd even been there.

One of his phones was buzzing and he pulled it from his pocket.

"Got your prize in sight," Sullivan said, clearly pleased with himself. "Only had to fuck an air controller to get it."

"You're as resourceful as Pullman claimed you were," Tyler responded. "But I'll only be impressed when you have her. Alive." He stressed the last word before he ended the call and tucked the burner phone back into his jacket. Carl might have a plan but Tyler would always make sure there was a backup one too and with the Hale brothers, it was a wise course of action to make sure he had all bases covered. He lifted his hand and flagged down a taxi, slipping into the back seat as his thoughts lingered on Kagan.

His former section leader was dangerous. There was no doubt in his mind that there was more than met the eye in the meeting he'd just over heard. With Kagan, only a fool thought they had him figured out. He'd been a section leader for a very long time, which translated into the blunt fact that Kagan had more connections than anyone knew. Tyler had taken to pledging himself to men like Jeb Ryland because Kagan wouldn't leave him alone easily.

Things had a funny habit of coming full circle. It looked like he just might be working with Kagan again.

Of course, that just meant that Tyler needed to make sure Kagan knew who the boss was. Tyler would make sure Carl knew that. The Shadow opps teams had to go.

"Gin?"

Ginger blinked and opened her eyes. She felt pinned to the bed, her limbs still heavy with fatigue.

"We've got to move."

She jerked all the way awake in an instant, and his grin faded as he cupped her bare shoulder.

"Easy, nothing's wrong. Precautionary only." He straightened up, letting her see that he was fully dressed, his chest harness back in place. "You have time to grab a shower."

"Right."

She rolled over and sat up, instantly regretting it. Her internal muscles were sore. Not that it should surprise her but her face went up in flames as she realized Saxon was watching her with those keen blue eyes of his.

Night sports . . .

Yeah, with Saxon, sex was definitely a serious athletic event. Not that she was complaining; far from it. She ducked into the shower while it was still cold, sucking in her breath as she danced in a little circle. Stopping when she caught sight of the razor Saxon had stuck to the tile with a small piece of duct tape.

They had a few minutes? The phrase had never made her blush before, but it did now.

"Moving" could mean a lot of things, and she still recalled him warning her that they might not get another chance to shower for a while.

There was the scent of coffee in the air when she finished toweling dry. It drew her out of the small bathroom and got her pulling her clothing on with quick motions before she took her boots with her into the outer room.

Two caplets of pain killers were sitting next to her coffee mug. She stared at them for a moment as she pushed her foot into one boot.

"You'll have to get used to me noticing details, Gin." He warned her softly. "It's what I do."

Ginger knotted the lace of the boot and raised her face so that she was looking at Saxon. "Maybe I want you to see me as able to keep up with you."

"You wouldn't still have that gun if I doubted your ability." He reached for a mug and drained it. "We need to roll."

He was in back-to-business mode. Two days ago, she wouldn't have noticed the stark difference.

It seemed an eternity ago now. The nights spent in his embrace too new, too blissful a memory for her to not notice the way he changed. It was for her benefit and yet it stung to see him able to do it so effortlessly.

*Oh, now you've gone and done it . . .*

Ginger managed to ignore herself by getting her other boot on and guzzling the coffee. She ended up panting because it was so hot, she was pretty sure she'd burned her throat.

Well, that might just be a good thing. It might save her from making an ass of herself by babbling all day and letting Saxon know she'd gone and fallen in love with him.

Stockholm Syndrome . . .

Maybe.

All she knew was she cared about his feelings a whole hell of a lot, and she didn't have anyone to blame but herself. He'd never misrepresented himself.

So she was just going to have to keep it together because there was no way she was going to toss her lapse in emotional discipline onto his load. No, it was her issue.

So she'd deal with it herself.

Vitus Hale woke easily and quickly. He grabbed his cell phone while he was still opening his eyes, his brain processing the information of it ringing while he was still coming out of slumber.

"You have company," Dunn Bateson said. "Half a mile out."

Vitus was on his feet as he muttered a "copy that" He discarded the phone in favor of his gun. He let out a low whistle that gained immediate reaction from Bram Magnus.

"Dunn says we have a visitor."

They moved down the hallway, pushing in the door to the suite Thais was in. The bed was mussed, a body beneath the satin sheets. But Vitus felt the cold kiss of steel against his neck while he was looking at that unmoving form in the middle of the bed.

"Honest mistake," Thais said as she identified him and holstered her gun.

Vitus sent her a glare. "You're the bait," he reminded her.

She offered him a flutter of her dark eyelashes before she stepped a few feet away from him. "Live bait can bite. Handle with care."

"I'm a married man."

"That doesn't stop many of them," she said with a hint of disgust that teased his curiosity. Thais didn't talk about her past; in fact, she didn't talk much at all, unless you counted her soft conversation that undermined most men's control, but that was just practice. He knew the difference, had run with the Shadow opps teams long enough to know Thais was just refining her technique. Like sliding a blade along a sharpening stone, a wise man did it as often as he got the chance because he never knew when the shit was going to hit the fan, and he would need to call on all of his preparedness.

"Pardon the intrusion from reality . . ." Bram interrupted. "Company."

"Dunn called," Vitus supplied.

"Coming down the ridge behind us, on foot. Looks like it might be a single man." Dare Servant filled in the missing information. "Dunn sure does like his privacy. The man has this place wired."

"Let's move." Bram Magnus's tone made it clear he was intent on intercepting their unannounced visitor.

"Maybe we should let him get his target," Thais said.

The three men looked at her like she was insane.

"Did you miss the fact that he's likely here to kill you?" Bram asked.

"No," Thais answered. "I just can't seem to overlook the slim opportunity that it might be Tyler Martin, and I would really like the chance to pay him back for taking out two of my teammates."

The three men shared her sentiments. For a moment,

they all let the idea breathe between them, craving the chance to actually let it become reality.

"Are you suggesting we allow him inside?" Dare asked. "If it's Tyler, he'll smell that trap a hundred feet off."

"Tyler wouldn't come out himself," Vitus said.

"I agree it's unlikely," Thais said. "And my idea was to slip out of the window and let him stumble on me as I tried to escape in a fit of panic."

"That's risky," Vitus informed her.

Thais rolled her eyes. "And here I thought I was working in such a mundane field."

"Be serious, Thais." Vitus reached out to grab her upper arm when she started to move toward her clothing that was laid out on top of a dresser.

She twisted with a motion that was graceful but deadly. She dropped her arm on the other side of his hand, forcing him to release her or have his wrist broken. Vitus curled his teeth back but it was half in respect because the woman knew exactly what she was doing. She was hand-to-hand lethal.

"I am always serious, Hale. I wouldn't have lasted very long on your brother's team if I wasn't." Her tone sharpened, as did her gaze. Vitus knew he was looking straight into the eyes of an agent who had as much resolve as he did when it came to doing what needed to be done.

He swept the other agents in the room, taking stock of his resources. "We'll let him go after that lump you made in the bed. He stuck his finger in Thaïs's face when she started to protest. "That's as much of a risk as I'm willing to take." He looked at his men. "Dig in."

Sullivan lifted a pair of heat sensing goggles up and watched his cohorts progress through the forest. Decent enough fellows; too bad they were fodder. It was nothing personal, just a job, and sometimes, a bait and switch was called for. Besides, the guy was dim enough to think no response from the cabin meant he was sneaking in.

Bullshit.

No one with enough money to afford a luxury forest vacation home failed to make sure there was security on the place. What Sullivan wanted to know was where the occupants would go from here. Of course, he couldn't be seen, so he'd found a man willing to sign on.

Fodder. Or maybe distraction was a better way to put it. No one was looking for him now.

Bram Magnus was at home in the darkness. Honestly, there were times he felt more relaxed under the moon than by daylight. He hated being hot. The desert was boiling by daylight, making it impossible to sleep.

But tonight he was wide awake, making his way carefully across the forest floor. He moved in controlled steps, closing the distance between him and their unannounced guest. The guy had purpose and knew where he was going. The moonlight shone off the pistol in his hand while providing enough light to show Bram that the guy was wearing a ski mask to conceal his features.

Bram quelled the rising excitement trying to distract him. If it was Tyler Martin, he needed all his wits if he planned to survive the encounter. Tyler Martin was one slippery fish.

The guy pulled up, contemplating the cabin. Bram eased into position, setting his shoulder against a thick tree trunk and leveling his gun.

"Hold it right there," Bram spoke clearly, shattering the silence of the night.

"Fuck!" The guy jumped, whirling around and squeezing off a round in panic.

Bram grunted, dropping and discharging his weapon
with the muzzle pointed at the guy's thigh. It was over
as quickly as it began, the echo of the gunfire fading as
Bram blinked. The guy was down but Bram didn't aban-
don his cover. It might just be a ploy. He waited, keeping his weapon trained on the figure as Vitus and Dare
closed in and grabbed the guy.

A moment later, Vitus was frowning. "Dead."

"Not a chance," Bram tightened up. "I only popped
him in the thigh."

"Straight through the heart," Vitus replied.

Bram replayed the fight through his mind, looking
for the error in his judgement. It had to be there because
Vitus was standing over the body, and he'd never be at
ease if the guy had a pulse.

"No way," Bram said as he holstered his gun. He took
a closer look at the body and found another hole. He held
up his hand, the slick presence of blood on his fingertips.

"Sniper," Vitus hit the ground as his fellow agents took
cover.

They were on the high ground, making them perfect
targets. Vitus made the call for them to move.

Fuck.

Sullivan put his long range rifle over his shoulder and
used the heat-sensing goggles again. He watched the three
men pick up the body and take it back to the cabin. It
didn't take long for a pair of four-wheel-drive vehicles
to emerge, making their way away from the cabin. Ricky
pulled his phone out, watching a pulsing beacon on the
screen. As he watched, it moved with one of the vehicles.

Fodder, but useful, because Sullivan could track the
beacon he'd attached to the guy before setting him on his

mission. The Feds were taking the body, which meant Ricky had a means of following them.

Yup. Useful. He couldn't ask for more. Nope. After all, he'd killed the guy, so there was only so much use to get out of a corpse.

# CHAPTER SEVEN

Saxon was back in mission mode. Ginger took a cue from him and spent the better part of the next few days looking at the scenery as they drove. He took her down winding mountain roads and then back up different ones, driving on what seemed an endless route until there were points she was pretty certain she'd seen the same tree twice. It was blending together because she was trapped in her thoughts.

She wasn't going to distract him.

She knew one thing for certain about him, and that was, Saxon would put himself between her and a bullet.

The horror of that idea nearly gagged her.

That left them in silence, the sound of the tires against the road the only noise. Saxon made good on his promise of no showers, as they made camp and packed it up again at the first glimpse of dawn. Two days later, when he pulled into a real campground, she felt like they had found one of the wonders of the civilized world. She happily disappeared into the showers. They were made of cinderblocks and had that musty smell of a locker room, but the water flowed from the calcium-encrusted showerhead, making them a small miracle.

The lukewarm water and shampoo restored her resolve to face down her husband. She found him tending to a small fire that welcomed her back with a cheery crackle. The deepening darkness brought a chill that was finding every bit of water left in her hair and turning it to ice. Saxon had made camp a good ways away from the other inhabitants of the campground. When she approached, she realized the spot was surrounded by a thick blanket of dead needles since it was so remote. They crunched under her boots as she crossed toward the fire.

"All right, I'll talk."

Ginger looked up to find Saxon lowering himself in front of her. He did it with all the strength she knew he had, stopping in a crouch just a foot from her, the mask he'd worn throughout the last few days cracking to give her a look at a man who appeared to be fighting to control his feelings.

"What's bothering you, Gin?"

She let out a sigh and shrugged. "Reality?"

He snorted. "Now you're the one who is going to have to explain, because that could mean a whole lot of things. So, talk to me."

She bit her lip instead.

Saxon muttered a word of profanity beneath his breath before he reached across the space between them and pulled her against his body. He rolled back onto the sleeping bags, taking the impact of their bodies hitting the forest floor before he flipped them over, putting her on her back as he settled above her.

"This is not a talking position," she informed him.

"It can be a very effective communications one," he

countered with a confidence that made her temper rear its head. She used her forefinger and thumb to press her bent finger into his sternum.

"I don't need to hear about you using sex to gather information."

He grunted and sat next to her. "Sorry."

Ginger rolled up and realized she was being a chicken. *Pathetic* . . .

"I know you're used to facing the odds, but . . ."

He reached right over and cupped her nape, using the hold to keep her in place as he kissed her.

She wanted to say something else, but it slipped off her mind when she felt him shudder. He rolled over, taking her with him. He settled on his back and pressed her head onto his chest. It was so damned tender, she felt the teasing burn of tears in her eyes, which just fueled her determination to make sure he didn't end up dead because of her.

"I don't know how to deal with you, Gin . . ."

It was a confession, one that stilled her efforts to move away from him. Ginger let the sound of his heart fill her thoughts. So strong, so steady.

"We've got that in common." The words just slipped out, like a dam overflowing. She seemed to have reached her limit for holding back her emotions.

"Yeah," he said in a husky tone that sent a shiver down her spine. It was far more than sexual. The idea of intimacy hung between them, both burden and gift.

"Don't love me, Gin." He flipped over. Ginger landed on her back with Saxon hovering over her. "I can let you go if you don't."

"Maybe I don't want to let you go," she answered, reaching up to flatten her hand against his chest.

"You're just reaching out to the only solid thing left

in your world." He sounded like he was fighting to push the words out.

She wanted him to lose that fight.

"So what if I am?" she gripped his shirt and pulled him closer. "Does that make our feelings any less sincere?"

"Less likely to last."

"By who's account?" she demanded. "So we didn't meet at a church picnic. So what if you have a way of making me feel like the good girl who ran off with the bad boy?"

He chuckled at her, rolling onto his back as amusement shook his body. Ginger sat up and got caught in a moment of wonder as she watched him in that unguarded moment. When he finished and opened his eyes, merriment sparkled in them. The sight was so stunning, it overshadowed everything else.

"Enjoying yourself?" he asked.

Ginger shrugged. "I get the feeling not many people have been privileged enough to see you snickering on your back like a sugar-hyped-out teenager," she offered. "It's sort of adorable."

"I'm bad, sure enough," he muttered as he reached up and boldly palmed her breast, cupping the soft mound and fingering her nipple with his thumb. It felt good. So . . . damned . . . good. She took a quick look around them and heard Saxon scoff at her.

"I wouldn't camp in the open, Gin." He tugged her down and flipped one of the sleeping bags over them. "Not when my job is to keep you out of sight."

She realized that he'd laid the sleeping bags out flat, making a bed of them. It allowed the one on top of them to cover them both as he settled next to her on his elbow and tugged the buttons on her shirt open.

"You planned a seduction?"

"And you sound like you enjoy knowing I did." He pegged her correctly.

He was stroking the swells of her breasts above the cups of her bra, sending ripples of sensation across her skin.

"Hummmm . . ." she offered as he leaned down and kissed one side of her cleavage. "I could be brought around to your way of thinking."

He lifted his head, locking gazes with her. "I'll have to convince you?"

She shifted, excitement making it impossible to lay still. Her clothing was bugging the crap out of her as she felt the rise of need inside her. Reality was, it had never truly been banished, no matter how hard she'd applied herself to suppressing her need for him. It didn't seem like she could separate it now. It felt like her hunger for him was merged completely with the very fibers of her being.

So there was nothing to do but let him lift her back as he went searching for the hooks of her bra strap. It was a relief to be free of the undergarment but she needed more. She found the buckle that secured his chest harness and worked it free.

It was a challenge to do it all under the cover of the sleeping bag. It was also ridiculous. Ginger felt her cheeks bulging out as she tried to contain her giggles while they twisted and turned and tried to keep the covers over them.

But everything vanished when they were both bare. Saxon settled on top of her, the skin-to-skin contact as mind blowing as it had been the first time. It swept away reason and the very foundations of thinking, reducing her to a pile of cravings that Saxon seemed to be the only one who could satisfy. It was in every stroke, every touch of his lips, all of the details of the way he held just enough of his body weight off her to keep from crushing her while letting her feel just how strong he was.

She cradled him between her thighs, lifting her hips to make sure his thrusts slid smoothly into her. It was hard, yet gentle, his pace slow until he felt her heart rate increasing. Still he maintained control, driving her insane as he refused to let her buck beneath him. He caught his weight on his elbows, lowering enough of it onto her to pin her. The result was a mind-shattering ride that left her gasping. Every thrust applied just enough pressure against her clit to keep her on the edge of climax, but kept her a hair's breadth from it. She withered beneath him, lifting up, fighting his grip as she tried to take what she craved.

"Not . . . yet . . ." he growled at her through his teeth.

"Saxon . . ." Her tone was pure pleading.

He moved his hands up, threading his fingers through her hair and gripping it as he hovered over her lips. "Just . . . want to savor . . . this . . . and you."

"Yeah." Just, hell yeah. She wanted the release, but she needed to cling to him even more.

Only a dim bit of red glow made it through the sleeping bag, but she felt like she could see him because all of her senses were ultra-sensitive. He was the only thing solid in her world, and she clung to him, feeling everything shatter as climax burst through her. A moment later he was straining toward her, rocking his hips against hers as he lost control. Nothing else mattered. She was pretty sure she wouldn't have noticed anything else anyway. She was too busy clinging to Saxon, too absorbed by the way he held her against him as though she was life itself.

Tyler grinned when one of his phones ran. He flipped it open and identified Ricky Sullivan's burner phone number.

"I flushed them out of the cabin,"

"What?" Tyler demanded. "I instructed you to sit on them."

"You told me to find the mouse, and she's not the one at the cabin," Ricky answered back with his normal jovial tone. One that irritated the hell out of Tyler.

"Someone switched out the bait," Ricky continued. "I wasn't born yesterday. I'm sending you some pictures and going to check in with Pulse. Tell him I'm getting close."

Tyler killed the call and waited for the pictures. He fussed with the resolution for a moment until he could make out Vitus Hale.

"Problem?"

Tyler looked up to find Carl Davis watching him from the doorway. Carl looked around before aiming a pointed look at Tyler.

"Seems Saxon's family ties are just as strong as they have ever been." He turned the phone over to Carl.

"Who do you have on their tail?" Carl asked.

"The Hitman Marc Grog thinks is working for his son Pulse," Tyler stated.

Carl flashed him a smile, one that chilled his blood. "Perfect. I'll lean on Kagan. Pick out a good location for us all to meet."

Carl's meaning wasn't lost on Tyler.

"Already have it. Bakersfield."

Carl made a motion with his hand to get Tyler to explain.

"A city that has been hit hard by military downsizing. Perfect location for you to announce your partnership with the high-speed rail project that all those planet-loving voters are in favor of."

Carl's expression darkened. "That's Dunn Bateson's

little gem. A high-speed train to Las Vegas. The oil companies will eat me alive."

"They're energy companies now. Have a few closed-door meetings to assure them they will be supplying the energy. Remind them that the Internet has made sure information flows freely, so they'd better get busy maintaining good images. Green energy is trendy, and the casinos will enjoy knowing they have a steady flow of customers who can drink right up until they depart," Tyler said. "California will be yours in the polls, and Nevada will follow. Most importantly, it's out of the way enough for Marc to be tempted to make a try for the witness because he'll think he's close enough to Mexico airspace to outrun the law."

Carl was thinking it through. He suddenly nodded. "You've got a good head on those shoulders Martin."

"I'll deal with Kagan."

Surprise flickered in Carl's eyes. "Doesn't he want you dead?"

"A lot of people do, but Kagan wants his Shadow opps more. By helping you get elected, I ensure that you can make sure Kagan gets what he wants most."

"I've already made that clear to him," Carl said.

"So it's time for me to make a visit to the man and make sure he knows you and I are a team, and that I am there to collect your payment or warn him to start getting his retirement portfolio in order."

Understanding dawned on Carl. "Right. Let me know what to expect for when his job no longer exists due to a presidential order."

Tyler nodded before turning and moving out of the room. There had been a time when he had reported to Kagan and enjoyed the idea of serving his country. It had twisted his guts to discover just how little justice there was in the world, but he'd wised up because the alternative was to live like Saxon Hale. Working mission after mission for a salary that would never get him what Carl Davis enjoyed.

Tyler wanted more, and he'd made sure he was going to get it.

"You're awake."

Saxon was playing with her hair. It was quiet all around them, the fire nothing but embers. But the moon had come out, a huge full moon that cast a beautiful yellow light on them. Saxon had pushed the top sleeping bag down from their faces and was watching her as he combed his fingers through her hair.

"You need sleep," she said softly.

She felt him tense before he leaned down and inhaled against her hair. "I think I need this . . . even more, Gin."

She shuddered. He felt it, noticing the details as he always did, but tonight she didn't feel exposed. No, all she felt was cherished. "I know the feeling."

His embrace tightened, telling her without words that he needed her. Was it just what she wanted to hear? Maybe. But at the moment he was there, stroking her, holding her, so she rolled over and straddled him, lifting her hips so that his cock could spring up between them. She lowered herself onto his length.

"I need this . . ." she muttered.

He held the sleeping bag over them, his face showing her that he was frustrated by the need to keep his hands on something other than her. She smiled at him, riding him with a slow motion that sent pleasure rolling through her like waves at twilight.

"Now who's feeling controlling?" he asked.

"What's good for the goose . . ." She lowered herself onto him, taking all of his length before she tightened her muscles around him and listened to him gasp.

"Is good for the gander . . ." he grunted out.

"So nice that we agree."

And they did. In that moment they were in perfect harmony, moving together with a fluid grace that was as beautiful as it was thrilling. The passion built, reaching a crescendo, and when it was over, she landed beside him, looking up at the night sky while they both caught their breath.

He didn't let her sleep, though. He turned and came up behind her when she rolled, closing his arms around her as though separation was unbearable.

"Do you want kids?"

Ginger had been half-asleep, floating away on the cloud of bliss produced by their lovemaking. "Yeah. I mean, family is the best. You and your brother share a bond."

"We do."

"That's the stuff . . ." She made a little sound of contentment. "The stuff life is made of."

He choked against her hair. But he thrust his hips forward, against her bottom. "You're a dreamer, Gin."

"Thanks for noticing," she muttered. "It's not bad to see hope in the world. Why else do you put your life at risk?"

"You see more of me than most, Gin," he muttered. "Not too bad." There was a note in his voice that warmed her heart. A touch of hope that might actually have been whimsical. She decided it suited the moonlight perfectly.

"In that case"—she had to stop for a yawn—"I'll claim this was all a dream in the morning."

It was after all. A dream. One of those that fit into the

category of unreachable because she knew it would take more than just her love to hold him. Saxon hadn't said anything about affection but she refused to dwell on it. Instead, she enjoyed the way he cupped her breast and settled into sleeping at her back.

A dream or maybe moon madness.

Whatever it was, she decided it felt absolutely perfect.

"What's wrong?" Ginger had waited until Saxon finished his call. She didn't remember the phone ringing, but she'd noticed when he'd crawled out of their sleeping bag haven. "Your expression tells me reality is just as much of a bitch as ever."

She got a little twitch from the corners of his lips for her sarcasm effort. Ginger rubbed her eyes and went over to the tailgate of the truck. A small camping stove was sitting there and she struck a match to light the burner.

Coffee . . .

Saxon came close, leaning against the side of the truck as she measured out the grounds and set the little pot over the flame.

"Someone made an attempt on the cabin."

She bit back the comment that sprang to her lips because she didn't want to stop him from sharing more information. His gaze lowered to where her teeth were set, making her snort.

"I didn't want to jinx the moment," she offered in explanation. "But, since my cover is blown, is your brother okay?"

Saxon tilted his head to the side. "This is our job."

"He's your brother."

Saxon nodded. "Vitus is fine, but it means someone managed to track the helicopter to the cabin."

"The world isn't as big as it once was." Ginger didn't

care for how vulnerable that made her feel, and she realized it was because she knew Saxon would protect her with his life. She just couldn't bear the idea of it.

"No, it isn't," Saxon agreed with her.

"So, maybe we need to go on the offensive," she decided in an attempt to fend off the wave of horror trying to knock her off her feet. "Stop all this hiding. Stand up to this guy and let the press fry his ass."

For a moment, a glint appeared in Saxon's eyes. "As much as I enjoy a straight-out fight, it's too dangerous."

"So is waiting around and playing hide-and-seek. If I wanted to be a prepper, I'd have married one. Trust me, there were offers," she exclaimed in frustration.

"You married me."

And he didn't want to let her have a chance to argue the point. He shot her a look that warned her not to debate the topic.

Ginger grinned at him. His eyes narrowed, and she watched him battle the urge to ask her why she was amused.

"I did marry you," she offered. "Slept with you, too."

That earned her a grunt before he moved over to their bedding and started rolling it.

Ginger turned around and peeked at the coffee even though she knew it wasn't ready because she had a huge, stupid smile plastered across her face.

So much for moon madness. The sun was shining bright, and she was still besotted.

Kagan still knew how to make Tyler wait and worry over what he was thinking. Tyler's former section leader was built like a linebacker, and the comparison didn't end there. Tyler had noticed the first time he met the man that Kagan had it in him to take out what was in front of him if he decided to do it. As a Section Leader, Kagan had always weighed the options better than others, which accounted for the number of years that he'd held the position. Hot heads didn't last long. They might enjoy a flash of popularity because they charged in when the moment called for it, but they tended to disappear when those they crossed got even through their friends.

No, the way the world was now, the men at the top liked a nice marching band, one that performed on cue. Tyler knew it, accepted it, and had crossed over the line to join them because he wanted a slice of the good life. Kagan clung to his worn-out desk, putting duct tape on his budget because he was still a lone wolf at the center of his soul.

That was what had Tyler waiting. Even a wolf learned to run with the pack when survival was on the line. Kagan knew that hard fact of life. He'd do what he had to in order to keep his teams.

"I'll pull Hale in with the girl," Kagan spoke at last but he shot Tyler a hard look. "Fact is, you shouldn't thank me for that."

Tyler heard the warning loud and clear, but he didn't care. Quite the opposite really, because he thrived in the world of shadows and secrets, always had. It was all a game. Knowing lives hung in the balance just intensified the rush.

"But not until I see something public on Carl Davis's part to prove he's intent on taking down the Raven." He leveled a solid look at Tyler. "It's a horse trade and my filly is top grade, so he better bring something worth letting her go. You're not the only one who knows how to get paid."

Kagan walked away from him, into the people walking through the park. He didn't blend very well with the moms and their strollers or the trophy wives in their expensive jogging attire. Another little detail that supported Tyler's dedication to Carl Davis. When the buzz faded after the first few assignments with the Shadow opps teams, an agent was often left with the bitter realization of just how easy it was to wipe one of their number off the face of the earth. Pledging himself to powerful men like Jeb Ryland and Carl Davis would ensure his survival. It was nothing personal, and Ginger Boyce was just collateral damage.

Or she would be soon. Even Kagan was embracing the fact that she was nothing more than a means to an end. There was a certain satisfaction in knowing that Kagan recognized the logic of playing in the big leagues with men who didn't have trouble dealing in lives. It meant Tyler wasn't the monster he sometimes wondered he was. No, it was reality, and he was just smart enough to ensure that he didn't end up one of the sacrificed.

Saxon's phone buzzed. Ginger was still hovering over the brewing coffee as she snuck a look at him. He tossed one of the rolled sleeping bags into the back of the truck before taking the call. She moved toward the remaining one, taking over the chore while he walked a few paces away. She didn't hear very many full words, but the sound of his grunts made it clear he wasn't happy.

He cussed when he ended the call, and she discovered him looking straight at her. She picked up the rolled sleeping bag and walked toward him.

"So?" she asked as she placed the bundle next to its counterpart in the bed of the truck.

"We need to join the team."

The journey was quiet but for a much different reason. Saxon was thinking. It hit her far differently than it had before. It was very personal now. He was thinking of her as his wife, not a witness. Not that impersonal creature that he'd been so ready to pass off to another team. She felt the difference.

Which just made her feel like she was on a cliff. One with a very long drop on either side with nothing but the jagged points of reality to land on.

"What the fuck?" Marc Grog demanded as his hidden office door was opened with the aid of a kick. A line of white powder was laid out in front of him as four men entered.

"Federal warrant," one of them announced as he held up the paperwork.

"The fuck you say!" Marc exclaimed.

"Call your lawyer," the deputy informed him as he flattened the warrant on top of the line of cocaine. "You're going to need him." The guy was enjoying himself and flashed Marc a grin. "Welcome back from the dead. A whole lot of people are going to enjoy knowing you're alive."

There were shouts coming in from all over the office. Profanity-laced statements of surprise came as over a hundred Federal agents began tearing the place apart. Marc shook his head, wondering if it was the coke, but finally recognizing that the agent hadn't bothered to bag the small amount of cocaine for evidence. Which only meant they felt they had much bigger fish to fry.

*Fuck Carl Davis!*

Marc was forced to collapse back in his chair and listen to his empire being pillaged and he absorbed the reality of knowing he had a lot of warrants in his name.

Yeah, fuck him. Marc started dialing his lawyer because

he wasn't going down without making sure Carl Davis paid the price for turning on him.

The team was tense when Saxon and Ginger joined back up with them. Ginger felt it rippling across her skin as Saxon took her into a house that looked and smelled like it hadn't been used in a decade. There was the scent of stale air peppered with thick dust that swirled around as they all moved across the carpet. A small puff of it rose into the air when Bram Magnus sat down on a chair.

"Just like home," he muttered. "Afghanistan," he offered when Ginger looked at him in confusion.

Saxon made eye contact with his man before he disappeared to call in. What followed was the longest five minutes of her life.

But what weighed on her the most was the fact that it just might be some of the few moments she had left.

"I don't like it any more than you do, Hale," Kagan said.

Kagan's words were echoing inside his skull.

*"Bring her in."*

"Without something concrete from Carl?" Saxon asked.

"I'll work on that, but don't forget who is in the power position, Hale. You can stay out, sure, and Carl can cut the cord to all of us. We have to deal with him. It's not giving me the warm fuzzies either, but stay out and he'll get you by undermining the entire department, which will leave your ass flapping in the breeze for the Raven to find. We need Carl to push the case through or all our teams risk exposure. It is the only option with any hint of success. Carl can block any attempt I make to convene a judge and hearing," Kagan replied.

Saxon cut the line, but his action didn't put him in the clear. Vitus was watching him, his expression dark because his brother knew his body language.

"Kagan has ordered me in. He wants to work a deal with Carl Davis."

"When pigs fly," Vitus snarled.

"Or when they are a stone's throw from getting into the White House," Saxon replied in disgust. "Marc Grog represents a lot of votes through his son Pulse. Seems if they aren't going to support Carl, Marc's going to discover that Carl will use him as a scapegoat and get the votes by bringing in a crime boss."

"Take credit for our work you mean," Bram grunted. "Damned fat cat."

"A leopard never changes his spots," Thais added, too much knowledge in her tone. "His kind knows no other way."

Ginger felt a chill go down her spine, Reality was delivering the punches with all the force Ginger had expected. She gripped her shirt sleeves to keep from rushing into Saxon's embrace. Reality was unfolding like a giant spider in front of them.

"I'm not going in." Saxon's tone was hard and determined. It sliced her to the bone because she'd never had someone willing to lay themselves out for her.

*Well, until you met Saxon Hale and fell in love.*

Yeah. She savored that thought for a moment, trying to let it sink in deep enough so that it would always be with her.

"It will cost you your shield and maybe your life." Vitus offered the information softly. The rest of the team seemed in agreement, looking at their leader like he'd lost his mind. "I think it's shit, too, but Carl Davis is ahead in the polls. As President, he could shut down the

Shadow opps teams. Kagan is covering our butts and the rest of his men. Without resources, it would only be a matter of time."

Vitus was disgusted. He shook his head and cussed as Bram Magnus joined him.

"The game," Thais stated softly. "It can always be relied upon to be unfair when you need it to be the opposite." There was a sickening sound of first-hand knowledge in her tone, the frustration of missions gone to hell in her past.

Ginger found Dare Servant looking at her, his eyes bright with the need to fight. "I'll go with you," he said firmly. "They can have my fucking shield if it doesn't stand for what I thought it did anymore."

"Take me in." She couldn't have held the words back if she'd tried. Saxon turned to her with a look that was designed to make her bend to his will, but she straightened up and shot him a hard look. "It's the only move."

"You don't know Davis. I do. I wouldn't give him any witness, and I'm sure as hell not handing over my wife."

There was a note in his voice that made her mouth go dry. She thought she'd seen him being dead serious before, but she hadn't, not truly. She was staring at it now and just in case she missed the severity of the situation, shifting her gaze just a smidge to the side allowed her to see the look on Vitus's face, and it was stone hard with the knowledge that Saxon wasn't blowing anything out of proportion.

Something shifted inside her. The last bit of insecurity she'd harbored crumbled as she realized she had what it took to step up and be his match. "Don't ask me to give less than you do. It would make me your pet, and in the long haul, you would never be satisfied by that sort of a woman. Don't ask me to stand by while I could do some-thing to protect you."

Her words brought him up short. He hated them, his complexion darkening. She watched the desire to ar-gue with her flicker in his eyes, but something else was there, the frank honesty that they'd shared under the stars and inside a concrete bunker. It was who he was and who she wanted to be—worthy enough to stand next to him.

"Call your boss back . . ." Ginger was on her feet, moving toward him as she caught Vitus turning away to give them privacy. It seemed such a long distance, and yet she was suddenly there, able to put her hands on him, unbearably conscious of the fact that it might be for the last time. "Let me face whatever life seems to think is my destiny."

"Gin." He grasped her hands, his grip too hard as he tried to get her to bend to his will. "There is nothing he-roic about this. Carl Davis is out for himself, and he will trade your life as cheaply as he does his socks. I can keep you off grid."

"And do what?" she opened her hands, breaking his grip only because he released her. She slid her hands along his pectoral muscles, soaking up the strength. "Live a shadow life? Separate you from the only thing that has been your identity? Your badge?"

"It's a fucking piece of metal."

She slowly shook her head. He reached out and cupped her nape, trying to still her argument.

"You're more," she said in a whisper.

"I can't do it, Gin." He pulled her closer, his frame shuddering.

"You have to, because I won't give less than you do. I wouldn't be worthy of you if I let you destroy yourself."

She heard him draw in a deep breath, her words striking their mark.

"It would be worth it for you," he said.

"Maybe in the short term." She laid her head on his chest, listening to the sound of his heart, trying to brand it so deeply into her brain that she'd never forget it. "But in time, I'd know I fell short. Don't ask me to live with something you wouldn't. You'd never let me shield you by giving up everything I was."

"Shit," he grunted, threading his fingers through her hair and holding the threads as his embrace tightened. "I love you." His voice broke. "I should have told you that . . . before . . . shouldn't have argued with you."

She wiggled free and lifted her head so that she could meet his gaze. "I'd have checked your forehead for fever. You thrive on trying to get me to adopt your way of thinking."

One side of his mouth twitched up. "Only because you're so damned cute when you bristle."

He let her go, and it felt like the air temperature had dropped twenty degrees. She shivered as she watched him pull out his cell phone and push a button.

"Tomorrow. Send me the details."

Saxon killed the call and reached for her. He closed his fingers around her wrist and tugged her along behind him. Ginger caught Vitus turning to investigate what they were doing but she didn't care.

They were married after all.

And there was no way she was going to give up her last night with the man she loved.

Saxon found Vitus waiting for him in the morning. It wasn't really sunrise yet, but Saxon tucked the bedding around Ginger and went to face the odds that were stacked up against him.

"She's okay," Vitus offered.

"She's nursing delusions of glory," Saxon bit out. "Tyler won't let her live."

"Seems I have something in common with Tyler Martin after all. I can't seem to reconcile myself to letting *him* live." Vitus answered.

Saxon cracked a half grin at his brother's dry humor but it was only for a moment because he was focused on beating the odds. "Carl Davis will want to milk this for all the free publicity he can, which gives us some time to undermine him and snatch the victory flag."

"She knows that," Vitus stated. "That's no dimwit you're hitched to."

From his brother, that was high praise.

"You didn't do too well when the logical thing was to turn over the woman you loved."

Vitus offered him a shrug. "I didn't, but Damascus knew it was the only way to eliminate the threats to us completely."

It was slim hope, which had never bothered either of them before.

Today, Saxon discovered himself feeling the bite more, the sting sharper, and for the first time, he was damned happy to be personally involved. How in the fuck had he lived life without actually being in touch with it? He shifted his attention to his brother.

"Let me take point. You have a wife now."

Vitus eyed him over the rim of a coffee mug, through the steam rising from it. Saxon was no stranger to his brother's assessment. Vitus took a long draw off the java before he lowered the mug and spoke. "Looks like you do, too."

Saxon felt his confidence shift like sand beneath his feet. When it came to the odds of the mission, he was rock solid in his belief that he would persevere, but not with Ginger.

"I don't have the right to assume she'd choose me when this is over."

His brother drew in a stiff breath. "I recall that feeling, but I know what I saw on her face when she was looking at you."

"First thing's first," Saxon said to cover his lapse in confidence. He couldn't allow it to undermine his thought process. Not when Ginger's life was on the line.

"I'm Kagan."

Ginger considered the man and decided he looked exactly like someone who worked with Saxon should. In fact, she glanced down at his massive hand to see if he was wearing a Super Bowl ring.

He wasn't.

But he did have on an undershirt, which drew her attention because people on the west coast didn't wear them. The guy had just come from a colder climate.

"I don't like this."

Kagan offered Saxon a single nod before he opened the back door of a car and pointed Ginger toward the inside.

Saxon caught her wrist, pulling her back. For a moment, she caught the scent of his skin, felt the brush of his breath against her ear. "Remember."

She looked up and locked gazes with him, her brain offering up a perfect recollection of the one thing he'd said that was branded into her mind.

*"I will come for you . . ."*

"Now, Ms. Boyce," Kagan insisted.

She'd worried that it would be hard to get herself to move, but the truth was she was eager to go because it meant Saxon and his team were going to be out of the line of fire.

*Like you know anything about Shadow opps . . .*

Okay, maybe not, but she knew she couldn't let them shield her when it would cost them everything. Sure, it sucked, on an epic scale, but life was often unfair so she was going to pull up her big girl panties and face the fact that fate had decided to grab her down in New Orleans. Maybe it was her fault for being so ungrateful for the vanilla life she'd had, her "just desserts" so to say. Life was deciding to show her what she'd been so foolish to whine about by taking it away and leaving her with the knowledge that she'd been in a mighty good situation after all.

Well, she didn't regret it, not a bit. She looked at Saxon as the car pulled away. He was everything she'd ever dreamed a man could be. The word noble had true meaning now because she'd seen it embodied in him.

She felt like she was gathering up the memories, all the bits and pieces of their moments together, and putting them into a box where the winds of change couldn't take them from her.

Because she knew for a fact she was heading into the worst of the storm.

But not alone. No, she had Saxon's promise and that was all the shield she needed.


"There is only so much I'm going to be able to do."

Marc Grog didn't get told what he didn't want to hear very often. His lawyer was sweating and lifted his arm up to wipe his forehead before the man sent him a hard look. "With an eyewitness to your activities in New

Orleans—and the fact that you faked your death to avoid an official investigation . . ."

"She hasn't testified. Maybe she didn't see *anything* . . ." Marc hissed.

It wasn't the first time his lawyer had heard him offering to buy someone off, but today, the man looked less than confident in that being an option.

"A Federal agent heard you order him to kill her because she'd seen your face," the lawyer continued. "It gave the Feds a link between you and the New Orleans underground. I don't need to lecture you on how important it is to remain anonymous."

"No shit," Pulse said from his seat in the corner of the office. The lawyer flinched but didn't back down.

"They have too much evidence. I'm surprised the judge allowed bail while knowing that you have a private jet at your disposal, but I suggest you use your free time *wisely*."

The hint was clear to everyone in the room. Marc's lawyer suddenly let out a sigh and stood up. "I'll need some time to go over the charges before I can answer any more questions. A few days." He gathered the sheets he'd spread out on the desk and put them into his leather case.

"Fuck." Pulse said the moment the door shut behind the lawyer.

Marc held up a finger. His son shut his mouth and stayed quiet while Marc walked through the door and out into the afternoon sun. Pulse kept step with his father until they'd rounded a corner and ducked into a menswear shop. The owner instantly disappeared into the office to kill the video surveillance system.

Marc went to the dressing rooms and started to peel off his clothing. Pulse fell into step beside him as the owner of the shop appeared with new garments. They left looking like two locals, blending into the foot traffic on the sidewalk. The Feds might think they knew everything, but Marc had made sure to tuck enough cash away to see him through in the event of crisis. He stopped at an upscale wine-storage business and used his code to unlock a temperature-controlled vault. Withdrawing a bottle, he took it with him until he had a quiet place to smash it and withdraw the cash that had been stuffed inside. There was a key, too, one he took to another storage business and used to retrieve the guns he'd stockpiled.

Finally, he looked at his son. "No one steals from us. No one talks."

Pulse nodded and grinned, showing off the two gold-capped teeth he had courtesy of boxing. "Dead mice don't squeak. Davis is heading to Bakersfield. Just a quick hop to Mexico from there."

Marc grinned. "You're going to have to run the business in the States from now on. Together, we'll build an empire."

Pulse smiled with victory. With anyone else, Marc would have been pissed, but his boy had earned the moment.

"Fucking pricks!"

It was definitely time for profanity. Ginger didn't much care that her nose darn near got caught in the door as it was being pulled shut. It was worth it to shout at the bastards who had been treating her like a cow for the last few hours.

She heard the door lock with a crunching sound that threatened to shatter her courage.

No.

She couldn't lose it. Saxon sure as hell would keep it together.

That thought only made her long for him more, so she turned around, hating the way her paper gown rustled. The sound was a blunt reminder of just how helpless she was. The only thing in the room was a small container in the corner. Its intended use was obvious since there wasn't a bathroom.

*Pricks!*

There wasn't an inch of her body they hadn't poked, looked into, or scanned. The two paper gowns she had on were her only garments as she started to shiver in the air-conditioned room. The lights suddenly flickered before going out, leaving her in the dark. Her heart accelerated, pissing her off even more because she knew they were trying to scare her.

So, she was going to refuse to crumble.

That's right. She held tight to that thought, like a candle flame illuminating the blackness around her. It showed her Saxon's face, where it was branded into her memory. Not the look that he'd had when she was taken from him. No, she recalled the moment when he'd been on his back, giggling like an adolescent on top of a sleeping bag in the middle of nowhere with no one watching them.

The memory calmed her heart. She sunk down with her back against the wall and hugged her knees as she cradled the memory, letting it take her into slumber because she had a feeling she was going to need all the strength she had.

"You're pissed at me."

Saxon turned slowly around to find Kagan and Vitus standing behind him.

"I'm reserving judgement until you explain your plan."

Kagan cracked a rare smile. "You're both good agents. I like that about the pair of you."

"So what's the plan?" Saxon pressed the issue.

"Carl Davis is planning to show her off tonight at the celebration gala." Kagan laid the information down. "He's taking credit for bringing the reign of the Raven to an end. The good people of the world can rejoice, be safe on the streets, and remember to vote for Davis."

"So nice of him to provide such a public service," Saxon growled. "How hard is it going to be to get into that gala?"

"Next to impossible now that Tyler has taken up post alongside his meal ticket," Kagan said. "If we don't have passes, we won't make it past the gate. Davis is here to generate support through the voters. The guest list is exclusive to those with ties to old family, money, or votes."

Saxon slowly grinned. It was mirrored on his brother's face. Kagan looked between them as Bram Magnus raised an eyebrow. "What am I missing?"

Saxon snickered softly. "Mother-in-laws have uses after all."

Kagan smiled and pointed at him. "You see it. I couldn't refuse to turn Ginger over to Tyler, but I would have done it anyway because you need to draw Marc Grog out or you'll spend the rest of your lives looking over your shoulders."

"You're using my wife as bait," Saxon growled.

"Life gave her a nasty hand when she managed to walk into that party," Kagan reminded him. "I'm taking the only chance I see at tying up all the loose ends while she still gets to live."

"Fuck," Saxon said.

"Tyler won't let any of you live," Kagan confirmed. "And Davis will shut down the Shadow opps teams the moment he's sworn into office if I don't play his game. I did. But what you two do, without my knowledge . . ."

Kagan's hint was clear.

"Miranda Delacroix will get us dialed into her escort," Vitus said.

"Marc Grog made bail," Kagan informed them. "No one has seen him for twenty-four hours."

"Then there isn't any time to waste," Saxon said.

It was do or die time and today, it was personal.

But that was working for him just fine.

Miranda was a well-established charity spokesperson. Her smile was pleasing and her hair perfect as the cameras flashed around her. She'd been born into political life and married into it, as well. She never missed a step when she caught sight of Saxon Hale hovering just beyond the range of the cameras. He made eye contact with her just once before he melted back into the masses who were gathered to attend the literacy rally.

Miranda read a children's book and posed with youngsters on her lap for the next hour but her mind was on the Hale brothers, and of course her daughter, Damascus. She was giddy by the time she was able to break away, eager for news from her son-in-law because if Saxon Hale was there, his brother Vitus wouldn't be far.

At least she hoped so.

Saxon might have come alone, and she'd see him, of course, because favors had to be repaid. However, in the case of her late husband's death, she'd have gone to prison for pulling the trigger. There would have been some satisfaction in letting his friends know that she wasn't the spineless creature they'd always applauded Jeb Ryland for wedding. However, she was rather grateful that Saxon had made sure she didn't need to spend any time behind bars.

Being free to share her daughter's life was better. The private security force that always surrounded her took her back to the hotel she was staying at. They checked her room before she said good night and went through the door to take up post there.

She waited and wasn't disappointed.

"Oh Vitus . . ." she whispered and lifted her hands to hug him. The burly ex-Seal didn't take it too well but he suffered without complaint. She winked at Saxon from where he was watching from the bedroom doorway.

"I'm afraid this isn't a social call, Ms. Ryland."

Miranda winkled her nose with distaste. "Call me anything but that bastard's name." She stepped back from her son-in-law.

"Gladly," Vitus offered.

"I knew you'd understand," Miranda insisted. "I owe you a great deal. It will be my pleasure to assist you in any way possible." Her tone made it clear she had a solid core lurking beneath the motherly public persona she presented when the cameras were around.

Saxon slowly smiled. "In that case, Carl Davis's gala ball, do you have an invitation?"

Miranda fluttered her eyelashes. "I'd better. That man would be a fool to snub me publicly." She moved over to a desk where her personal items were laid out. Selecting her cell phone, she swiped the screen and tapped in her passcode before maneuvering through her inbox.

"Yes. I do," she confirmed. "It would have been amusing if it wasn't there."

"Except we need it," Saxon said.

"Well then, I will let my assistant know I have decided to attend." Miranda tapped in a message and sent it. "I normally take four in my personal escort."

Saxon was nodding. Miranda watched him smile with satisfaction before she directed her attention toward Vitus.

"Now, tell me something about my daughter. Anything at all. A happy moment."

Vitus's professional mask cracked at the mention of his wife. "She tested the smoke alarms last week. Making dinner."

Miranda let out a peel of laughter that she smothered with her hands before the men at her door decided to investigate. "My poor baby is just like me."

The lights in her cell came on making Ginger jump. She growled when she landed on her backside in a jumble of arms and legs because half her body was numb and the floor slick. There was a click before the door opened.

She straightened up, leaning against the wall as a man entered the cell. She'd thought she was cold before but now, her blood chilled even more because she recognized him. She had a perfect recollection of him breaking Kitten's neck and letting her body drop onto the ground like a bag of trash. He racked her from head toe and she ordered herself not to shift. She was practically naked, and the fact that he seemed to want to rub her nose in it just made her hate his guts. Well, if he was there to kill her, she wasn't leaving the world wailing.

"Tyler Martin," he suddenly called out like they were meeting in an upscale hotel lobby. The dude even extended his hand.

Ginger scoffed at him. "Yeah, I remember you, and I'd just as soon not touch you."

His lips twitched, but what she noticed more was the way his eyes remained full of triumph.

"What is all this designed to get you?" She opened her hand wide to indicate her surroundings.

"Nothing too terrible," he responded. "In fact, it's the

one thing you already agreed to do. Testify against Marc Grog."

The glimmer of victory was still in his eyes, sending a ripple of alarm down her spine.

"And you just thought I needed to be locked in a freezing cell to help me understand . . . what?"

He offered her a half shrug. "The cell is a means of making sure you aren't carrying a bug inside your body. The Hale brothers know their business, but so do I, and you will be under my control completely now. Since you're cleared, I can offer you more comfortable accommodations."

He remained standing between her and the door for a long moment, making it clear he controlled her life.

"Boy, you measure up pretty short compared to Saxon."

Sure, it was a stupid thing to say, but it certainly was satisfying. Tyler frowned, her words hitting a soft spot. He appeared surprised to feel the sting.

"A little more time to consider your circumstances then."

He flashed her a smile before he left, and she heard the door lock. A moment later the air conditioning kicked on full blast. Ginger sunk down and hugged her knees to her chest.

She wasn't giving up.

Saxon never would, and she sure as shit wasn't going to fold.

# CHAPTER EIGHT

There was poking and prodding and then there was another form of poking and prodding. Ginger glared at the stylist messing with her hair but the man only rolled his eyes and went back to making little tsking sounds while using a comb to tease up her hair. It was a lost cause, one she'd accepted years ago, but the man seemed loath to cry surrender.

Likely that was due to the pair of burly men standing just a few steps behind him. Oh, they were there to keep an eye on her but she decided that it wasn't personal as Carl Davis treated everyone like a piece on a chess board. She was being dressed and fluffed for his gala celebration dinner where she was expected to play her part as the rescued damsel.

That part was sticking because Saxon and his team deserved the credit.

Not that anyone cared.

"Well, I believe I've done as much as humanly possible," he exclaimed dramatically.

"Thank you," Ginger purred before abandoning the chair while the stylist rolled his eyes again.

He turned and looked at the two men. "She's just so *large* . . . and honestly, real beasts like that just don't stay where they should . . ."

Ginger felt her temper simmering but held it in check. There were bigger fish to fry tonight, and if she didn't keep her focus, it just might be her sizzling on the grill before dawn. She wasn't stupid. Tyler Martin was watching her like a hunter, just waiting to make the call on when was the right time to drop her.

She was going to have to make sure she made that harder than the man anticipated. Saxon certainly would. One of the men cleared his throat, and she realized he was holding the door open for her.

Show time.

"Step one inch out of line, and it will be the last mistake you make."

Tyler Martin had a savage grip on her arm. His fingers were digging in, promising her a bruise as Carl Davis made a speech about making America safe through the efforts of Shadow operation teams. "Don't think I'm your biggest worry. Marc Grog is hunting you."

"Bring it," she hissed under her breath.

She caught his lips twitching up a moment before he looked past her to listen closely to what Carl Davis was saying.

"And to that end . . ." Carl held his hands up to quiet the applause. "I want to introduce you all to a very special lady. One who has stepped up and refused to be silenced by fear. As you all know, the underworld boss known as the Raven has been riddling our fair nation with his thugs and crimes. This lady came face to face with this monster and is willing to brave the death mark proclamation he is so well known for putting out on those who testify against him. Ms. Ginger Boyce."

"You're on." Tyler Martin escorted her toward the front of the room as the people gathered there cheered. Carl Davis never really turned away from them, reaching out to place his arm around her shoulders as cameras flashed. The fakeness of it all made her recoil and step back onto Tyler's shoe.

"She's shy," Carl proclaimed, gaining a round of amusement from the assembled guests. "But not when it comes to justice . . ."

And just like that, she was back to being nothing more than a prop. Tyler Martin kept her in place as Carl talked some more.

"Help me in raising a toast to the end of the Raven!"

There was the clink of glasses before everyone happily went back to the business of enjoying the lavish spread laid out by Carl Davis and his supporters. Waiters carried full trays of wine glasses through the crowded room, and those in their expensive evening attire happily lightened the load of those there to work the event.

Tyler suddenly reached out and grabbed her arm. She gasped as pain went shooting up into her shoulder because of the way he twisted it. Carl took a step toward his man.

"Miranda Delacroix is here," Tyler said softly.

But it wasn't low enough that Ginger didn't hear the concern in his tone. Hope burst inside her and right on its heels came fear, the same bone-deep feeling that had sent her walking away from Saxon.

"The Hale brothers won't be far behind," Carl said under his breath. "It's for sure that bitch doesn't support me."

Tyler was pulling her back as Carl waved. Ginger was

torn. The moment had arrived, but she worried her lip in indecision as she tried to decide if staying in public was a better plan. The music changed as she was making ready to fake a rolled ankle and hit the floor to keep Tyler from taking her into some corner and killing her. The live band suddenly broke into "Blue Suede Shoes."

She instantly opened her mouth and released her lower lip.

"Good girl," Saxon remarked under his breath. There was a tiny microphone hidden in his bow tie. "We're in business. Move to second position."

Saxon was in motion, moving away from the gathering as Carl Davis and Tyler used an exit concealed behind the podium. Vitus was there, falling into step with the Secret Service escort. Tyler pulled Ginger along, moving to a location he'd selected before the event started.

Saxon was counting on his former lead to operate according to his training. Tyler didn't disappoint him, moving Ginger into a back service area that was locked down while Carl Davis was there.

Inside, they would be alone without any witness. Carl ordered his escort to stay outside the door.

"Ease up," Ginger groused. "Some of us are wearing heels."

She earned a grunt for her effort. Tyler Martin kept muscling her along until they were inside a half-lit storage area. Her heart started accelerating and the memory of the way Tyler had snapped Kitten's neck was replaying inside her brain like a bad horror movie. She was poised on the edge of panic, the need to escape overriding everything else. Time felt like it was speeding up along with her heart rate, making it impossible to think things through because her thoughts were spilling over the boundaries of her mind.

She drew in a deep breath and tried to grasp the threads of her composure.

*Think!*

Otherwise, she was going to get cut down like a startled doe.

"I hope you have a plan to deal with the Hale brothers," Carl said.

"She's the bait," Tyler remarked. "Sullivan says Grog is here."

Ginger suddenly turned on him, jabbing at his throat, the way some of her prepper friends had taught her. He recoiled and struck her across the face in response. She went reeling but that pleased her because she was out of his reach.

"Don't be too proud of yourself." Tyler Martin leveled his gun on her.

Ginger stayed on the floor for a long moment. She hoped she was doing a decent job of looking scared to death. It afforded her a few precious moments to look at her surroundings.

"A little mouse makes good bait . . ."

Ginger stiffened as another part of her nightmare rose up near her. Marc Grog came out of the shadows, a gun in his hand. Her dress was a long one with a tulle slip. She reached down and slowly slipped her shoes off while Marc boldly walked toward Tyler Martin. Carl shifted off to the side, out of the line of fire.

"Even when you hamstring me, you're still playing along with my tune." Marc looked around the storage room. "Couldn't have picked a better place to take care of business."

She watched Marc shift the aim of the gun toward her.

Those moments were the longest of her life as she tried to move but it felt like she was weighed down and stuck to the floor. She heard each of her heartbeats, felt her muscles straining to perform and get her out of the line of fire. Her eyes widened as she saw the flash of fire at the end of the gun, and she waited to feel the bite of the bullet.

It never came. There was a blur of motion, a man moving between her and the bullet as she finally managed to push herself into action. She came up and off the floor and then landed hard on her face as she stepped on her dress. But she was sliding across the concrete, being pulled by Bram Magnus. She stared into his face, confused because her mind wasn't processing details fast enough.

But when her brain kicked in, what she heard was the fight going on behind her. She whipped her head around to see Saxon grappling with Marc, the pair of them struggling over control of the gun.

And then she lunged back toward them because Saxon's shoulder was covered in blood.

"Shit!" Bram cussed as he went after her and caught her around the waist. The agent proved himself worthy of being on Saxon's team by slinging her up and over his shoulder as though she weighted about as much as a gallon of milk.

"No . . . wait!" In some part of her mind, she really did realize Bram was doing the most logical thing. But in the other, all she saw was Saxon fighting for his life. It was a horrifying moment, time slowing down again to allow her to see Tyler Martin leveling his gun and pulling the trigger.

"Saxon!"

She felt like the word was torn from her soul. Vitus

was suddenly there, returning fire as Bram passed him and dropped her in a heap against the far wall. She struggled to get on her feet and then it was over.

Silence surrounded them, the scent of gunpowder mixing with fresh blood. It was gut wrenching, her stomach heaving, but she resisted the urge to throw up because she need to see Saxon. She ended up making it only to her hands and knees and looking through Bram's feet. Saxon's face was turned toward her, his eyes closed, while Marc was sprawled on his back, his lifeless eyes staring at the ceiling. She must have let out a cry because Bram turned around and hooked her around the waist as she tried to pass him again.

"Let me go!" she hissed trying to tear his arm away.

"You're my primary responsibility," Bram informed her as he locked her arm up, making even the smallest motions impossible. "Tyler is unaccounted for."

Vitus had skidded to a knee beside Saxon and pushed two fingers against his neck. Ginger held her breath as she waited. He suddenly nodded. "Thais!"

There was a patter of stocking-clad feet as the female agent came into sight. She'd kicked her heels off, too, and didn't hesitate to drop down next to Saxon in spite of the ripping sound that came from her evening gown. Vitus shifted his focus to Bram, giving the man a nod before he was gone into the shadows with another man flanking him, both of them with their weapons drawn.

"Okay, it's clear now," Bram said as he released her. She made it across the space between them in record time, her skirt going over Saxon as she slid in like she was hitting third base. Ginger started to jerk it back but Thais had other ideas.

"Good. Use it to put pressure on the wound," Thais ordered her as she was pressing buttons on her phone.

At last her brain didn't let her down. She was in motion the moment Thais's instructions were past her lips. Ginger gathered her skirt up and shoved it down onto Saxon's shoulder as Thais flipped open a knife and cut it away at the waist.

"Fucking hell!"

Saxon's profanity was sweeter than anything she'd ever heard. He jerked and tried to buck her right off him but she used her body weight to keep pressure on his shoulder.

"Magnus!" he growled. "Get your target under cover."

"It's clear." Bram got on his knee so that he could make eye contact with his boss. "Marc is dead."

Bram jerked his head to the side. Saxon rolled his over so that he could see the body. Ginger watched a flicker of satisfaction appear in his eyes before he was wrapping his fingers around her hip.

"I'm fine," she said softly. "You kept your promise. You came for me."

He nodded once before looking back at Bram. "Martin?"

"Your brother took off after him. Bastard slipped out."

There was suddenly the pounding of footfalls, that unique tone of dress shoes hitting a hard surface as members of the Secret Service came to Carl Davis's aid. There were guns everywhere, but there was no way Ginger was going to raise her hands. Bram was flashing his badge, using his body as a shield while he argued with them.

None of it was able to penetrate her focus on Saxon.

Nothing mattered beyond him at all.

Nothing.

Saxon wasn't dying.

At least, if he was, he was doing it his way. Bram pushed her up into an ambulance beside him against the paramedic's warning and shut the door before he pounded on it twice to let the driver know he could roll. It was a bumpy ride as the flashing lights on the top of the emergency vehicle made for an eerie disco sort of setting.

At the hospital though, she discovered that all of Saxon's men had followed them. The emergency crews shoved her back and Saxon let out a snort as he flipped right over and caught Vitus in his sights.

"Right," Vitus muttered. He reached out and settled a hand on Ginger's shoulder. Saxon contemplated his brother for a long moment before he relaxed and let the doctors roll him onto his back again.

"He'll be all right?" she asked.

Vitus didn't answer her but the worry in his eyes chilled her blood. She felt numb as a nurse guided her into another treatment area to clean up the cuts and scrapes Ginger hadn't had time to feel.

Honestly, there was nothing except Saxon.

Two days later, Ginger woke up and blinked.

"What are you doing?" she demanded as she kicked at the blanket she'd slept under. Vitus had managed to get a cot delivered to Saxon's hospital room.

"Getting dressed," Saxon informed her.

He already had his pants on and had shrugged into his shirt. His wound was still fresh enough that the effort of moving his shoulders had made him groan.

"You are going right back to bed, as the doctor instructed you."

He pushed the last button through its hole and tucked the tail of his shirt in while sending her a look that she recognized.

"You're damned frustrating. Know that?"

His lips twitched, but there was tension in his eyes that

stilled her words. Suddenly, being playful with him wasn't sitting right. The reason was clear. He was crawling back into his shell, resuming his life, and she hated it because he was leaving her, but there was still part of her that was just so damned happy to see him alive.

Even if it meant he was going to walk out of her life.

"The doctor really did tell you to rest."

He was finishing his tie, watching her as he perfected the knot and tightened it. He took a moment to look at himself in a mirror that was attached to the inside of the closet door before he turned to face her.

She felt her belly knot, but she stood steady, ready to face what her actions had brought her.

"I am not going to declare my love for you wearing a hospital gown and lying on my back."

Ginger blinked, stepping back because she was just having too hard a time grasping what he'd said.

Saxon caught her chin when she started to look away. "We're discussing the elephant in the room, Gin. So stop trying to avoid it."

Sure, she could have stepped away from him but that would be pretty low of her considering the guy was sporting a gunshot wound that he'd received while protecting her. But standing in place left her feeling like she was in the middle of a shopping mall on Christmas Eve, buck naked.

Saxon's lips slowly curled upward. She knew this grin. It was pure determination, a promise that he fully intended to get his way.

Damn if that didn't hit her straight in the heart.

"What I can't do," he stated firmly, "is deal with a future without you in it."

Ginger stepped back as he walked toward her. "Um . . ."

He pressed a fingertip against her lips to silence her retort.

"What I won't do . . ." he continued as he caught the waistband of her jeans to hold her in place so that his next step brought them into contact.

*Oh . . . yeah . . .*

"Is walk out of your life without making very sure that I tell you I want to stay."

She was melting, her reasoning standing no greater chance against him than ice against spring. "But . . . it's not love and I love you and you're just feeling sorry for me."

She was rambling, but every word was pure truth. Just as it had always been when it came to him, her composure was worthless.

"Wrong. I'm feeling sorry for myself." He stroked her cheek with the back of his hand, his eyes filling with an abundance of emotion that fed the glow warming her heart. "Because I am going to be the most pitiful creature on the face of the planet if you leave me."

"You don't know how to play that role."

He snorted. "You bring out a lot of firsts in me, Gin. There's no doubt in my mind that I am going to be reduced to begging if you don't accept the fact that I am completely dependent on you." He pressed his fingertip back against her lips when she started to argue again. "That's love, honey. The type that isn't ever going to go away because it's bone deep. So, even though we're doing this a little backwards . . ."

He withdrew a step and hit his knee, keeping a grip on her hand as he held her gaze. "Will you . . . remain my wife?"

"It would serve you right if I said yes."

Saxon was off his knee and wrapped her into an embrace that was almost too tight, except that it wasn't because she needed to feel him against her, like her very life depended on it.

"How sweet."

Ginger smothered her amusement against Saxon's tie as Vitus's voice came from behind them. Saxon lifted her chin and studied her face for a moment. "See? You're already getting used to my brother and that is a mark of a keeper."

Vitus made a sound behind them that made it pretty clear he was flipping his brother off.

"Tell him to go back to bed." She turned and aimed a smile at Vitus. "He won't listen to me."

"If that's the case, I haven't got a chance in hell. Besides, he's been lying on his tail long enough."

Right on cue, Saxon walked out of the door and grasped her hand on the way. He seemed to know where he was heading, Vitus falling into step with them as Saxon found an exit door and the motion sensors opened them wide for them.

Ginger snorted, earning a grin from Vitus. "Don't worry, I'm actually just trying to get him in my truck before he realizes I'm taking him home where our Mom can nurse him back to health."

Saxon stopped and turned to face his brother. "Payback is a dish best served with double gravy."

Saxon took his foot off the doorstep of Vitus's truck as he caught his section leader moving across the entryway of the hospital and sent a look toward his brother before he went to see Kagan. His section leader stopped beside a mobile scan unit that was bid enough to hide his face behind.

"I realize I'm not your favorite person right now," Kagan stated the obvious. "Maybe you could factor in that if I hadn't listened to you and assigned her to a protection team, you wouldn't be so happy right now."

Saxon conceded the point with a soft grunt. Kagan nodded.

"Had to let it play out, Hale. Carl Davis is poised to win this thing. I didn't like it any better than you."

"But we all do what we have to in order to survive?" Saxon asked.

"We do," Kagan said. "As Commander in Chief, he could end the Shadow opps teams."

There was a long moment of silence.

"So what now?" Saxon asked.

"Now?" Kagan offered him a rare smile. "Looks like you're going to play house, so expect assignments to be more mundane in support instead of the field."

"Agreed." There was a time that word would have stuck in his throat, today, it was the easiest agreement he'd ever given.

Kagan flashed him a grin and shook his head.

"Have some kids, they'll keep the in-laws from driving you insane," Kagan advised with a smirk. "I'm resettling her parents next to yours."

Saxon choked.

"No need to thank me," Kagan insisted as he pulled a folded map out of his pocket. "Wedding present for you."

Saxon took it and looked at the circled location. It was only a few miles from his parents' home.

"The old missile silo?" he asked.

"Your new office. Oversee the renovations to start with. Let me know when you have it up and running. The new world is smaller, so we need to have some rabbit holes to watch for our prey. I'm sending your brother along with you. We'll have to discuss team members at some point. Captain Magnus is going back to Afghanistan."

"Right," Saxon agreed, but there was a tingle on his nape because he had the feeling Kagan hadn't placed the cherry on top of the sundae just yet. Kagan didn't disappoint him.

"And brush off your dress uniform. The president will be awarding you a Medal of Honor for preventing the assassination attempt by the Raven on Carl Davis."

"Like fuck," Saxon hissed.

Kagan offered him a crusty laugh. "You're more like your brother than you admit."

Kagan started walking, melting away into the corridors of the hospital. Saxon knew that the video cameras wouldn't have a trace of him, the map in his pocket the only tangible evidence of his visit.

"Getting that medal will suck." Vitus advised him.

Saxon turned and cussed as the wound on his shoulder sent searing pain through him. Vitus was leaning against the wall, grinning at him.

"It will be a media circus." His brother was leaning against the wall, unashamed of listening in.

"Works for me." Saxon replied.

Surprise flickered in Vitus's eyes. Saxon sent his brother a grin. "I'll take it because it means Ginger is alive. Nothing else much matters beyond that."

Vitus nodded, but his expression remained serious. "With the notable exception of Tyler Martin being alive."

Saxon offered Vitus the map. "We have some renovations to oversee before we'll be in position to go after him but we know where to look."

Vitus shared a smile with him, one Saxon felt warming his insides. Ginger was everything he needed, which meant there was no way he was going to leave Tyler Martin out there.

"Miranda Delacroix to see you, sir."

Dunn Bateson was surprised, but he rose and let it show on his face as Miranda came into his office. She flashed him her media-covered smile that came with sparkling eyes. He waited until she'd sat down before resuming his position in his office chair.

"Thank you for seeing me without an appointment," she began.

"Family doesn't need an appointment."

Miranda's façade melted, leaving behind a genuine smile, one she reserved only for her children.

"You know, I never wanted to give you up," she sighed. "I was so young, you deserved more from a mother."

"I've never sought an apology because I'm rather glad you didn't let your family clean me up like spilt milk."

Miranda's face took on a hard, determined expression few people had witnessed. "My father may not have approved of my relationship with your father. But there was one thing he understood, and that was that you were your father's blood and any man worth anything will fight for his blood. The only condition was that I agree to never admit to giving birth to you. Agreeing was the only way I could ensure you lived. My father would have done something unspeakable if I hadn't promised."

"Old memories now." Dunn shut her down gently but firmly. "Let's live in the moment."

Miranda lifted her eyebrow, looking more like him than Dunn had ever realized she might. He chuckled softly as he realized she'd smoke-screened him, too.

She offered him a flutter of her eyelashes before she

got down to business. "I've spent too many of my years waiting for my turn to be myself. But mothers do those sorts of things."

Dunn nodded. "And now that you're an empty nester?"

"I am running for Congress."

Dunn sat for a moment, considering the media support Miranda would have from years of playing the good wife. He threw his head back and laughed.

"A candidate for our children," she elaborated. "A clean planet is my priority."

Dunn came around the desk and hugged her. She laughed against him, reveling in the ability to touch her son.

When he set her back, there was a wicked gleam in his eyes, the same one that his father had that stole her heart so many years before.

"Count on my full support, Madam Delacroix."

"Exactly why I am here."

"Fuck!" Carl Davis barely made it into his office before he exploded. "That damned bitch!"

Tyler Martin watched his boss pacing. Carl pointed at him. "She's going to win, know that? Between the Delacroix family ties and her popularity among the voters, it's a done deal."

"You're going to win, too," Tyler Martin remarked. "Unless you take your eye off the ball and screw up your image."

Carl stopped and drew in a deep breath, rocking back on his heels. "Right. The big picture."

"Miranda has a couple of skeletons, like the rest of us," Tyler continued. "She killed Jeb Ryland. Makes me wonder what else she's got stashed behind that mother of the year cloak she wears."

"Good," Carl exclaimed. "Dig up something, in case she gets in my way."

"In the meantime, make a good show of being friends with her. She'll bring in some votes."

Carl nodded. "What about that contract killer?"

"Sullivan?" Tyler answered. "I sent him on a trip that he won't return from."

Carl nodded. "In that case, looks like the only thing to do is show up and watch Saxon Hale get a medal for saving my life."

Eight months later . . .

"To think . . . both my boys have the Congressional Medal of Honor."

Saxon's mother was cooing. Ginger watched with morbid fascination as all five and a half feet of Athene Hale managed to ride roughshod over her full-grown sons. Behind her, their father was watching the moment with an expression that told Ginger he was fighting the urge to laugh hysterically.

"Can I get out of this monkey suit, Mom?" Saxon asked at last.

Athene fluttered her eyelashes, betraying the fact that she was messing with her kids. "All right, I guess I've had my fun." She put aside the cell phone with which she'd been taking pictures and turned to wink at Ginger. "At least until that baby is born."

Behind his mother, Saxon sent Ginger a smug smile. The second they made it to their suite, her husband turned her around so that he was hugging her from behind. She heard him snort against her hair as he nuzzled against it and framed her rounding belly with his hands.

"Still not sorry that you decided not to wait?"

"Nope." She tried to wiggle out of his embrace, but he stroked the mound of their growing child, and she quieted, as she always did, marveling at the way he stroked her belly. His big hands so gentle, it made her eyes sting with tears. Somehow, she'd never truly understood the word "cherish" until now.

"Me neither," Saxon whispered in a tone that was touched with awe and had been ever since he'd realized she'd conceived.

The baby moved, making her smile as she felt like the motion was a direct link with life. It was something she desperately needed, to help her believe that somehow, fate had delivered a happy ending.

It was deeper than love. It was intimacy on a level she'd never felt before, the way he held her, making her believe she was treasured beyond measure.

"I admit, I love knowing that you're mine."

"I am," she whispered, taking his hand and moving it to where their child was kicking. "We are."

And for the first time in her life she realized it was time to apply the cheesiest words ever penned in a love story to her own life.

"And they lived happily, ever after . . ."

"I'm working on it," he whispered. "It's going to be my life's work."

Read on for an excerpt from Dawn Ryder's
next *Unbroken Heroes* series

# Take to the Limit

Coming soon from St. Martin's Paperbacks

"Jesus . . . ." A bag of trash hit the concrete but Jaelyn surprised him by controlling the rest of her emotions. Her eyes flashed wide but returned to normal faster than he'd have given her credit for. He'd never pegged her as having much nerve. But she stared back at him, steady as could be.

Impressive . . .

"I'm sorry Magnus, I didn't see you."

Her voice trailed off as she heard a soft laugh and recognized it as her sister's. Magnus watched her face, wanting to know if she knew what her sister was about. Jaelyn turned toward the sound and frowned.

"Your sister is busy," he informed her dryly.

"But you're her boyfriend . . . oh never mind," she bent to pick up the trash bag but only made it half way there before straightening. "Look . . . I'm really—"

"Sorry? Don't be," he shrugged "Better this way."

"I can't see how."

His temper was sizzling and another soft laugh drifting on the night breeze, turning up the heat. "It's simple enough. I'm shipping out at daybreak and it looks like I'm doing it a single man. No strings attached."

"But you won't have anyone to kiss you good-bye," she whispered.

He chuckled but it wasn't a friendly sound. "Are you volunteering?"

Jaelyn looked shocked but not as outraged as he expected. He wanted a fight and was being an ass, but a flare of hunger entered her eyes, deflating his initial surge of temper. Leaving him poised on the edge of something volatile, something he felt like he'd known had been simmering inside him but had been ignoring. For all the right reasons of course but tonight, there was a boundary missing between them. That knowledge set something loose inside him.

"Your sister seems to have vacated the post of being my girlfriend, so kissing me good-bye is now an open opportunity for you. Sounds good to me."

He pushed away from the wall and wrapped his arms around her. He was being presumptuous at the least, a huge prick at the worst, but the flicker of heat in her eyes drew him to her. Maybe it was plain old desperation to cling to the living before he shipped out to a place where life was cheap and easily smashed.

*Like hell it was that simple . . .*

Whatever had broken free inside him was growing, stretching, as it gained freedom. It was hungry and needy, as well as uncontrollable.

Magnus trapped her arms at her sides, sliding one hand up her spine to capture her nape before claiming his kiss. He needed to hold her, needed her to feel his strength. A soft gasp got muffled between their lips as he pressed a deep kiss against her mouth. He forgot what his intentions where when the taste of her swept through his brain, knocking his better judgment out cold.

The only thing left was the feel of the woman in his arms. The way her lips moved beneath his, the way her body curved to fit against his, it was mind numbing and exhilarating at the same time. She was warm and soft and he teased her lips with a sweep of his tongue because he needed to know what she tasted like. The thin, summer dress she wore was nothing but a frail barrier between her hard nipples and himself. He slid his hand around and cupped one breast, feeling its weight and brushing his thumb over the puckered tip. The soft sound she made snapped him back into focus.

What the fuck was he doing?

He opened his arms, fighting that thing inside him with every ounce of self-discipline he had. All he wanted was to press her against the side of the house and keep pressing until he was deep inside her.

God . . . he craved her . . . .

Jaelyn staggered back a pace, her respiration agitated, her eyes wide.

That was why she tasted so good. She was everything pure, everything his hands were too dirty to touch.

"I had no right to do that." But he wanted to do a whole hell of a lot more.

His jeans felt too tight, his cock swollen and demanding. Her taste clung to his lips and he forced himself to walk away before he lost his grip on his discipline.

Before he took what he wanted . . .

"Hold it right there Bram Magnus."

Surprise made him stop. The husky sound of her voice something he'd never heard before. Or expected to.

But he liked it. Liked it a hell of a lot.

He turned to face her and felt his arousal spike when he found her standing only a pace from him. There wasn't a hint of outrage on her face, only a glimmer of something in her eyes which promised him hell.

He liked the look of that too.

"I believe the idea was for me to kiss you good-bye." She closed the gap between them, captivating him with the way her hips swayed. She stepped up to him and settled her hands on his chest. "Which isn't what just happened."

She stroked him. Moving her hands up and over his collarbones to his neck. It was slow, so damn slow he wasn't sure he could remain still but it was worth the effort. Her touch sent shivers down his spine, the kind he hadn't felt since he'd been a raw youth in the troughs of his first love.

When her hand reached his head she rose onto her toes to complete the kiss but he was still too tall. She gently pulled on his neck and he had no problem complying with her demand.

Shit, he could take orders from her all night so long as she was touching him.

This time their kiss was sweeter but not because it was slower. It was in the way she explored his mouth, teasing him with soft pressure while tracing his lower lip with the tip of her tongue before thrusting shyly inside. That was his undoing. He wrapped his arms around her and captured her neck so he could turn her head to suit his desire. The kiss became hard and blistering hot. Control vanished as he fit her against him, pushing her back into the shadows and against the warm stucco of the house. He ravished her mouth with his lips and tongue. She moaned, the little sound pushing him further over the edge as she arched up against him, pressing against his cock and trembling when she felt the hard proof of his desire.

He pulled his head back, stroking her back as he detected the ripple of reaction. Her eyes were wide but her lips open as she panted.

"I shouldn't have started this."

"Well, I've decided to finish it." She surprised him with how determined her tone was. Her fingers fisted into his shirt, pulling a handfull of his chest hairs in the process. The little tingle of pain intensified the moment, feeding the savage side of his nature that was all too close to the surface.

"Jaelyn—"

"Shut up." She surprised him again, actually stunned was a better way to put it. She was the sweet sister. The family supporting, apron wearing, sibling who always embodied the model of a good girl.

But there was one hell of a woman hiding inside her.

He cupped her jaw, holding her head in place as he studied her gaze. It was hot enough to blister him, giving him a peek at the woman he'd never taken the time to notice she was.

Hell, maybe he'd ignored it because he'd been stupid enough to chase her sister. A hundred missed opportunities flooded his brain as he watched the way her face turned sultry with the help of her lips still being wet from his kiss.

"Jaelyn—"

She reached up and wrapped her fingers around his wrist. She tugged his hand away from her face and slipped away from the wall of the house. He felt like she was ripping herself away from him, the beast inside of him raged against the loss.

But she tugged him behind her, pulling him across

the driveway, along the garage door to keep away from the light the street lamp generated. She kept going to the second garage that was offset from the main house, her grip tight on his wrist. A stair case led to the upper level, where a loft apartment was located. There was a jingle of keys as she pulled them from her pocket and fit one into the door. With another tug, she pulled him inside and shut the door behind them. There was a clink as she dropped the keys on the small table next to the door and leaned back against it like she was suddenly undecided about what she was doing.

She steadied herself with a deep breath before reaching behind her. The unmistakable sound of the lock turning filled the room.

The little click felt like it severed the bounds between what he was expected to be and what the beast inside him wanted.

God help him, he was dying for her. The taste of her, the feel of her against him. He wanted to savor every second, memorize it, and brand it into his brain.

He pressed his hand against the door above her head, his body curving over hers as he drew in a deep breath. The delicate scent of her skin and hair filled him, setting off a need that threatened to destroy his plan to savor the moment.

"Touch me." He ordered roughly.